CU01572692

Published in Great Britain by
L.R. Price Publications Ltd, 2021
27 Old Gloucester Street,
London, WC1N 3AX
www.lrpricepublications.com

ISBN:

FOR MY SISTERS

Where should I go? - Alice.
Depends on where you want to end up.
Cheshire Cat.

TO SILVERDALE CLOSE

Boris and the Fatberg

Pat Stevens

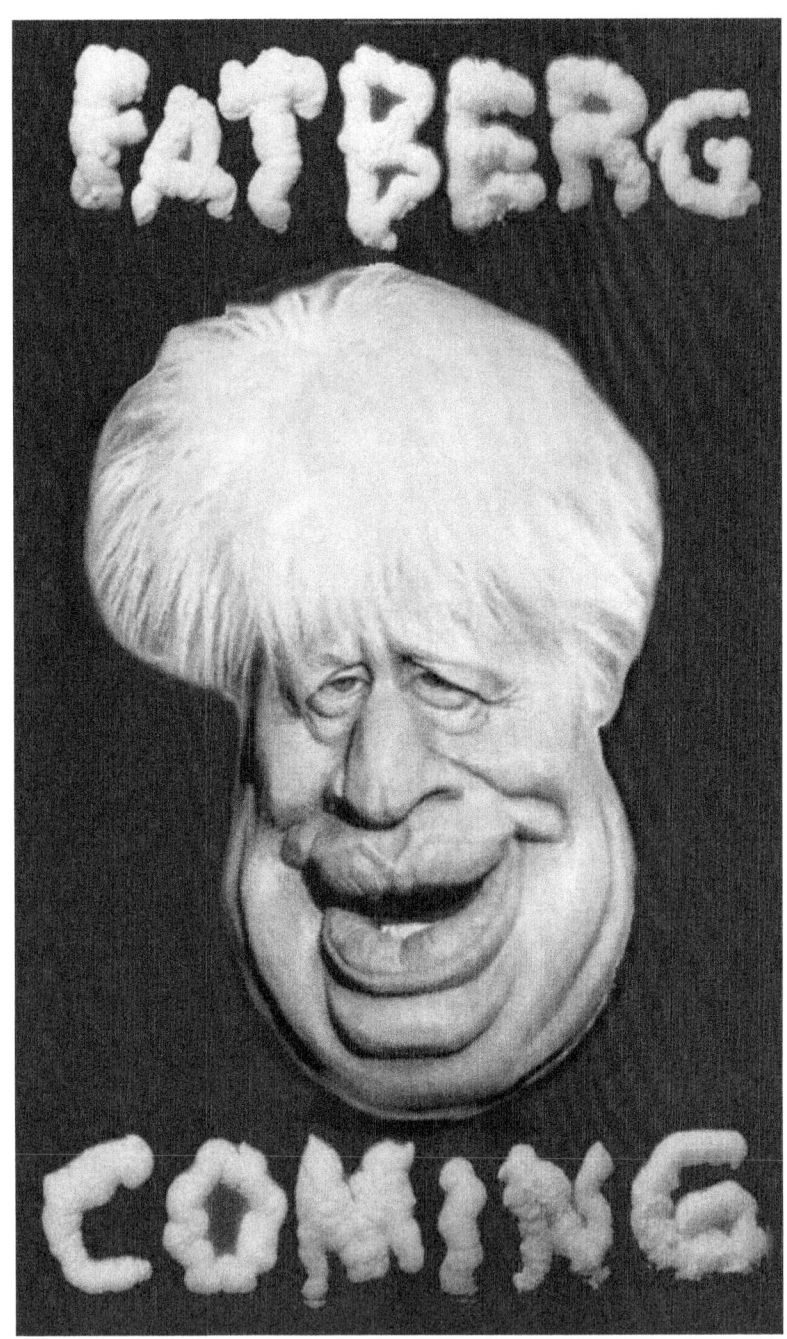

Contents

May 2010

Popular Science

The **What's New** magazine

LONDON WATER

It's a monster! My night with the fatberg busters

In this Issue— **Is the Fatberg alive?**

Fatberg Autopsy

This book recounts the deadly triple threat that recently plagued London, a lethal pandemic and an evil entity spawned by a fatberg in a subterranean sewerland, almost as smelly as the Whitehall political sewer festering above it? Although they are not in any manner chemically linked, before the curse of Covid-19 came the feared living fatberg, so perhaps it's best to begin our story there.

Professor Peter Watercloset had been invited to the Whitechapel fatberg autopsy, because he was a renowned expert in the field; there was not much the professor did not know about sewage. Fatbergs are a congealed mass of fat and discarded plastic blocking British sewers. It was during the B.B.T. televised autopsy that Peter Watercloset discovered something that could potentially wipe Whitechapel off the map. Beside the morass of waste plastic and cooking oils, fatbergs also contained nitrates and phosphates.

These chemicals caused eutrophication: an increase in the chemical activity required for life? But, famous T.V. journalist Harry Hack just laughed.

"Living fatbergs, Peter?" Harry guffawed, when the professor disclosed his fears. Harry was a British Broadminded Television top dog, and it was this renowned newshound who had set up the B.B.T.'s *Fatberg Autopsy.* Peter Watercloset disliked Harry Hack, so he would normally not attend any B.B.T. event. But his good friend Evil Neville asked for an invite – and the ravishing Dr. Zee Garbo would be there. So would any red-blooded male.

Evil Neville was not a scientist, but a neighbour of Peter Watercloset, who wanted to see the fatberg. Dr. Garbo was part of the influx of Polish immigrants who are rebuilding the decaying London metropolis, which Polish pilots had saved during the Battle of Britain. Zee Garbo was a science lecturer at the Słupsk School of Sewage, a division of the Pomeranian University, but had been netted by overseas pommies to help rid London of fatbergs.

It was reminiscent of the 1858 "Great Stink", when London had the foul habit of dumping sewage directly into the Thames River – not a good idea, for human waste contains suspended solids which adversely affect the environment. Wastewater contains nitrogen and phosphate fertilizers, which encourage the growth of algae – this in turn blocks sunlight and fouls the water, while decomposing bacteria consumes oxygen, killing fish. The Thames became an open sewer, bereft of wildlife, which London used for drinking water - cholera was rife.

One of the worst epidemics, in 1853, killed 10,000 – though small change now, when compared to Covid-19. It was believed that miasma from the Great Stink spread cholera, when in fact the true cause was bacteria in the water, not the odious stink. The 1858 "Great Stink" was not nearly as stinky as that caused by the Tory party in 2020, but we'll address that later. For back in 1858 the Londoners were reeling in the streets, scented lace handkerchiefs at nostrils, something must be done

"The book of nature which we have to read is written by the finger of God."

SIR MICHAEL FARADAY
(1791-1867), founder of
Electronics and Electro-magnetics

With
Pen
in Hand

"I traversed today by steamboat the space between London and Hungerford Bridges, between half-past one and two o'clock. It was low water, and I think the tide must have been near the turn. The appearance and smell of the water forced themselves at once on my attention. The whole of the river was an opaque, pale-brown fluid.

In order to test the degree of opacity, I tore up some white cards into pieces, then moistened them, so as to make them sink easily below the surface, then dropped some of these pieces into the water at every pier the boat came to.

Before they had sunk an inch below the surface they were undistinguishable, though the sun shone brightly at the time; when pieces fell edgeways the lower part was hidden from sight before the upper part was under water. This happened at St. Paul's Wharf, Blackfriars

Bridge, Temple Wharf, and Southwark Bridge. Near the bridges, the feculence rolled up in clouds so dense that they were visible at the surface, even in water of this kind. The smell was very bad and, common to the whole of the water, it was the same as that which comes up from the stinking gully holes in the streets.

Having just returned from the country air, I was perhaps more affected by the smell than others, but I do not think that I could have gone on to Lambeth or Chelsea, and I was glad to enter the streets for an atmosphere which, except near the stink-holes, I found much sweeter than on the river.

I have thought it a duty to record these facts, that they may be brought to the attention of those who exercise power, or have responsibility in relation rivers. There is nothing figurative in the words I employed, or any exaggeration. They are the simple truth.

Professor Michael Faraday, Royal Institute

FLVM'N' · VINC'LA · P°SV'T

Sir JOSEPH BAZALGETTE cb
Engineer of the London Main Drainage System
And of this Embankment

FIRST FATBERG FIGHTER

Sir Joseph William Bazalgette.

28 March 1819 – 15 March 1891.

Also designed Hammersmith Bridge.

So, engineer Joseph Bazalgette was called in by city planners to create an underground complex of sewers, to divert the sewage flowing through London. Bazalgette and his team built 82 miles of intercepting sewers, parallel to the River Thames, and 1,100 miles of street sewers at a cost of £4.2m. Work started on the scheme in 1859 and was complete by 1868.

It was a major achievement for its time, as there were few Polish workers around in those days; Bazalgette drove his drunken Irish slave labourers to the very limit! 318 million bricks were used to create the underground sewage system, and more than 2.5 million cubic metres of earth were dug up. Originally built to serve two-and-a-half million people, the sewers served four million by completion.

Joseph Bazalgette's prescience may be seen in the diameter of the sewers, for he doubled the necessary diameter, his foresight allowing for an unforeseen increase in population density, with the introduction of the tower block.

With the original planned pipe diameter, London sewers would have already overflowed in the 1960s, rather than coping until the present day as they have. Then came a major increase in plastic usage, which created gigantic fatbergs.

Quarried under Whitechapel in 2010, and named for London's mayor at the time, the Boris Johnson Tunnel proved too narrow, just as Professor Watercloset had warned, now the tunnel was blocked.

So, the Fatberg Autopsy continued.

"Look: a whole KitKat! Time for a break," Harry Hack cackled. He was a big Boris fan.

"I wonder if he'll eat it," Evil Neville boomed, in his clarion Brian Blessed voice, and they all laughed as they examined the fatberg, which exuded a Great Stink of its own. The KitKat was safe.

Across the U.K., the cost to extract fatbergs exceeds £80m a year. Taking a closer look at the putrefying beast was a smelly business, but it offered clues to Londoners' habits, which could perhaps lead to solutions.

London Water was tasked with extracting the sludgy behemoth, and publicity hungry journalist Harry Hack arranged for British Broadminded Television to film the autopsy.

In the dank, smelly basement of B.B.T. Head Office, teams dissected segments of the Whitechapel fatberg as if it were a subterranean cadaver. In front of B.B.T. cameras, scientists sorted syringes and mangled plastic into trays; the sewers of iconic sewage-seer Joseph Bazalgette were revealing their smelly secrets.

Modern-day Bazalgettes named Peter Watercloset and Zee Garbo, as well as to the myopic media journalist Harry Hack were fascinated by the autopsy. As a top London news reporter, Harry Hack had a probing investigative mind.

"This is interesting," Harry Hack chirped, as he gingerly fished out a used condom.

"Why not try it on, Harry?" Came the barb from Evil Neville, as Harry poked around in the stinking morass, more interested in finding unusual items than in scientific research.

"Ah! A syringe! A bloody sanitary pad!" So it went, as they dissected the fatberg, and Dr. Zee Garbo turned her pert nose up in disdain – not at the smelly fatberg, but at Harry. As they analysed the contents of the supersize fatberg, discovered beneath the streets of Whitechapel in east London. They discovered that cooking fat was the biggest contributor, making up 90% of the sample.

"The fat sticks to sides of the pipe, then plastic wet wipes come down and stick to the fat. Other fat comes down and sticks to the wet wipes, and that adds to the mass of the Fatberg," Professor Peter Watercloset explained to the layman, Evil Neville. It was true that plastic was the main catalyst for fatbergs. Typical items found in the fatberg included condoms, sanitary towels, nappies, cotton buds and wet wipes, all of which had some form of plastic base.

"Some wet wipes, including brands labelled as 'flushable', are unable to disintegrate in a sewer," Doctor. Zee Garbo observed.

"Manufacturers don't follow the rules," she lamented, and the media were tardy in spreading the message. She then glanced meaningfully at Harry Hack, feeling that B.B.T. Television could be a help in spreading the message: *"Don't dispose of plastic in toilets."* But, Harry Hack seemed more interested in finding odd items?

"Look, a huge dildo!" Harry cried.

Then, fearfully, he said: "The fatberg moved!"

This caused Professor Watercloset to look more closely at the quivering Brown Blob oozing from the fatberg. It did indeed seem to be twitching, and there was a faint, green mist rising from it.

"There are life forms in the sewers. I wonder if it's possible…" the professor mused.

"Please, Peter, you're letting your wild imagination off the leash again," Harry Hack chortled.

The professor said no more, but Dr. Zee Garbo could see that he was worried: was it possible that life was forming? The chemical composition of the fatberg naturally showed most street drugs, but also a high concentration of prohibited gym supplements: there was evidence of Hordenine and Asterix, which can be found in performance-enhancing sports drugs.

Professor Watercloset separated the Brown Blob which oozed from the fatberg, and placed it in a bowl for a separate study; he was convinced it was a rudimentary life form. Water is a basic requirement for life to arise – any life based on molecules requires a liquid solvent to move them around – and there was plenty of water in the sewers.

Water has many unique physical and chemical properties, which makes it well suited to support the complex chemistry required for life. Sadly, there was presently a lower life form interrupting the study: the giggling idiot Harry Hack kept thrusting his dildo under the nose of Evil Neville; the journalist was close to getting a clout from Neville's walking stick. They finished the autopsy and, after ditching uncouth journalist Harry Hack, the other three repaired to a nearby coffee shop for a civilized chat.

"Why did you decide to come out of retirement, Peter?" Zee Garbo asked, curiously. Peter had retired from university lecturing, to settle into a retirement in the comfy Whitechapel Bright Side Suites.

"The advent of a fatberg fascinated me," Professor Watercloset confessed, with a smile.

"Must be the smell," Evil Neville put in, and they both laughed. Peter and Zee were professionals, used to the smell. Lovely Doctor Zee Garbo attending the fatberg autopsy had been a motivator to attend.

Peter studied her as she sipped coffee. She was a

woman in her sixties, who had retained the beauty of youth; the few lines in her face conferred character not age. They were kindred souls, neither had married, choosing instead to devote their lives to studying sewage. Peter Watercloset was intensely attracted to Dr. Zee Garbo, but the long distance between Poland and England thwarted any serious relationship.

Now Zee was seconded to the London Water Board, so the two sewage experts had run into each other at *Exercise Cygnus,* held at the Imperial College, in London. Professor Watercloset and Dr. Zee Garbo had struck up a close friendship, after they both attended the conference of epidemiologists, to study what Britain would look like seven weeks into a pandemic. The study, codenamed *"Exercise Cygnus",* was a three-day, cross-government practice run, it found that Britain would be overwhelmed by a pandemic. The exercise flagged a shortage of personal protective equipment, morgue capacity and critical care beds,

"The UK's preparedness and response, in terms of its policies and capability, is currently not sufficient to cope with extreme demands of a severe pandemic, that will have a nationwide impact across all sectors." Exercise Cygnus.

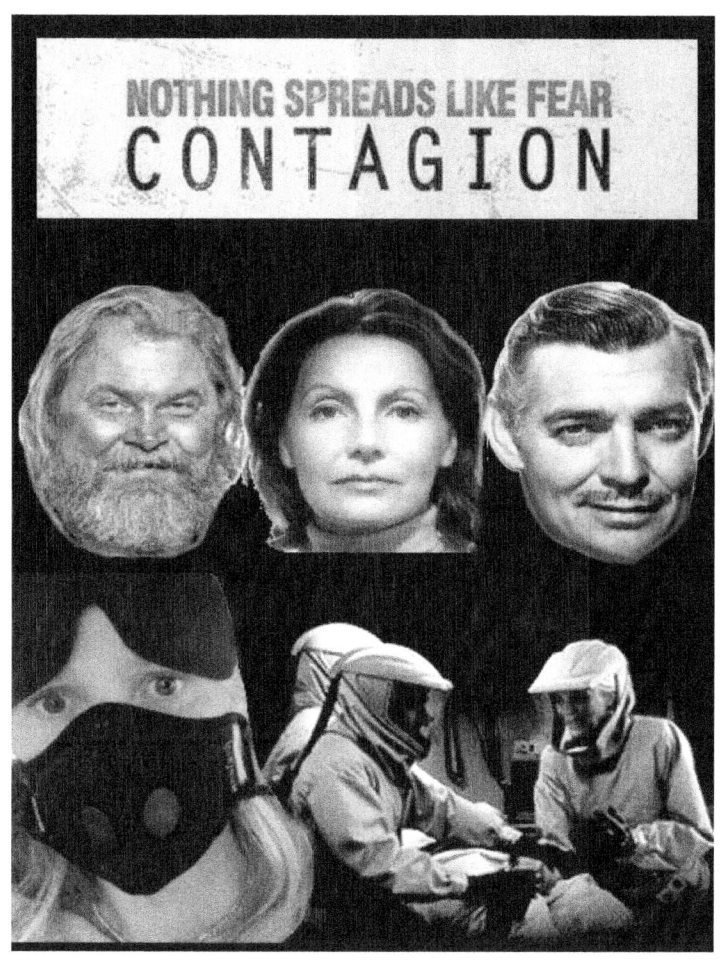

Coinciding with *Exercise Cygnus* was the film *Contagion.* Little did our heroes know back then that they'd be leading stars in a future real-life pandemic, which would echo the thriller, that charted transmission of a virus across the globe, as scientists sought a vaccine to avoid a total economic meltdown. In 2021, Gwyneth Paltrow would share an inflight snap on Instagram, well masked up and joking about her role in the 2011 film *Contagion,* which had been eerily prescient. While *Exercise Cygnus* revealed to government that a pandemic would bring the N.H.S. to its knees. Social care was a particular area of concern, as care homes are mostly privately run, making it difficult to test patients moving from hospital to care homes, in order to clear hospital beds.

Exercise Cygnus had critically established that, with a pandemic, governments must move quickly to lock down, or the virus may spiral out of control, so the Cygnus findings were handed to the Conservative Party government. The ruling party was also known as "Tories", a word derived from the Irish *tóraidhe*, meaning "pursue", which was given to the royalist cavaliers of King Charles I, fleeing roundhead troops during the 1649 occupation of Ireland by Oliver Cromwell. Before the end of the book, Tories would be hotly pursued by all three of our heroes, when living fatberg Boris Johnson ignored the research of *Exercise Cygnus* and turned his country into a sewerland. Fortunately for the world, Professor Watercloset would stumble over the *"Covid-19 Prophecy"*, providing clues to stamp out the pandemic and the living fatberg nightmare, along with inept politicians who failed to control both. Someone had to seize the reins, for venal politicians like Boris Johnson would prove woefully incapable of saving his people in a time of great danger, and Professor Peter and Doctor Zee would emerge as heroes. Despite the mutual attraction, they kept it strictly professional, as they chatted over coffee and explored the idea Peter had ventured during the autopsy. It seemed farfetched, but the Whitechapel sewers were a strange place, hence the many legends.

"Do you really think that the fatberg could assume a life form?" Evil Neville asked, for the implications were immense. The professor thought long and hard before he answered.

"Well, obviously not intelligent life, but there are

25

many life forms in sewers," Peter replied, carefully. What worried him was the performance-enhancing sports supplements Hordenine and Asterix.

"Hordenine and Asterix represented more than half of the pharmaceuticals we found in the fatberg sample," Peter Watercloset pointed out, worriedly. Asterix is used for muscle gain, and is on the World Anti-Doping Agency's prohibited list. Dr. Zee Garbo echoed his concerns, for she was a trained chemist.

"Asterix could promote lipids in the membranes of bacteria, made up of straight-chain fatty acids, which are ester-linked to a backbone of glycerol-3-phosphate. The lipids in the archaeal membrane could grow a backbone of glycerol-1-phosphate linked to isoprenoids." It was extremely scientific, but actually true. At this, Evil Neville raised his hands and said: "I'm off, folks. This is out of my league." Evil was a biker, not a scientist. As he picked up his cane and left, Peter continued with Zee.

"Scientists from the University of Groningen and Wageningen University have created the life form you mention, with a mixed membrane, yet they discovered it stayed stable." They sat silent for a while, as they absorbed the implications.

Was it an exaggeration to say that London was under dire threat? As Harry Hack had observed, the prospect seemed laughable. Yet, fatbergs coming alive and attacking the city was not what worried them; Peter had stated that intelligent life forming was unlikely. But, the fatberg had oozed a brown substance emitting an eerie, greenish hue. This iridescent green sheen could be an atavistic substitute for sunlight, the source of energy for life on Earth, like a monster blind worm the Brown Blob might develop, then seek to escape the sewer.

"Something to think about," Zee worried.

Unlike short-sighted journalist Harry Hack, Dr. Zee did not sneeringly laugh off the concerns of Professor Peter Watercloset, the doctor was an intelligent woman. While Harry Hack gave himself great airs, but he was in fact a clown – even his Savile Row suit could not disguise this.

Peter and Zee parted company and he drove through the suburbs of Whitechapel, to the luxury Bright Side Suites in Ripper Street. He'd purchased an apartment there because he loved the area. It was vibrant and animated, with a pulse of life which belied its dark history, like the infamous murders of Jack the Ripper in the late 1880s. In the latter half of the 20th century Whitechapel become a Bangladeshi suburb, bringing a new ambiance to the area, which became famous for Bangladeshi restaurants.

Every April, the Bangladeshi community held a *Boishakhi Mela Fair* for Bengali New Year, and a popular *Curry Festival* every September. But, the 1970s and '80s saw a massive decline in Whitechapel, due to the closure of the docks; it slumped into becoming an area with high poverty rates, accompanied by unbridled crime. *The Blind Beggar* pub is where Ronnie Kray murdered George Cornell in front of witnesses, and was also the location of William Booth's first sermon, which led to the creation of the Salvation Army, who assisted the poverty-stricken.

Then, another salvation fortuitously arrived, when the Crossrail train line was announced and a flurry of construction projects kicked off. Whitechapel was due to become an important transport hub, so hardworking Polish tradesmen set to work, and Whitechapel Station was renewed for Crossrail. Royal London Hospital also closed, then reopened behind the original site, in a brand-new building costing £650m; the old site was repurchased by the council to open a new town hall.

Whitechapel today figures prominently in London's art scene, after the Whitechapel Art Gallery underwent a renovation with support of £3.26m from the Heritage Lottery Fund. As the neighbourhood improved, it gained citywide and even international visibility. By the early twenty-first century, Whitechapel began to figure prominently in London's punk rock/skuzz movement. The main focal point for this scene was the Rhythm Factory bar/restaurant nightclub. This scene included musicians the likes of

The Libertines, Zap!, Nova and Razorlight. Now the area, with its art and music scene that Peter Watercloset loved so dearly, was under threat from an invasion of fatbergs, and the professor was determined to do something about it. Harry Hack of B.B.T. Television had asked Peter to appear on his interview show, *Hurt Talk*, Peter accepted the invite encouraged by Evil Neville.

"Get onto the T.V. and tell your story," he boomed. Evil Neville was a Scotsman, with a voice designed to carry over the Highlands without benefit of audio electronics. Yet, the legendary biker was a man of rare good sense. A friendly neighbour at Bright Side Suites, he often came over, to chat with his good friend Professor Watercloset. The sensible Dr. Zee Garbo also felt that Professor Watercloset should appear on *Hurt Talk*, so Peter took their advice, but he would come to regret it.

British Broadminded Television was housed at the top end of Ripper Street, where Peter lived, for B.B.T. had taken over the old Abbey Mills pumping station.

They picked up the abandoned pump station for a song, refurbished the upper floors for offices and studios, and made money on the side by hiring out the basement section for film sets. The spooky appearance of the building and the slight rotten eggs smell, made the ancient structure an ideal location for modern journalism, and also for Hollywood scary movies which was rather ironic.

In the 2005 movie *Batman Begins*, Arkham Asylum was actually Abbey Mills pump station. Designed by Joseph Bazalgette and built in 1865, with its elaborate, Byzantine-style architecture, the pump station was called the "Cathedral of Sewage". The rotten eggs smell in the B.B.T. building arose from the basement, where manholes still led down to the ancient sewers. It was in this basement that the fatberg autopsy had been carried out.

Now a journalistic sewage smell would be exuded, for another type of autopsy was about to begin: one where top dog interviewer Harry Hack took Professor Watercloset apart. Peter was filled with trepidation as he approached the B.B.T. building, for it was a foreboding place, with tendrils of green mist arising from the ground. Yet Peter was cheered by the thought that he would bring truth to the TV viewers of Britain, why should they remain innocent of what lurks in the shadows, how can they live in the world if they don't understand how dark and brutal it can be. That was his inspiration, but the cynical Harry Hack of B.B.T would soon quench his ardor.

B.B.T. Television

Harry Hack shuffled down the gloomy corridor of B.B.T studios, and was almost knocked down by a slavering, white-haired old man, chasing a terrified young girl down the corridor,

"Uncle Jimmy so loves children," Harry gushed.

"If they're old enough to bleed, then they're old enough to stab," Sir Jimmy giggled evilly, as he cornered the screaming girl. He was a renowned wit and completely open about his paedophilia, because Sir Jimmy Savile was a neoliberal hero and therefore untouchable. Though Harry Hack was the razor-sharp host of *Hurt Talk,* the T.V. interview show where guests were known to wet their pants, Harry refused to believe the rumours cascading around Sir Jimmy. The British tradition of the protectors of free speech also being the censors of speech was long-established, so the liberal media swung in behind Sir Jimmy and fiercely protected him. Neoliberals were the modern, landed gentry of Great Britain. The prophetic novel *Animal Farm* described it thus: *"All people are equal, but some more equal than most."* The great English writer George Orwell was born among the English liberals – instructive for a writer or animal?

"No one believes more than Comrade Napoleon that all animals are equal. He would be only too happy to let you make your decisions for yourselves. But, sometimes you might make the wrong decisions, then where would we be?"

So, Harry Hack ignored the screaming girl being hotly pursued by Sir Jimmy; he had more pressing matters on his mind. For, Harry was about to conduct a truly bizarre interview. That blithering idiot Peter Watercloset wanted to air his views on *Hurt Talk*. The subject of fatbergs coming alive should be good for a belly laugh, and Harry wanted to make the best of it. As one the station's top hatchet men, Harry Hack usually made mincemeat of his guests, and this was an opportunity to show his mettle. Hack thought on it as he leant over the coffee machine, his baggy trousers hung like coal sacks off his bum, while his scruffy jacket scrunched up into a sort of tweed brassiere. Harry was the type of man you could dress in a Savile Row suit yet he'd still resemble a Whitechapel urchin, and his manners were as shoddy as his clothes – as he now demonstrated in his opening of the fatberg interview. Professor Peter Watercloset was a highly distinguished man, so he needed to be taken down a peg, and interviewer Harry Hack specialized in unpegging people.

"Sooo, Professor, you are saying that the fatbergs under Whitechapel will spring to life and attack thousands of people, wiping out the population of London, or perhaps even Britain?" As was his wont, Harry Hack started *Hurt Talk* with his usual gross exaggeration and icy sneering sarcasm. Professor Peter Watercloset realized immediately that he'd made a mistake in agreeing to the interview, as the professor tried to introduce some logic to doubting Harry. It was like feeding pearls to a drunken swine, what Harry Hack didn't understand didn't exist, and that included a mountain of things for the TV journalist wasn't the brightest of men.

"I'm not saying a 130-tonne fatberg will come to life, but its chemical composition could possibly spawn a smaller life form," Peter hedged. What worried him was the performance-enhancing sports supplements in the fatberg. "Hordenine and Asterix chemicals represented over half of the pharmaceuticals we found in the fatberg during the autopsy," Professor Peter ventured, tentatively.

"They are just dead chemicals," Harry sneered.

The professor tried again: "Asterix is used for muscle gain, so there's a possibility it may bind to an androgen receptor, thereby creating selective anabolic activity as a result." The professor explained his concerns rather lucidly, but Harry Hack was not impressed. He put his head back, guffawed, then snarled back, nastily.

"Big words, Prof, covering small ideas," Harry sneered, and the liberal London audience lapped it up, watching Harry mock bigshots.

The loud laughter rankled but Peter kept cool. "The chemical Asterix promotes muscle growth. If it can intensify protein synthesis and build muscles, then it could possibly kick-start a life form."

Seeing that he was momentarily out of his depth, Harry Hack turned to his lapdog audience. "Any comments on this utter claptrap?"

"LET THE PROFESSOR TALK!"

For a moment, Harry Hack thought Brian Blessed was in the crowd, but it was Evil Neville, with Dr. Garbo. The boom handler approached with a mike, which Evil Neville didn't really need.

"Professor Watercloset is correct in his assumptions. Bodybuilders have proved that the chemical Asterix can improve lean muscle mass. It also exhibits an acid-base effect, which allows it to bond with carbon and make amino acid – nucleobases which build D.N.A. and R.N.A." The heart of Peter Watercloset leapt, for the speaker was none other than the beautiful Dr. Zee Garbo, so Harry turned to ridicule and mockery. "Maybe Fatberg the Ripper will strike, or the Black Sewer Swine will escape." Harry switched the interview into burlesque comedy, by quoting Whitechapel urban legends.

Perhaps Harry Hack's behaviour was a result of his father being an anarchist, which had an opposite impact on the son who toadied to any form of authority. Harry had worked in television all his life, and he viewed B.B.T. with a religious reverence. Highlights of Harry's luminous career included numerous attempts on his life, and being punched in the stomach by then Prime Minister Harry Wilson; in truth, there was something so "hittable" about Harry.

"I can't stand the bugger," Wilson had snarled.

This type of violent dislike had dogged Hack, especially during his service as a war correspondent. In 1989, he avoided bullets at the Beijing Tiananmen Square massacre, and in 2003 Harry was badly injured in Iraq, when a U.S. warplane deliberately bombed him. Yet, Harry Hack was unafraid of attacks directed at him. He laughed in the face of danger, because Harry admitted to using hallucinogenic drugs, in fact he was high as a kite at the interview. After the show he rushed to his dressing room, which was better stocked than your average chemist, the mind-blowing drugs gave him a really hazy view on life. He passed a studio from where *Jim'll Fix It* was broadcast, and Harry momentarily paused. Because Cub Scouts were being featured and Harry had once been a Cub himself. Sir Jimmy had finished with the girl and now concentrated on the boys, who were crouched in a ritual circle, while chanting the traditional pledge to Akela – the wolf pack leader in Rudyard Kipling's *Jungle Book* – adopted worldwide by the Cubs as their war cry. Akela is also the name of a well-known dog food, which those poor Cub Scouts actually were, under the artful ministrations of the perverted Sir Jimmy Savile.

The wolf howl at the end was Sir Jimmy's own idea, and just to make sure the Cubs hit the right pitch for the howl, Sir Jimmy would crouch and squeeze their tender testicles. As you can see in the adjacent picture, the technique worked perfectly to perfect the howl, although Cub Master Jimmy may have had other motives – he was a depraved sort of fellow.

I'll do my best, Akela!!

Howooooooooooooooooooooooo!"

The renowned journalist Harry Hack watched entranced at his hero Jim "fixing it". Harry was a great fan, for Sir Jimmy was a national icon, which is why the scurrilous rumors really irritated Harry. *Jealousy makes you nasty,* Harry Hack thought.

He respected Uncle Jimmy's work with the Cubs. Harry had been a Cub Scout himself. In fact, Harry had risen to the lofty position of Queen's Scout, and not many boys achieve that.

Harry Hack was a British T.V. correspondent from the old school; it had been a long time since Harry attended school, but the iron rules of English schools were deeply embedded. Harry Hack was there wherever the news presented itself, no matter what the danger was; he was that type of drugged-up Englishman. Harry Hack had been trained in the school of hard knocks, as a Queen's Scout, he had once actually been presented to the Queen.

Sadly, on the greatest day of his young life, the fly buttons on his trousers were open. The shame of that still haunts Harry Hack to this day, the newspaper photo clearly showed his open fly and the look of disgust on the Queen's face, for his soiled underpants were truly repulsive to look upon. The young Harry Hack had forgotten the Scouts' motto, *"Be Prepared"*. In 1907, Baden-Powell, an English soldier devised the Scout motto: *"Be Prepared"*. He published it in *Scouting for Boys* in 1908, Baden-Powell wrote that Scouts must *always be in a state of readiness in mind and body to do your duty.* After the open fly episode, the motto was now engraved on Harry Hack's memory, every journalistic assignment was planned with military precision. This famed war correspondent was now always prepared, he adjusted his World War II German helmet in the mirror, put on his body armour with the many patched holes. Harry Hack was ready for action.

"We're covering Chelsea Flower Show, Harry" his cameraman sighed, noting the patched body armour, it was bloody ridiculous.

"TERRORISTS ARE EVERYWHERE!" Harry hollered. This war correspondent was fully prepared; never again would Harry Hack be caught short; he had learned his bitter lesson.

Ever since those supposed cross-coordinates and missile strike in Iraq, Harry took no chances, and even wore body armour in the bogs. Assassins were everywhere! For, Harry Hack was not just an interviewer, but a behind-the-lines war correspondent, in the fashion of Winston Churchill. Just like his hero Boris Johnson, he considered himself a modern-day Winston Churchill, who was Harry's role model. He twisted the speeches of Churchill to present him as a Euro-sceptic Brexit imperialist, and moulded himself on his hero.

Just like Churchill penetrated Boer lines in South Africa, Harry infiltrated enemy lines in Zimbabwe, to bring news to censored B.B.T. viewers. The Zimbabwe regime had banned British Broadminded Television, so Harry the spy blacked his face and entered Zimbabwe disguised as a ZANU war veteran. But, when he opened his mouth and spoke Queen's English, in his fruity accent. Harry was mistaken for Robert Mugabe, the Anglophile dictator, and badly beaten by an enraged mob.

To honour his fearless reporting, Harry Hack was granted the Royal Garter of Heinous Hacks. This was a high honour indeed, for the award was presented by

Queen Elizabeth herself. Branded on his memory was the fiasco of his previous royal appointment, this time Harry prepared meticulously for the high point of his career; on no account must there be a repeat of the infamous "open fly" incident. The Royal Garter of Heinous Hacks was a great honour, the celebrated war correspondent nervously checked his fly for the umpteenth time, brushed his teeth until his gums flowed blood. He even changed his tighty-once-whitey undies, a rare occurrence for Dirty Harry.

As 'fountain of honour' in Great Britain, the Queen has the sole right of conferring titles of honour, in public recognition of service. There are many awards but the Royal Garter of Heinous Hacks, has been blown up by journalists as greater than the Victoria Cross. Harry stood proudly in Buckingham Palace – a genuine war hero, about to be honoured for courage under the boot – and this time Harry had everything under iron control. Harry Hack glanced around at the royal portals and his heart pumped with pride, to think that he was the centre of attention in this magnificent place. His hand surreptitiously swept down to his fly, to ensure that it was closed; it was safely shut, so he relaxed. He popped in another mouth mint for, like most newsmen, Harry suffered terribly from bad breath. Because everything that emerged from his mouth had a truly odiferous aroma, a smell very similar to a fatberg in fact?

The ceremonial Royal Garter of Heinous Hacks went off like clockwork… until Harry Hack bowed down to receive the traditional tapping of the sword on his shoulder, Her Majesty lifted the sword and the nervous Harry let out a resounding fart. And, by resounding, we mean really loud, like a yard of Velcro being ripped, or a sheet of bubble wrap torn apart. It clanged through the palace like a thunderclap. Harry crouched there, shamed and rooted in shock at his appalling blunder. Then Her Royal Majesty the Queen of England imperially took command.

"Stop that!" hissed Her Highness.

"Certainly, Mum, but which way did it go?" The shell-shocked Harry Hack blurted out.

The Harry Hack fart was the only recorded instance of someone farting in front of Her Majesty Queen Elizabeth II, but there are historic records of flatulence in the court of Queen Elizabeth I, who ruled from 1558 until her death on 24th March 1603. The most famous fart was emitted by the 17th Earl of Oxford, Edward de Vere: in making a low obeisance to his beloved Queen, he let out a resounding clapper.

Edward de Vere, Earl of Oxford
* * *
12 April 1550 – 24 June 1604

FARTYPANTS

Poor Edward de Vere was so abashed, he went to travel for seven years. On his return, the Queen said: "My lord, I had quite forgotten the fart." Queen Elizabeth I was forgiving about farts. When an archbishop let one rip, and in a panic coughed and dragged a foot across the carpet, Queen Elizabeth I responded magnificently:

"My lord, you needn't find a rhyme."

Rumours abounded that Sir Walter Raleigh was much admired in the court, for the awe-inspiring explosiveness of his farts, which Elizabeth and her courtiers found absolutely hilarious.

Yet, the British press studiously ignored the Harry Hack fart. In fact, I'll bet this is the first you heard about it. Besides, B.B.T. had no wish for the press to zone in on their affairs; there were matters the press had best ignore about the national broadcaster – and thus far they dutifully did, as is the U.K. media's manner. Yet a foul smell continued to hang around Jimmy Savile, the B.B.T. director who worked on *Jim'll Fix It* and *Top of the Pops* blew the whistle about Savile having sex with underage girls, but was blithely ignored. The director claimed that he walked into Savile's dressing room one day and caught him having sex with a "very, very young girl"; both quickly pulled up their pants, she was just one of many. The director reveals that his bosses just shrugged it off when he told them what he'd seen. He says it is wrong of B.B.T. executives to claim nobody knew what was going on, "everyone would've known about Savile."

There was a rank stink fouling B.B.T. – smellier than Harry Hack farting in front of the Queen, and the newspapers knew that was just the tip of the fatberg. Why did the Mayor of London not take a stand, British Broadminded Television headquarters are situated in London, at the end of the day they dell under the watch of Boris Johnson? Everybody in London knew of the depravities of Jimmy Savile, yet nobody had the guts to speak out, was Boris Johnson too busy covering up his own misbehavior?

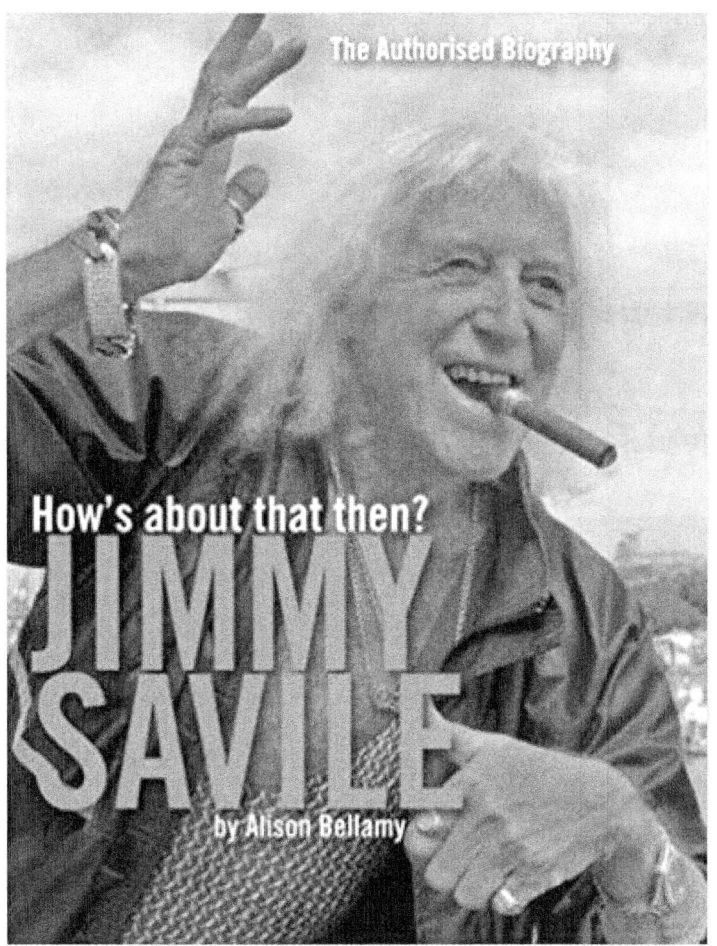

"*This is the remarkable story of a national icon, who appeals to people across all generations and from all walks of life. It is written by close friend Alison Bellamy, with the full support of Sir Jimmy's family and friends.*" 10 June 2012.

The cowardly London press shifted uneasily, for they knew British Broadminded Television were sinking into a Whitechapel sewerland. The women were competent professionals, but the men were international laughing stocks, yet two-thirds of the highest-paid stars were men? The corporation was stuffed with male prima donnas with gigantic egos, who demanded huge salaries, despite their pitiable incompetence.

"Ladies Last," was the B.B.T. credo. Arrogant stars like Harry Hack were paid millions – on average five times the salaries of women in comparable jobs, who were really more competent performers. British Broadminded Television worshipped misogyny religiously, and openly tolerated overt sexism toward women, it's no wonder starstruck children were treated as sex objects. When national broadcasters who are supposed to represent the people, cover up for individual deviants, then something is very wrong. What would it take to awake London, already there was an awful stink in the sewers?

2000 Savile interview by Louis Theroux.

Louis Theroux: *Jimmy, why do you say in interviews that you hate children?*

Jimmy Savile: *We live in a very funny world. It's easier for me, as a single man, to say "I don't like children." Obviously, I don't hate 'em.*

Louis Theroux: *Why would you say that, then?*

Jimmy Savile: *Because it puts a lot of salacious tabloid people off the hunt.*

Louis Theroux: *Are you saying: "Is he/isn't he a pedophile."*

Jimmy Savile: *Oh, aye, how do they know whether I am or not? How does anybody know whether I am? Nobody knows if I am or not. That's my policy and it's worked a dream.*

BBT
BRITISH BROADMINDED TELEVISION

£2.2 MILLION

£ HALF MILLION

IN BRITAIN A WOMAN BELONGS IN THE HOME

 £16,513

Pay gap for CEOs & Directors

54% of male senior managers received a bonus	38% of female senior managers received a bonus
£22,687 average bonus for senior men	£13,699 average bonus for senior women

British Broadminded Television were engulfed by scandal upon shame; a tsunami of disgrace where minor personalities acted like demi-gods. For the scandals had spread internationally, when on a popular quiz show witty panelists joked about the atom bomb attack on Hiroshima, forcing management to issue an apology to Japan.

This was followed by a gaffe from motoring show *Low Gear*, where hosts called Asians "slopes" and African Americans "niggers"; when a producer dared to object, he was badly beaten up by a thuggish presenter. Amazingly, the station bosses tolerated this thuggery, and *Low Gear* motored merrily on, an ode to egoïstic liberal behaviour.

Boorishness was one thing but paedophilia another, B.B.T. staffers were becoming increasingly uneasy, with Uncle Jimmy and his perverse gang of paedophiles. Who openly raped innocent children, not only in T.V. studios but at hospitals, where Uncle Jimmy did charity work. Then the seething volcano erupted, the Louis Theroux interview was followed by the shocking *Operation Yewtree* operation, how did it happen right under the nose of the British press?

Who were strictly regulated by a Press Complaints Commission; if there was a press cover-up for Jimmy Savile, the P.C.C. would crack down hard? Harry Hack comforted himself with that thought, but he really should have looked deeper, for matters were not really what they seemed in in the liberal kingdom of Sewerland.

Because in 2012, the Leveson Inquiry found gross irregularities in the British media. The P.C.C. was scrapped and replaced with a press regulator backed by law, and not dominated by censuring editors and newspaper owners, to prevent further unsavory Jimmy Savile-style cover-ups.

"The sinister fact about literary censorship in England is that it's largely voluntary. Unpopular ideas can be silenced and inconvenient facts kept dark, without the need for any official ban." George Orwell

The sad truth is that British Broadminded Television censored news, while proclaiming their belief in free speech. George Orwell put it succinctly;

in his novel *1984* he called it "doublespeak": *"the power of holding two contradictory beliefs in one's mind".* Orwell himself was adept at *doublespeak*, because he wrote out of his own experience, eventually becoming one of the liberal controllers. In 1949, George Orwell assisted Celia Kirwin of the Foreign Office in compiling a communist list, naming 37 writers and artists considered unsafe.

Including actors Charlie Chaplin and Michael Redgrave, along with Orwell's writing rival J.B. Priestley. In the forthcoming chapter *Covid-19 Prophecy,* Peter Watercloset combines Orwell books with a Gematria, to try break this censorship. For the tradition of protectors of free speech, also being censors of speech is long established in the UK, and sly B.B.T were experts at the art. When *Operation Yewtree* stunned the nation, there was no doubt that B.B.T. management had turned a blind eye, to the hundreds of paedophile sexual depredations.

"It's absolute nonsense! Sir Jimmy would never abuse children; he's a staunch Catholic!" Harry Hack defended his idol, for it was true that Sir Jimmy regularly attended confession – perhaps to swap contact details for underage girls with priests? The Catholic Church also turned a blind eye, the primate of the Catholic Church in England and Wales Cardinal Murphy O'Connor, acted like a *true* primate by protecting abusers. His Scottish counterpart Cardinal Keith O'Brien, was an outspoken critic of homosexuality, yet he abused young men in his service. While in Catholic Ireland, 35,000 children were sent to Church-run reformatories, where they were systematically abused.

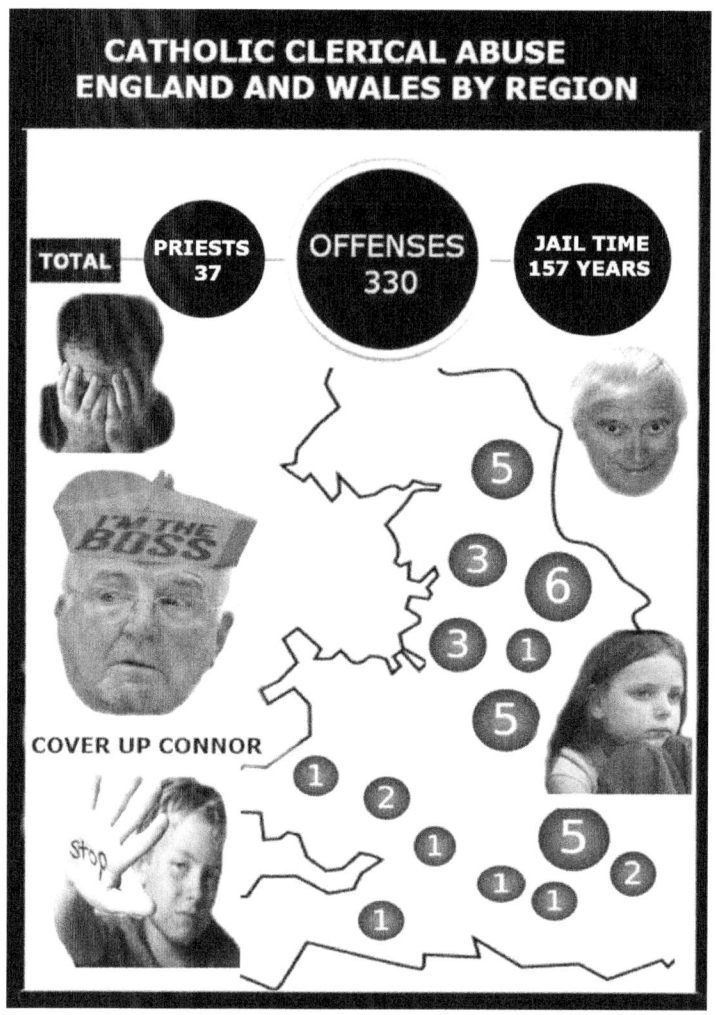

This map lists 37 cases of priests who committed sexual crimes against children, broken down by region, as defined by the *Roman Catholic Dioceses of England and Wales*. Yet, this falls far short of real numbers. Many claims never came to court, for some priests died and others absconded, or were deemed too old to stand trial in court.

The Church Office for Protection of Children and Vulnerable Adults (COPCA), has to date detailed 302 sex abuse allegations made to the Church since 2003, so covering up is an established Catholic practice. Apostle Paul noted that it was better to marry than burn, Cardinal Murphy O'Connor would have done well to teach this, rather than protect unmarried priests who vent frustrations on children.

Yet the Anglican Church, where priests are allowed to marry, appear to share the same predilection as Catholic priests. It would take until 2018 for the Archbishop of Canterbury to initiate an inquiry into the sexual abuse of children within the Church of England. The inquiry is currently considering the case of Peter Ball, the late Bishop of Gloucester, and investigating whether there were inappropriate attempts by people of prominence to interfere in the criminal justice process, after Peter Ball was first accused of child sexual offences.

16/11/93 - Ball to Charles
Life continues to be pretty nasty for me for it seems that my accusers still want to continue their malicious campaign. Luckily they are beginning to show some of their fraudulent plans.

11/12/94 - Charles to Ball
I saw the Archbishop the other day and he told me he is trying to bring you back to a public ministry. I do hope this will be all right and suit you, if and when it happens...

A bishop must be blameless, the husband of one wife, vigilant, sober, of good behaviour, hospitable, apt to teach."

1 Timothy 3:2.

Bishop Peter Ball was imprisoned for sexual abuse of eighteen young men, and the present

Archbishop of Canterbury, Justin Welby, has asked former Archbishop George Carey to leave the ministry, due to his handling of the case. While shamefaced Prince Charles admits he should rather have defended Sir Cliff Richard.

All of this British Broadminded Television were blissfully unaware of, until *Operation Yewtree* began in 2010 and dozens of B.B.T. staffers were charged, only then did the arrogant TV station realize the sewerland they were now in. In a desperate attempt to divert attention from the scandals, the beleaguered B.B.T. spent a total of £28m on silencing clauses in staff contracts. The Director-General was fired with a severance package of £1.3m; it seemed that B.B.T. rewarded people handsomely for failure?

So, to disprove this perception, the service set about sharpening the performance of their top stars. Harry Hack was their top earner as the host of *Hurt Talk,* which required a hard man as an interviewer, yet Harry bore the defeated look of a downtrodden Whitechapel tramp. For in truth the stations top journalist was a broken man, the growing revelations about Jimmy Savile shook him, for Harry genuinely believed the shocking rumors were false.

Surely the Press Complaints Commission, would crack down on any press cover-up, but the 2012 Leveson Inquiry revealed the P.C.C to be as effective as blind, toothless sheep. What then of the esteemed Catholic Church, his hero Sir Jimmy was a committed Catholic, which didn't mean that much? The host of *Hurt Talk* slouched around like a beaten dog, and his interviews were now tame and listless.

B.B.T dressed Harry in severe suits topped by military-striped neckties, and layered mascara around his eyes to make him look fiercer. But, Harry still resembled a benign Billingsgate fish porter.

"It's hopeless," management muttered.

Then, advertising came up with a dazzling advert which would make Harry Hack look far fiercer: the idea was to run a backdrop of large animals fighting, with Harry Hack standing in the foreground, with a ferocious look on his face.

"Ready, Harry," his cameraman advised, as two bison viciously cracked heads in the background, and Harry Hack frowned fiercely in the foreground.

"If you gotta go, GO!" the cameraman sighed.

"Go where?" a perplexed Harry queried.

"To the bogs, you look like you're dying to pee."

They then tried it with two lions scrapping, while Harry Hack did his killer look. "How's that, eh?" Harry gasped proudly, as he screwed his eyes into a murderous expression, clenched his teeth until his fillings ached… then let out a loud fart.

"Almost, Harry; just a bit fiercer!" the cameraman cajoled, and Harry Hack let rip. "Fierce" was too weak an adjective to describe the look on his contorted face. In fact, two typists walking by fainted when they saw Harry's fierce face.

"How's that for fierce?" Harry gasped.

"Especially the fierce smell, Harry," the cameraman gagged, pinching his nose as the rank smell hit him, while fierce Harry Hack walked bow-legged but proud to the bogs.

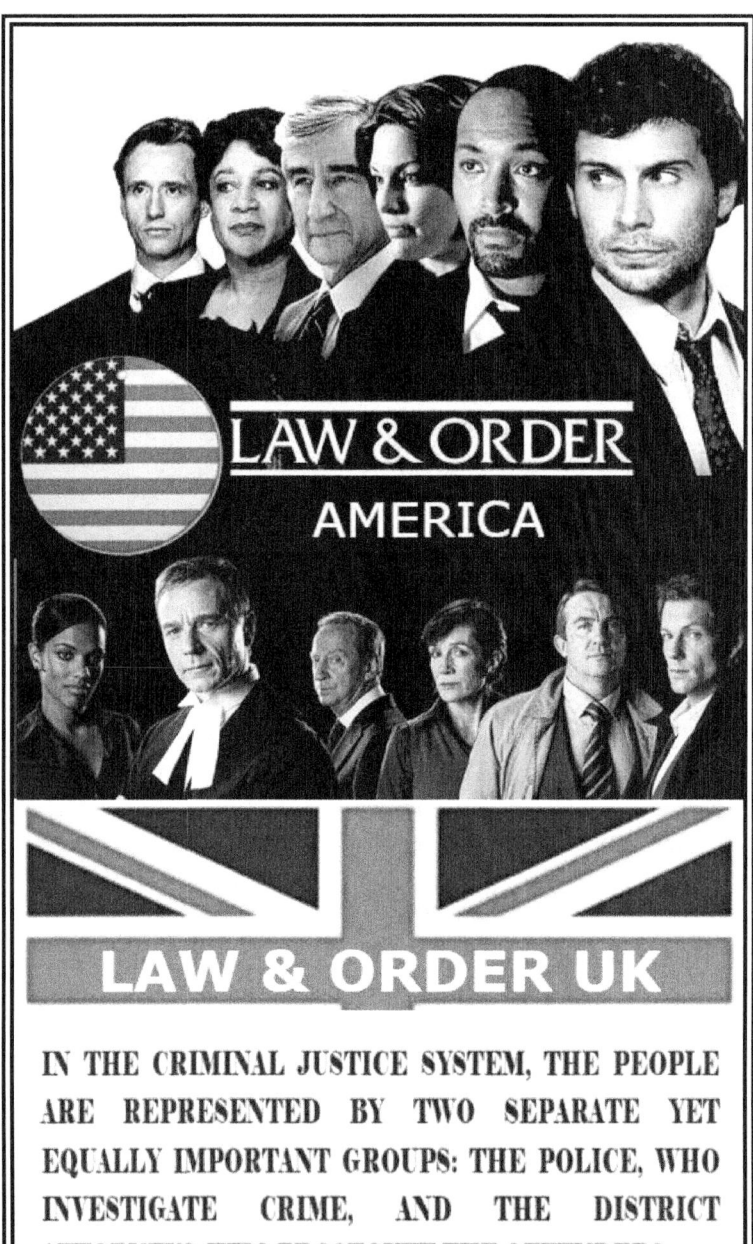

IN THE CRIMINAL JUSTICE SYSTEM, THE PEOPLE ARE REPRESENTED BY TWO SEPARATE YET EQUALLY IMPORTANT GROUPS: THE POLICE, WHO INVESTIGATE CRIME, AND THE DISTRICT ATTORNEYS, WHO PROSECUTE THE OFFENDERS.

Halls of Justice

Law & Order is a television franchise created by Dick Wolf, originally broadcast on the American *N.B.C.* channel; all of the shows deal with some aspect of criminal justice. In 2019, the U.S. hit show *Law & Order: SVU* announced its 21st season, which made this sex crimes series the longest-running live-action series in history, for *SVU* overtook *Gunsmoke* and *Law & Order*, which both ran for 20 seasons. In 2009, *Law & Order U.K.* kicked off and ran until 2014. It was the first American drama television series to be adapted for British television, with scripts copied from the parent series.

All the various franchises share the principle that the law belongs in the hands of police and prosecutors, and not pretentious entities like British Broadminded Television. To avoid intrusion, there's a "sub judice law" regulating the publication of matters under consideration by a court. This prevents pushy politicians or arrogant journalists from becoming judges, and triggering a breakdown of law and order. Yet, as the comedian Lenny Bruce once observed, *"in the halls of justice, the only justice is often in the halls,"* and so it sometimes is.

The head of the Crown Prosecution Service in Britain was Keir Starmer (Q.C.); he would hold this role from 2008 to 2013, and for his fine work be appointed Knight Commander of Bath in the 2014 New Year Honours List. He would then be elected as an M.P. to the House of Commons in the 2015 general election, and thereafter play a vital role in this book – but we're getting a bit ahead of ourselves.

For, right now, a fatberg threatened London, so Dr. Zee Garbo and Professor Watercloset approached the courts, to force the myopic mayor Boris Johnson to act. When invoking a public interest matter, the credentials of those making assertions are vital, and in this regard the two applicants were supremely qualified; that they were acting in the public interest was also established, as there was a great danger. Yet, getting the courts to act on a matter of public interest was a time consuming and costly business, and the two fatberg fighters did not have unlimited funds.

Professor Watercloset and Dr. Garbo received no succour from the courts, so they took the advice of comedian Lenny Bruce, and sought assistance in the halls of justice – where, curiously, they found a loyal Scots ally. For, an unusual man is about to enter the story, without whom it would not have continued...

Britain does not have a written constitution, like America, so English law develops from decisions of courts, which set "precedents" binding future decisions. If Jimmy Savile stood in the dock, he may have received 100 life sentences; a precedent set by judges is a life sentence for each victim. Savile could have been stopped if police had acted earlier, the official report into what police knew and critically failed to do makes for rather grim reading. Despite 450 police reports and the revealing Louis Theroux interview, the police claimed there were only seven potentially actionable cases. Yet, there was a long list of complaints from people who tried to report Savile, but failed to get the police to record their reports. Had the police joined B.B.T. and the Catholic Church in the Orwellian game of censorship?

The reluctance of police to act would be echoed in 2019, when devious Boris Johnson played fast and loose with the law – but that lies in the future. Let's get on with our sewer story, with Peter and Zee encountering a similar reluctance in the courts to force authorities to act against the deadly fatberg, and how in the halls of the courts Peter met a useful Scottish ally to assist them.

Professor Watercloset had been called upon to do jury service, which would grant an opportunity to observe the law and to meet a fellow crusader for justice. Peter was aware of gossip swirling around B.B.T., yet justice can only be affected when culprits are brought to book. There is an old saying in English law: *"Don't make a monkey of the law,"* which both Jimmy Savile and Boris Johnson did.

This monkey saying originated in the town of

Hartlepool when, back in the Napoleonic wars, a monkey was wrongfully convicted and unlawfully hanged by the English, which had a profound impact on English law. The essence of English common law is that it's made by judges sitting in courts, applying both common sense and knowledge of legal precedent (*stare decisis*), to the facts that are set before them.

Precedent is an extremely important foundation of English law, and the hanging of a monkey in Hartlepool established a vitally important legal precedent. The whole thing started when a wave of panic hit Britain during the 1850s, because the devious French had introduced the world's first ironclad warships, sparking fears of an imminent French invasion. Many ports were given naval gun batteries. Hartlepool got nine naval guns, which were placed at the Heugh; the nine-gun battery can still be viewed there today.

A psychosis of fear entered Hartlepool, as they waited fearfully for Napoleon Bonaparte to invade, which may have led to the unfortunate business with the French monkey, because the dark mood matched the great storm raging at sea. The children were all playing "catch boney" on the windblown Fish Sands of Hartlepool, while the fisherman debated if they should launch their boats, and brace the great storm raising massive waves.

Then, much to the delight of the Hartlepudlians, a huge, French ironclad warship named *Chasse Maree* foundered in the howling storm. All hands, as well as feet, were lost in the sinking, except for one lone survivor – but he didn't last too long. Resplendent in a blue French uniform, the ship's mascot washed up, coughing and spluttering on the English shore. Unfortunately for him, the mascot was a monkey.

Now, the Hartlepudlians didn't travel much, and they'd never seen a monkey before – nor even a Frenchman, for that matter – so they naturally assumed that the strange creature they captured must be an enemy French sailor (if you've ever seen a Frenchman, you'll understand the mistake). Although the monkey did not have a string of garlic around his neck, or the traditional black beret and striped T-shirt, the French facial features caused the tragic blunder. The Hartlepudlians interrogated the monkey for hours, but could make no sense of the babble it spoke, so they naturally assumed it spoke French. Because of its insistence on speaking French, they gave the monkey an English beach trial, unlike a bench trial it has no judge. Seeing he could not speak English – or even French, for that matter – the accused mounted a poor defence.

The English accusers knew the Frenchman was a spy – the little ferrety eyes and twitching nose was a dead giveaway – but the Frenchman appeared to be of high rank; the smart blue uniform bespoke a man of some standing, yet the arguments he put forward were gibberish, and the razor-sharp Hartlepool chief prosecutor cut the defence's chattering to pieces. On the balance of probability, the people found the monkey guilty of being a French spy, and sentenced him to hang from his spying French neck. Now the story takes a strange turn, some sources say the monkey pulled himself up onto the gallows, escaped the rope and later married a Hartlepudlian lass. Others say that as the monkey tried to escape the mayor took charge; grabbing the monkey's feet, the mayor hung on until the Frenchman breathed his last. Justice thus served, the mayor repaired to the free house for a yard or ten of ale, it may have happened that way? On the other hand, there are many accounts of a daring monkey escape, so who really knows?

Whatever happened it remains a fact, that in 2002 H'Angus Monkey ran for Mayor of Hartlepool, did that sly monkey escape hanging and interbreed with Hartlepudlians? Which may explain why in May 2021, his moronic monkey relatives all voted for the Tories, as lamented at the end of the book? The story didn't end there, though. Other sources say that the curator of London Zoo was sent to investigate – a learned man, familiar with both Frenchmen and monkeys. The body of the hanged Frenchman was exhumed and a post-mortem carried out, whereby the curator declared it a monkey not a Frenchman.

News of the Hartlepool horror spread through the kingdom, to this day Hartlepudlians don't like to talk about it. The English are a law-abiding folk, so the top legal minds in England came together and decided that, hanging trials would henceforth be judged by *beyond reasonable doubt* and not on the balance of probability. Yet, despite this, it remains true that to this day both monkeys and Frenchmen avoid Hartlepool like the plague. This is sad, for in 2002 H'Angus Monkey was elected mayor, so French monkeys are safe,

Because the unfair hanging forced British law to begin using more jury trials, at least one of the twelve should know what a Frenchman looks like, and also because it's enshrined in history. The 1215 *Magna Carta* founded the jury system in English law. It was the first document to put into writing the principle that the king and his government are not above the law. In 2020, Labour opposition leader Sir Keir Starmer would forcibly remind Boris Johnson, that neither were the prime minister and his Tory toffs!

In the T.V. show *Judge John Deed,* the actor Martin Shaw fought for separation of powers between government and the courts. The *Magna Carta* was an historic forerunner of this principle, by moderating heavy royal taxes and introducing a jury system. The charter brought the law closer to the people. Early English jurors acted only as expert witnesses, providing information on local affairs, but they were gradually used as adjudicators. Under King Henry II, the jury became an important tool, moving from reporting on familiar events to judging evidence of those locked in disputes. Juries are important in the justice system, but they deal with only a few cases today; minor offences are tried in magistrates' courts, where juries do not sit. Serious offences are tried in the Crown court, but juries actually decide only a small percentage of criminal cases, though still amounting to 30,000 trials per year.

There is talk of saving money by sending more cases to magistrates' courts, and also of juries being phased out, as it will enable judges to hear serious cases more quickly. Whatever the future of juries in English law, the halls of justice did bring Peter Watercloset together with a Scotsman who would become a staunch ally, in the fight against the fatberg. This one was about to kick-off, it would literally be a fight to the death so brace yourself for it, but first there was jury duty to be performed,

"Trial by jury is the cornerstone of our justice system. It is more than an instrument of justice and more than one wheel of the constitution; it is the lamp that shows freedom lives."

Lord Devlin 1905 to 1992

It was not the first time Peter Watercloset had done jury service, but it was his first time at Whitechapel Crown Court, where a case was coming up of great personal interest to him. The judge was well known for his passion for separation of powers between the government and courts, so he'd bumped heads with uppity London Mayor Boris Johnson, who considered himself above the law.

The jury was a cross-section of Whitechapel community: a stunning brunette, who was apparently a model – she certainly had the looks. The middle-aged blonde was equally beautiful, though in a more mature way; she strongly reminded Peter Watercloset of lovely Dr. Zee Garbo. Whitechapel is nicknamed "Banglatown", so there was naturally a Rasta and also a Bangladeshi lawyer, to bring greater balance to community representation. Nobody understood the talkative Chinese fellow in front, yet he kept babbling on determinedly, and there was also the inevitable "Jury Queen". Without waiting for jurors to vote, she declared herself forewoman, and was determined every felon who came her way would be incarcerated for a very long time indeed. It was fortunate that the rest of the jury were more balanced, though the priest was showing signs of growing agitation, for he hated being there. The main concern of the priest seemed to be affront at having to do common jury service – sadly for the priest, everyone was now eligible; judges, lawyers, doctors, journalists and bishops are all required to do jury service. Under the Criminal Justice Act 2003, all registered electors in England and Wales aged between 18 and 70 must serve on a jury if summoned, except people with a mental illness and those convicted of an offence.

"I supplied a most compelling reason," the priest insisted, that he felt he should never be required in law to be in a situation of passing judgment on others. Yet, the court insisted the priest do jury service, while the Chinese fellow could have got off because of a lack of English – but he was a zealously patriotic Chino/Englishman. He was also rather stubborn, which he proved in the first case, which involved a pretty young girl with a drug habit. She was accused of theft and there was no doubt she was guilty, but the Chinese juror had fallen deeply in love with her, and was determined to prove her innocent.

"The judge will go easy," the lawyer juror assured, for she was a drug addict, but the Chinaman was in love with the accused and her defence barrister, which was hardly surprising, considering the looks of the two ladies. The defence counsel and the accused were both beautiful women, though in vastly different ways, which demonstrated how disparate women can be. There was a wildness about the accused girl, who looked older than her years, no doubt as a result of her lifestyle. Yet there was a cool sereneness about the defence council. She was the epitome of a highly cultured woman; her beautifully modulated voice and calm demeanor showed this.

In most American states, a unanimous jury decision is required, but a British judge will sometimes accept a majority 10/2 decision. So, unable to achieve unanimity, the judge gave them this option. Fiercely, they fought it out in the jury room. Finally, they got it down to 9/3, it was late in the afternoon and the judge wanted a verdict. The young girl was not a major criminal, and the theft had been a cellphone and small change, so the lovelorn Chinaman got his verdict.

The Jury Queen was inflexible, but others folded and the Chinese juror smiled. You must not let your emotions rule you in a jury box, and you don't vote innocent just because you are tired and want to go home. But people are human, after all, and the judge accepted their innocent verdict with a smile. He could have overturned it, had he so wished, but they were finished for the day. While the Chinaman hung around, hoping to meet his love, Peter repaired to a pub, where he told nobody of his jury experience, because it is totally against the law – even if this story is fictional and has no basis whatsoever in fact.

The following day, they were back for case two (jury duty in the United Kingdom is for two weeks, so you are expected to sit on more than one case). The next case was more complex, for it involved assault. The accused was a respected local businessman, whose family sat in the gallery; they were on tenterhooks, for a guilty verdict could ruin his career. The case involved an altercation with another member at the golf club, which had unfortunately turned violent; the accuser had photographs to prove it. They were the clincher, for they showed his bruised and lacerated face. The Jury Queen snarled.

"The attacker must go away for a long time. This is utterly barbaric," she snarled, as she studied the photos. But Peter Watercloset was not convinced, and he listened closely as the prosecutor and defence lawyers spoke. It appeared that the accuser had struck first at the accused, who was apparently a martial arts enthusiast, so he got the better of the fight.

"There's not a mark on him. Look at the face of the other man," the Jury Queen snarled.

"That's simply because the accused is better at fighting," the juror in the white trench coat pointed out. He was a private detective. "The photos show the result of only two defensive blows."

The accused's career was saved by a just verdict, and it was a triumph for the jury system. Peter Watercloset felt good about the innocent verdict, and about the system which had administered justice, but the Jury Queen was infuriated.

"There's no justice in this country! I was once mugged, you know!" And there was the rub: she wanted to get back at all criminals.

Thank heavens the other jurors were more balanced. So, the verdict was innocent, and the accused's family cheered in tearful relief. Though, the next day the Jury Queen got her way with a guilty verdict, because this involved smuggling cellphones into prison in hollowed out shoes. There was a certain sympathy in the jury for the accused youth; he looked so young and vulnerable, standing alone in the dock in his ill-fitting, borrowed suit. The hearts of the blonde and brunette went out to the poor kid.

"We can't put him in jail," they both wailed, but the vengeful Jury Queen snarled, angrily.

"My muggers also looked young." Yet the wily detective backed the Jury Queen.

"Smuggling cellphones into prison is a serious offence," he contributed and all agreed, this time it was a guilty verdict, and they were proved correct. Because when sentencing the judge added something they had all missed. In the prison visiting room, the shoes with cellphones inside were swapped for another pair, also hollowed out. The accused was planning to do it again, so Peter was satisfied with the verdict, for they'd stopped an ongoing crime. The next case presented a problem, because if any of the jury members know the party to the hearing, they must inform the court of a possible bias.

"NOT GUILTY, YOUR HONOUR!"

The Brian Blessed voice of Evil Neville reverberated across Whitechapel Courthouse, he was the ally met in the halls of justice. After a week sitting on hard, wooden benches, the buttocks of Professor Watercloset were sore, but the last trial made it all worthwhile. It was both a coincidence and a handy convenience that Peter Watercloset sat on the jury which was to try Evil Neville. Peter realized there may be a conflict, the accused was a neighbour and friend, so he approached the court clerk.

The judge called for the juror and asked if he felt he could decide fairly. Peter replied he believed that he could, so the judge allowed him to remain – with a small smile on his face, because this was an interesting case. Evil Neville had declined the services of a lawyer and asked to defend himself, the judge agreed, on the condition that Evil Neville moderate his voice, or those around him would be forced to wear earplugs. His voice was fine for calling from the Scottish highlands, but far too strident for the small confines of a courtroom

"They may take our lives, but never our pension!"

It seemed as though a strong wind from the craggy Scottish mountains wafted through that Whitechapel courtroom, as the tough Highlander Evil Neville leant on his cane and began his defence. His long, white beard and rugged face gave him the look of a fighting clansman, which Braveheart Evil Neville was.Evil Neville began his defence with immortal lines from the film *Braveheart,* and the heroic story he told showed how brave he was, for Evil Neville had defended Bright Side pensioners against thugs.

Professor Peter Watercloset was aware of the battle, for he resided at Bright Side Suites, so the judge should really have reclused him from the jury, but he was a wise judge who had his reasons. The judge was concerned with the number of youth offenders he had imprisoned. England had one of the highest rates of youths in custody in Europe, second in absolute numbers only to Turkey. The overall juvenile prison population in 2011 was close to the high level of the early 1990s, for there'd been a shift from detainees on remand to sentenced prisoners.

Perhaps because the minimum age of criminal responsibility is set at 10 in England; in Europe 14 or 15 is more usual, with Belgium as high as 18. In America, not all states have a minimum age, while in New York and Massachusetts it's as low as age 6.

So, Evil Neville was well within the limit at the ripe old age of 70, but in this case, he was accused and the youth were the accusers – as well as being wimpish whiners. The accusers were a gang of youths on mountain bicycles, who preyed on pensioners at Bright Side Suites, and Evil Neville had fought back. The judge was hoping that the youths had learnt a lesson and would cease their criminal activities, because there were far too many young people charged with crimes. The total number of proven offences committed by youths last year was 176,511, with a cost of approximately £4bn annually.

Something drastic had to be done, and Evil Neville had taken a lead. The gang of louts terrorizing the old folk had been stopped in their tracks, by a mobility scooter group who called themselves the Old Farts Club. Using mobile phones to keep in touch, they patrolled the streets of Whitechapel; when a mugging went down they were there. Encircled by six fast scooters, the mountain bikes proved no match; using walking sticks as their swords and broomsticks as knights' jousting lances, the Old Farts mowed down the knaves.

With large, knobby tires and low gear ratios, mountain bikes are fine on mountain trails, but in the cobbled lanes of Ripper Street they were outmaneuvered by the scooters. For these were no ordinary mobility scooters; they had all been tweaked and souped-up by artful expert Evil Neville, whom you'll discover was a motorbike fundi. There are far too many young people under 18 in jail in Britain – 2,040 boys and 1,787 girls – and that's perhaps why the judge allowed Peter Watercloset on the jury; the judge had no sympathy for louts.

"He beat us silly," the first sobbed.

"Didn't give us a chance," said number two.

"Real hard fists," snivelled number three.

People influence people, and nothing influences a person more than a recommendation from a trusted friend."

Mark Zuckerberg.

The judge was disdainful of youth gangs, he had no sympathy for loutish bullies, so the judge just smiled and said contemptuously:

"You are young men who harass old people. When they objected you attacked a crippled old man and he beat up all three of you." That about summed it up, but still the youths cried.

"It wasn't fair; he's bigger than us!" This was true; Evil Neville was a big man. As former leader of a Glasgow biker gang, he knew how to fight; his legs weren't good, but he could stand and punch.

Thanks to the Old Farts Club, the mountain bike gang had ceased their criminal activities around Whitechapel. But; they bided their time and soon cornered old Evil Neville alone. He smiled with joy as he climbed off his mobility scooter; he was looking forward to this. With his back to the scooter, they had to come at him from the front, and that was their undoing, for Scotsmen punch hard – especially men who rode in a Glasgow motorcycle gang.

Biff, bang, boff and it was over; the three ruffians slunk away. The louts should have left it there, but one kid's father was a barrister, he realized as the case unfolded that paternal love is no substitute for evidence; it was patently clear that Evil Neville had merely been defending himself. Even the vindictive Jury Queen recognised this, and the vindicated Evil Neville walked away a free man. With the trial over they could now meet socially, so Peter bought the Scotsman a drink, to thank him for sorting the delinquents; that's how the friendship blossomed.

Professor Watercloset probed the history of this unusual man. What intrigued Peter was his open Anglophilia; Scotsmen are notoriously averse to the English, yet Neville sported a Union Jack on his mobility scooter and fanatically supported England rugby? The 2011 Six Nations Championship was won by rampant England, and both Evil Neville and Peter Watercloset were over the moon, they were also in fits of mocking laughter. When last year's champions France were beaten by lowly Italy, despite this Italy still received the Wooden Spoon given to the last team in the championship, which saved Scotland from that awful embarrassment. Evil Neville was disdainful of the Scotland rugby team, and more scathing of the current devolved Scottish Parliament, and the Scotland first minister – whom he wanted to replace with Nicola Sturgeon.

"Alex Salmond is a salacious sex addict." Curious statement for a Scotsman to make, yet it turned out to be eerily prophetic?

During his seven-year residence at Bute House, the jowly, boozy Alec Salmond turned the magnificent official home of Scotland's first minister into a raucous bachelor pad and wild drinking den. His touchy-feely approach to women would result in nine charges by separate complainants. No wonder Evil Neville was disdainful of Scotland, yet there were aspects he greatly admired.

Girl Friday to First Minister Alec Salmond was a feisty Glasgow solicitor named Nicola Sturgeon, she was backed by Evil Neville as a lady on the rise, for the enigmatic Scotsman was far more influential in politics than Peter Watercloset knew at that time. All they ever spoke about was motorbikes and rugby, now with the need to raise awareness about the fatberg threat, Evil Neville opened up more and spoke of his backing Nicola Sturgeon.

Her day would soon come because following the defeat of the *Yes Scotland Campaign* in the 2014 independence referendum, Alec Salmond would resign and Nicola Sturgeon be elected unopposed as Scottish National Party leader, and then become First Minister of Scotland.

A bitter foe of Boris Johnson she was vehemently opposed to his no-deal Brexit, thanks to the political drive of Nicola Sturgeon Scotland voted by 62% to remain in the European Union, which they may still do if they win an independence referendum? This feisty lady will play an important role in the book, so watch out for her, it's really easy to do.

Old Farts Club

The three greatest motorcycle stunt riders of all time are incomparably cool Steve McQueen, who did all his own stunts in *The Great Escape*, with the exception of the final jump over a 6ft barbed-wire fence; this was performed in the 1963 film by Scottish stuntman Evil Neville, then in 1966 an American stuntman copied the stunt and the name, and *Evil Knievel and His Motorcycle Daredevils* became world-famous.

Over the course of his career, Evil Knievel attempted more than 75 ramp-to-ramp motorcycle jumps. In 1974, he failed an attempted canyon jump across the quarter-mile Snake River Canyon, in a steam rocket named Skycycle X-2. Evil Knievel died of pulmonary disease in Clearwater, Florida in 2007, aged 69, and was inducted into the Motorcycle Hall of Fame. He certainly deserves his many accolades, but the pioneer of canyon jumps is never mentioned?

Doughty Scotsman Errol Neville picked up the nickname "Evil" from a motorbike gang in Glasgow. Errol was the black sheep of an eminent Scots family, who left the fold to pursue his dream of stunt riding, through the crags of the Scottish Highlands. Canyoning in Scotland is today a fast-growing, adrenaline-filled adventure sport – one of the most adventurous things you can do on your trip to the Highlands – but Evil Neville brought a whole new aspect to the sport.

Canyoning involves using jumping techniques, abseiling over small waterfalls and scrambling up and over boulders; Evil Neville did it on a highly modified Norton Atlas motorcycle. Like Evil Knievel, he wasn't always successful, and on one jump he missed badly; smashing hard into the gorge wall, he rolled down the rocks into famous Loch Ness, and the badly damaged Norton motorcycle came tumbling after him. The adjacent photograph shows Evil Neville, dragging his broken Norton bike through the Loch Ness shallows, the press went into a feeding frenzy?

Evil Neville became famous for his canyon jumping, on his powerful steel steed. The Atlas motorbike featured Norton's famous featherbed frame, and bike fanatic and mechanic Evil Neville bored the original 497cc Dominator engine out to 750cc, while the engine was fitted with a 376 Amal monobloc carburettor, giving 55bhp at 6500 r.p.m. With Norton's four-speed gearbox and heavy-duty clutch, the bike was perfect for canyon jumping, and Evil Neville sought out the hardest canyon jumps.

Evil Neville was a born 'n' bred Scotsman, with a passion for English rugby, for he'd cried too many tears at Murrayfield Stadium in Scotland, and at London's Twickenham Stadium the Scots had not beaten England since 1983. Their fierce rugby rivalry is named the Calcutta Cup, which England have won 70 times and Scotland 40. The Six Nations is the four U.K. home nations plus France and Italy, and England hold the record for wins in the Home Nations, Five Nations and Six Nations, with 28 titles.

Since the Six Nations era started, back in 2000, only Scotland and Italy have failed to win a title, which broke the stout Scots heart of Evil Neville. Each year he watched Scotland and Italy strive to swing the scales, to avoid the dreaded "Wooden Spoon," given to the nation coming last. In 2003 the England team became the only Northern Hemisphere side to ever win the Rugby World Cup. Evil Neville cheered loudly alongside English friends as he watched captain Martin Johnson proudly lift the coveted Webb Ellis Cup.

He would again watch England play in the final in 2007 and in 2019, where this time – thanks to Prime Minister Boris Johnson – they lost. Evil Neville wore a Union Jack on his helmet, in respect of the United Kingdom; unlike the sly mayor of London, he never belittled Scotland, whereas Boris Johnson was openly derisive of the Scots. *Conservative Home* would feature an article in 2014, claiming that Scotland remaining in the United Kingdom was *"a catastrophe for England."* A wild rabble who'd been conquered by England then granted massive over-representation, with 60 seats in Westminster Parliament, and disproportionate control of the U.K. budget. Yet, the Jocks insisted on administering their own affairs, through a devolved Scottish Parliament; the next picture shows how well sex-obsessed Scotland handled that! *"How can you take a nation seriously,"* Boris noted, wittily, *"who allow their history to be depicted through a film made in Ireland, by the drunk, Hollywood-based Aussie Mel Gibson?"*

Yet, this is perhaps fitting, as most trappings of Scottish culture are phony, adding to the disdain of Boris Johnson. Ireland wore the long léine before the Scots had the kilt, the traditional dish "haggis" was first mentioned in a seventeenth-century English cookbook. The legends of clans and tartans were created by the romantic writers like Sir Walter Scot, while bagpipes came from Ancient Rome via Turkey, and whisky was invented by alcoholic Irish monks.

The Scottish Parliament
Pàrlamaid na h-Alba

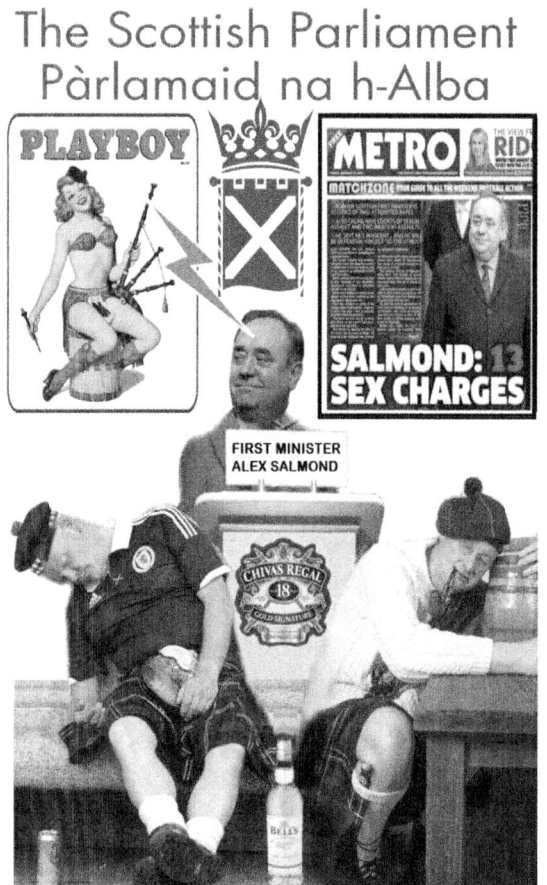

Evil Neville had reached the age of seventy, so he bought an apartment at Bright Side Suites. His many motorcycle accidents had taken a heavy toll on his legs, so nowadays he operated a mobility scooter and not a Norton Atlas. As you may have guessed, it was a pretty special, souped-up mobility scooter; the modifications made by Evil Neville were top of the range, and the envy of his geriatric fellow riders, for these mods included L.E.D. lights, indicators, a horn, disc brakes and, of course, a fancy sports seat.

Performance wasn't too bad, either, with a 200cc engine sending the rider down the road and to the local shops in good time. But, with this scooter it was all about the look; aesthetic changes, like the chrome skull in front, made this a ride to be proud of, and bound to catch the eye, which it certainly did. Soon Evil Neville was pressed upon to alter other scooters.

That was when the residents of Bright Side Suites formed their own mobility scooter gang, and Evil Neville was naturally the leader; with his Brian Blessed voice and long, white beard he was top choice. The Old Farts Club would soon be called upon by the desperate Professor Peter Watercloset and Dr. Zee Garbo, to perform heroic deeds which made them folk legends and earned the thanks of every London denizen, for destroying an evil life form spawned in the Whitechapel sewerland. But that would come later. More recently, the Old Farts Club had taken it upon themselves to rid Ripper Street of a gang of youths, who preyed on pensioners. Vigilantism should only be used in the last resort, but it does become justified when the government cannot enforce the law, through lack of resources or often impractical, liberal laws. Despite many pleas to the police, nothing effective had been done to curb the delinquents, so the Old Farts vigilantes formed.

Established community members who acted with definite goals, not with the intention of random violence, they were a last resort because of a failure of law systems. Citizen's arrests are legal in the U.K., so under the Police and Criminal Evidence Act of 1984, you can arrest a person who is committing an indictable offence, when it is not practical for an official police constable to make the arrest. So, the Old Farts Club had cleaned up the mountain bike gang, and soon they'd be going after the vicious spawn of the fatberg, which would prove to be a far deadlier battle than cheeky juveniles. The London authorities and media had scoffed at the fears expressed by Professor Peter Watercloset, so it was again up to the Old Farts Club to protect Whitechapel, which was rather ironic: a Scotsman defending English turf which closely resembled a part of faraway South Asia. Whitechapel is not called "Banglatown" for nothing; it is the beating heart of London's Bangladeshi-Sylheti community, and is famous for its curry houses.

Peter's favourite was the Rhythm Factory with its recent refurbishments, a cafe/bar/restaurant and also an art space, this was a 400-capacity club for a great London night out. Its mismatched chairs, cool little tables, couches, local art and a front chillout area, with relaxing vibes and beats, make Rhythm Factory an intimate night-time venue. The club manages to pack in some really good DJs and bands, featuring breakbeat, dance, drum and bass, disco, electro house, hip-hop and rock! The Rhythm Factory packs the crowds in without ever feeling overcrowded, so you can properly enjoy live gigs.

Dr. Zee Garbo fell in love with the club after a visit with Professor Peter Watercloset, and they were now seen there often together. Yet, their relationship still remained strictly professional; it was the threat of the fatberg which had brought them together, and how to handle it was the main thrust of their conversation. The problem lay right underneath their feet, for outside of Whitechapel the other fatbergs all tested benign – what was it that encouraged such growth.

"We can't expect help from cynical Harry Hack or B.B.T.," Peter observed wryly, as he tucked into his delicious *chingri malai* – a curry made from prawns and coconut milk, flavoured with spices.

"Harry Hack's sole purpose in life is to be a caution to others," Zee Garbo observed, pithily. She was vegetarian, so Bangladeshi food suited her, for vegetarian recipes are popular in Bangladesh. They often dined at the Kolapata – perhaps the best Bangladeshi/Bengali restaurant in London, with authentic Bengali dishes using traditional ingredients. The Bengali curry was as hot as was the conversation, for it centred around the myopic journalist Harry Hack and his failure to see the danger of fatbergs.

"If the authorities won't take action, we'll have to conduct an investigation by ourselves," Dr. Zee Garbo said, grimly. She was a determined woman, and her position at London Water gave her access to maps of the sewers under Whitechapel.

"We must check all manhole covers, there's thousands of them in Whitechapel," Zee said, for if the fatbergs exuded some life form, it would seek the sun and the manhole covers would be the way to go.

Peter sighed. "Why doesn't B.B.T. believe us? The scientific evidence is incontrovertible," he lamented. The skepticism of Harry Hack, that the fatberg could develop a Brown Blob life form, is pretty silly when you consider the solid scientific evidence; even the layman can see the pattern in the scientific chart overleaf. Everyone knows it's possible for organisms to change during evolution; what drives the new forms is not genes themselves, but gene regulation turning genes on and off.

THE BROWN BLOB

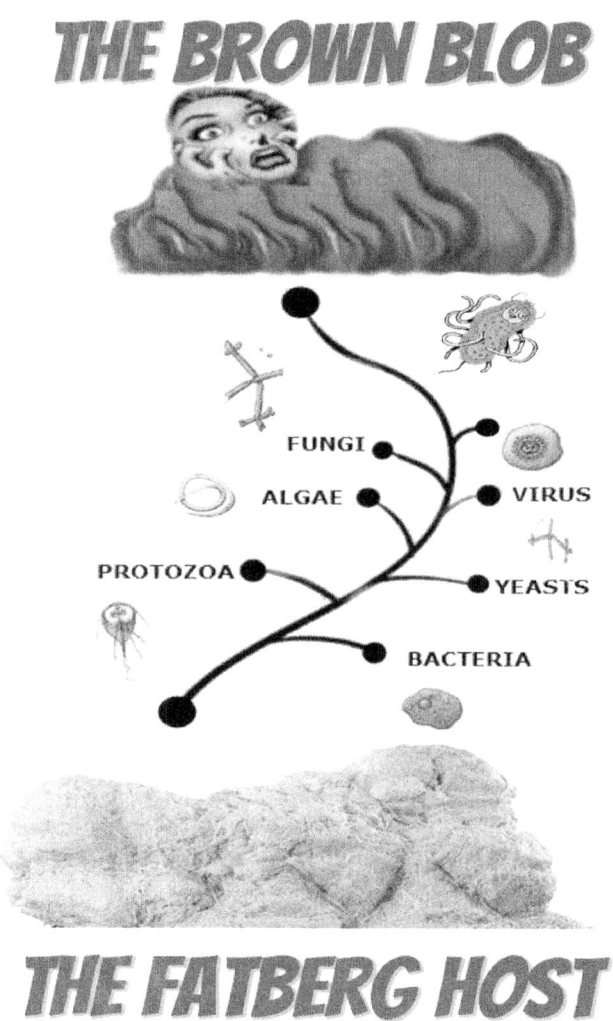

FUNGI

ALGAE

PROTOZOA

VIRUS

YEASTS

BACTERIA

THE FATBERG HOST

New studies have identified the kind of gene regulation most likely to cause evolutionary change: protein transcription enhances the metamorphosis of genes and regulates gene expression. New forms of regulation are crucial for new features of life. Ask yourself what distinguishes the body plan of humans from that of sea urchins: the answer is new kinds of regulation, which turn the correct genes on and off at the right time. Now consider the presence of body-building chemicals found in the fatberg. Asterix is used for muscle gain, so there's a possibility that it may bind to androgen receptors, thus creating selective anabolic activity. There was therefore no doubt that the monster fatberg presented a deadly serious threat, but myopic British Broadminded Television ensured that Peter and Zee were ignored by authorities. It's amazing how blinkered people are! It's even possible that some readers are skeptical of the scientific information in this book, so they may snigger at the possibility of Brown Blobs developing. I ask these readers if they have ever heard of

117

physarum polycephalum: literally the "many-headed slime". This is a slime mould that inhabits moist and shady areas, such as decaying leaves and logs. This protist may be easily seen without a microscope. Polycephalum is yellow in colour and eats fungal spores, bacteria and microbes; it has been shown to exhibit characteristics similar to those in single-celled creatures and eusocial insects. Let me warn you before you turn the page, that the information you find there will be life changing, as it will alter your perceptions of the planet you live on.

Hopefully you will suspend all your infantile doubts, what will amaze you is the incredible intelligence shown by the *physarum polycephalum* when hunting food; Dr. Zee Garbo was part of a team of Polish researchers who proved that polycephalum can quite easily solve the "Shortest Path" problem, as shown in the maze photograph. When grown in a maze, with oatmeal at two spots, polycephalum retracts from everywhere in the maze except the shortest route to the food.

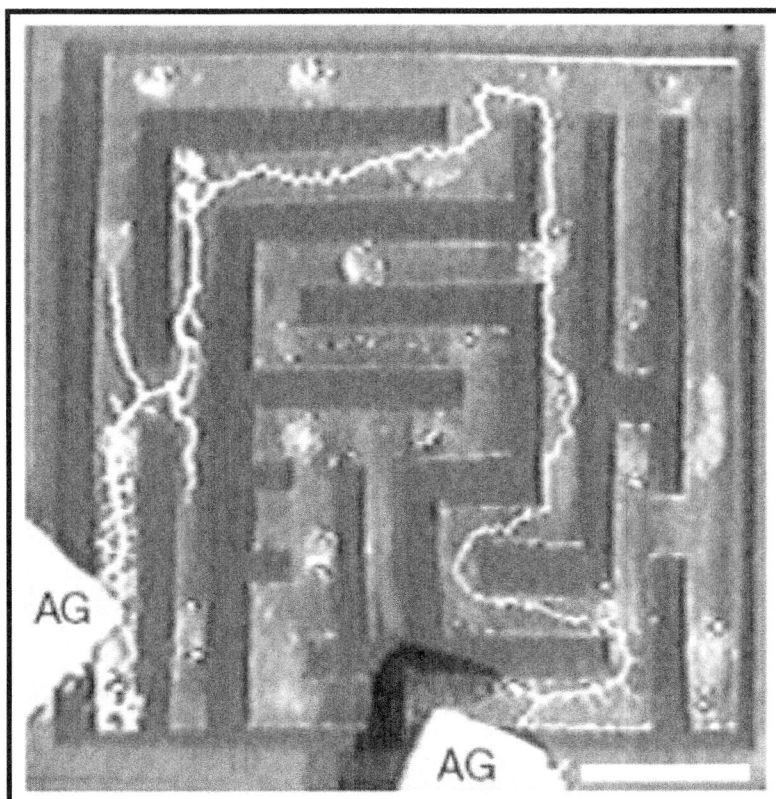

COULD YOU FIND THE SHORTEST PATH ?

Yet, if presented with more than two food sources, the chart shows polycephalum easily solving the complicated transportation problem: the amoeba quickly produces efficient transport networks in its search for food.

"It's brighter than Boris," Zee chuckled.

The amazing book *Physarum Machines* shown overleaf, claims that because physarum reacts in a consistent way to external stimuli, they are the ideal substrate for future and emerging bio-computing devices. Imagine a future programmable biological computer, which can be implemented in the vegetative state of a slime mould, programmed by the spatial configurations of attracting and repelling gradients. So, if a thinking slime mould capable of computing is conceivable, surely the possibility exists of an intelligent Brown Blob being spawned by the gigantic fatberg in Whitechapel sewers?

I trust this has sorted out the doubters, who now realize that this book is based on solid scientific evidence, and is not just a skillfully written parody,

The shady career of Boris Johnson is only an historic overlay, to the heroic story of Professor Peter Watercloset and his lovely lady friend Dr. Zee Garbo who, with the assistance of highland Braveheart Evil Neville defeated the fatberg and humbug bumbling Boris Johnson.

Yet let's not get too far ahead of ourselves; that would come later. Right now, it was time for urgent planning. A meeting was called in the conservatory of Bright Side Suites, with the five members of the Old Farts Club, where their leader Evil Neville revealed his plan of action on the whiteboard:

"ATTACK !!! ATTACK !!! ATTACK !!!"

The Brian Blessed voice blasted through the conservatory, the white beard of Evil Neville quivered and the rafters rattled – it was that type of voice. But it also asked awkward questions.

"Why is it only Whitechapel we are checking? Surely there are fatbergs in other parts of London – in fact, throughout the U.K.?" was the question that Evil Neville asked.

"I can't speak for the whole of the U.K., but in London my tests revealed that outside of Whitechapel the fatbergs all appear benign," Dr. Zee Garbo answered, rather guardedly.

"What do you mean by benign, Doc?" Evil Neville probed. There was an awkward silence from the doctor. It was difficult to explain to laymen how life could form in a sewer fatberg, or why it only appeared in some places? It was true that the problem seemed to be centered only in Whitechapel; outside of this area the fatbergs did not show any signs of developing prokaryotes including bacteria and archaea, which are two of the domains of life.

"It's certainly puzzling," Peter mused.

"It's really strange," Zee agreed.

Why was it that the emerging life formed by the fatberg, only appeared right under British Broadminded Television studios? It was almost as if the fatberg thrived on evil, did the depravities at B.B.T somehow sustain the fatberg, would it come alive and threaten the whole of London?

"ATTACK !!! ATTACK !!! ATTACK !!!"

Evil Neville only knew one way.

ATTACK
ATTACK
ATTACK

"What will we actually be checking for on our patrols?" Evil Neville asked, and the other members of the gang nodded heads, what was the objective?

"Do not try to attack a Brown Blob," Doctor Garbo advised. "Your task is surveillance, by observing the sewer manhole covers: look for green mist arising." Zee then produced a map, showing all the manifold manhole covers of Whitechapel, and they all studied it.

"You've all seen *The Blob*, so look for something like that," Peter jested lightly, referring to the 1958 cult horror film, which had starred Steve McQueen in his feature debut. The storyline concerned an alien amoebicidal entity crashing to Earth inside a meteorite; The Blob then devours citizens of a small town, growing larger and more aggressive.

"So, how can we kill the fatberg blob?" Evil Neville boomed. It was a good question, since in the film they had tried everything, but The Blob was impervious to bullets or even electric shock.

"They finally killed The Blob with cold," one Old Fart observed.

"I don't think that will work here," Dr. Zee Garbo countered. Then, she added: "Observation is your mission, not attack."

"We'll do a grid search," Evil Neville boomed,

and a plan was formed, the Old Farts mounted their scooters and rode into history.

Whitechapel still had some manhole covers from legendary Thomas Crapper (1836-1910). This appropriately named Victorian purveyor of sanitaryware was a great self-publicist; to this day, his name remains a big part of the sewer lexicon. Unfortunately, the Crapper Cover was not the answer, for the residue of dinner once successfully put behind us can cause a build-up of explosive methane in the sewers, unless they are ventilated.

William Crimp (1853-1901) was responsible for bringing stink pipes to the streets. The swifter air movement overhead dispersed noxious gases more effectively than gratings on the ground, the Crimp stink pipes allowed for proper ventilation of sewers and safe dispersal of explosive gases. Which was all very well, but if a Brown Blob did come alive, the manhole covers would not keep them off the streets.

Some manhole covers were 5ft in diameter, and although it may break up, the residue of a Brown Blob squeezing through there could be highly dangerous. The larger manhole covers would have to be zealously observed, and Professor Watercloset had a surveillance team at Bright Side Suites who could do this. So, the Old Farts Club rode into glory, and conducted themselves with military precision.

"Section two, proceed," came the order.

Think not that these were ordinary mobility scooters, for canny Evil Neville was not an ordinary man; he was a world-renowned motorcyclist. With specialist motorbike engineering knowledge, which he lavished on the mobility scooters, the results, as you can imagine, were truly spectacular!

They operated in shifts and conducted sporadic sightings of the manholes. The idea was not to watch a single manhole constantly, but short checks over a period of time. For this task, the mobility scooters were marvellous. They all had vehicle cellphone boosters, which the Old Farts operated like a two-way radio system.

"Scooter Two, come in. Seen anything?" Evil

Neville would boom. With the vocal range of Brian Blessed, he didn't really need a radio, but he used it anyway, for it reminded him of the old days. In fact, Evil Neville was loving it; he was back with his motorcycle gang in Glasgow, riding out grandly with the "Hills Angels". This time it was an Old Farts Club with their tweaked up mobility scooters, prepared in the workshop of Evil Neville, street gangs or fatbergs they were ready for anything.

"Seen any green mist, Scooter Three?" bellowed Evil Neville. Thus far, that was the only overtly suspicious activity coming from the fatberg, and strangely, it only occurred around manholes serving the British Broadminded Television studios?

Doctor Zee Garbo collected some green mist and analyzed it: there were low levels of developing prokaryotes in the mist, but in concentrations too small to sustain life for too long. It was a stalemate, there were signs that the fatberg was developing a life form, but not enough proof to present to the doubting authorities – it was terribly frustrating.

"What's our next move?" Zee asked.

"You and I are going surfing," Professor Peter grinned wryly, and Dr. Zee wryly reflected that he was always full of surprises.

"Sounds great," she said, uncertainly.

Surfing in Sewage

"But a diversion the most common is upon the Water, where there is a very great Sea, and surf breaking on the Shore. The Men, sometimes 20 or 30, go without the Swell of the Surf and lay themselves flat upon an oval piece of plank about their size and breadth. They keep their legs close on top of it and their Arms are us'd to guide the plank, they wait the time of the greatest Swell that sets on Shore, and altogether push forward with their Arms to keep on its top. It sends them with a most astonishing Velocity, and the great art is to guide the plank so as to always keep it in a proper direction on the top of the Swell, as it alters its direction.

If the Swell drives him close to the rocks before he is overtaken by its break, he is much prais'd. On first seeing this very dangerous

131

diversion, I did not conceive it possible, but that some of them must be dashed to mummy against the sharp rocks. But just before they reach the shore, if they are very near they quit their plank and dive under 'til the surf is broke, when the piece of plank is sent many yards by the force of the Surf from the beach. By such like exercises, these men may be said to be almost amphibious."

Lieutenant James King

First Lieutenant

H.M.S. Discovery

Written by Lieutenant James King this was the first ever written account of surfing, he was made first lieutenant of *H.M.S. Discovery* and given the task of completing the journals of Captain James Cook, killed in 1779 by Hawaiians after an argument over a stolen boat. No more surfing for Captain Cook but modern surfing began in 1885, when three teenage Hawaiian princes took a break from boarding school and came to cool off in Santa Cruz, California, where they surfed the mouth of the San Lorenzo River on redwood boards. In 1907, George Freeth was brought to California from Hawaii, to demonstrate surfboard riding as a publicity stunt, then in 1909 Burke Haywood Bridgers and a colony of surfers introduced surfing to the East Coast.

Yet, what has surfing got to do with sewage, you may ask, and what is Professor Watercloset doing surfing with a cellphone on the cover of *Surfer Magazine*? All is about to be revealed, for surfing nowadays has a lot to do with sewage. Surfing in contaminated waters can make you really ill, which is why Surfers Against Sewage sit on a European Commission panel, checking the quality of surfing water, *Safer Seas Service* is a cellphone water quality app, protecting water users from pollution. Professor Peter Watercloset sat on both boards.

Safer Seas Services alerts water users when sewer overflows discharge untreated human sewage into the sea, and when water quality is reduced by diffuse pollution, at 330 beaches across England and Wales.

This is the first and only national service to inform you, in real-time, when untreated human sewage and diffuse pollution is impacting water quality at your favourite beach. *Safer Seas Service* allows you to make an informed decision, about how you use the sea.

Untreated sewage and wastewater frequently discharge from sewer overflows right around the U.K., sometimes significantly reducing water quality. When this reaches dangerous levels, the *S.S.S.* operator is notified by participating water companies and issues a sewage alert, so surfers and other beach users can avoid this potentially harmful pollution. Consider that during the 2011 bathing season *Safer Seas Service* issued 353,329 free mobile-phone real-time messages, warning users of reduced water quality.

Swallowing water polluted with bacteria causes gastroenteritis, so that answers the question of what sewage has to do with surfing. Without the organizations mentioned above you may be surfing in sewage, and that could make you very ill indeed. Which also answers the question what Professor Watercloset is doing with a cellphone, while surfing on the cover of *Surfer Magazine*: obviously, it was an advert for the mobile app supplied by *Safer Seas*.

As a board member, Professor Watercloset was asked to speak at the Bournemouth Sewage Conference. This would give him a chance to discuss, with educated professionals, his concerns about the threat of the Whitechapel fatberg. As another interested party, Peter had asked Zee to accompany him, so they'd booked into Royal Bath Hotel, where the conference was held – separate rooms, of course (they were both old-school), but that would change on this trip. Peter naturally also planned to do some surfing; he would hire a board and hit the ocean, he surfed whenever he had the opportunity. Bournemouth surf isn't big, but its surfers are clever, securing for themselves an artificial reef break, in a place which rarely ever gets the decent, big waves.

Peter didn't mind the conditions but the crowds got to him, so he preferred to surf at the secluded Canford Cliffs, up the coast,

"I'm going surfing," he grinned at Zee as he drove, and she smiled gaily back, her hair flying free in the wind, out of the open convertible MG TF. They were enjoying the short break.

Peter Watercloset came to surfing through his

interest in cleaning up the sea. He learned to surf and fell passionately in love with it. Zee would discover it was not a hobby, but rather a religion. Surfing gave Peter a sense of upliftment, and a feeling of closeness to the ocean, which nothing else could engender.

The first time Peter paddled out past the break and did a turtle roll, he was filled with a sense of accomplishment that nothing in his life thus far had given him. To get in position to catch the unbroken waves, you have to paddle out past where the waves are breaking, and to do this you do a "turtle roll", also known as an "Eskimo roll". Surfers who ride shortboards use a duck-diving technique, which is sinking your board under the wave, then riding through underneath the wave – this is all well and good for short boards, but hopeless for long boards, because duck-diving a 12-foot board in 6-foot surf will only give you a battering; it's best to go through with a turtle roll.

As the wave comes near, you flip the board over on top of you, with the fins facing upward. Then, pulling the board down toward, you grab hold of it near the middle and keep your body vertical, so that it acts as a sea anchor; this serves to counter the force of the wave. Once the wave has passed, you flip the board back over and climb aboard, smiling to yourself after having pulled a perfect turtle roll, then you float with your fellow surfers, waiting for the perfect wave. Once you are out there it is so peaceful, as you sit on your surfboard enjoying the view, noticing how bumps start to form on the horizon.

You watch how they roll in and change shape, and you try to get a sense of where the wave will break, whether it's surfable or not, and where you must be to catch the wave. Then, you see your wave moving in and you manage to turn your board, so you are trimmed across the face of the wave. You feel all the power of the wave, pushing toward you and backing off slightly, before surging forward again, and you ride the wave all the way into the beach. Just make sure you have the right size surfboard, different sizes for different weights, as the table shows.

7'6 - 8'6   8'6 - 9'2   9'2 +

Up to 85kg   Up to 90kg   100kg +

Each time you are out there you learn something new. Your surfing improves with every wave you catch, as you learn to read the ocean better. The joy of surfing is many things – there's the challenge of it and the mental side – but when a person becomes a surfer, they nearly always also become an environmentalist. Although Professor Peter Watercloset did it the other way around: he was an environmentalist first, then surfing increased his passion to defend nature. It was almost like a committed marriage, reciprocated love.

Every time Peter walked along a beach some ancient urge rose: he wanted to shed shoes and clothes, and run shouting, screaming at Heaven that this was beautiful and must be saved. The cove where Peter loved to surf was rocky, with only a small patch of beach to exit, but he was a skilled surfer and the rocks presented no problem. He hired a four-wheel-drive vehicle to get there, so the cove was deserted, and that's what he loved about it: the lonely sand and sea, with no footprints on the beach, frequented now by only a few circling gulls, who became interested when they saw Zee open the picnic basket, as Peter prepared his surfboard.

The sea swelled into crests of white foam, its waves crashing on the sand, and Peter entered the sea with his surfboard before him. Zee watched as he caught some smallish waves, then came a big break and he rode it right onto the beach. His broad, brown chest dripped water, as he reached for the towel next to Zee.

"That's enough for now. I won't catch another one like that in a hurry," he grinned, as he sank down beside Zee, and tucked into the picnic basket between them. They ate in comfortable silence; there was no need for words, for both knew a volcano was about to explode: a long-suppressed need was now about to erupt. This would not just be sex it would be love-making, we have sex with someone who can satisfy us physically, but we make love to someone who can satisfy us soulfully. We have sex to satisfy a hunger, which is nothing, but survival, but we make love to feed our souls. To fill a void that has been there a long time, that longs for partner we can wake up with, to spend the morning with and perhaps - the rest of your life? Suddenly, they were in each other's arms, entangled in the wash and oblivious to the surge of tide, rippling the beach and covering their bodies.

Then, breaking apart, they ran up the beach to a drier spot. Zee lay down on her towel and Peter dropped beside her,

"I never knew it could be like this," she gasped. "No one ever kissed me like you do," she whispered, eyes brimming with love. The thunder of the waves and the trembling bodies – the looks of hunger in their eyes… it was here to eternity for both of them. Afterward, they were strangely shy, as they gathered the plastic picnic utensils scattered by the waves.

"No plastic in the ocean," Peter grinned, for that was the theme of the speech he was giving tonight, on the harmful environmental ogre called plastic, which blocked Whitechapel sewers and created a gigantic fatberg. Now plastic was threatening to block the ocean, but Professor Peter Watercloset would once again speak out.

They drove back to Bournemouth to return the hired four-by-four, then they returned to the Royal Bath Hotel, for Peter to ready himself for his speech. He looked so handsome in his tailored, grey suit that Zee felt her heart hammer. When Peter began his speech, the crowd listened entranced, for the professor was a skilled public speaker. Peter Watercloset was also an exceedingly handsome man; his looks have been compared to the movie star Clark Gable.

By 2050 there will be more waste plastic in the sea than fish. Unless industry cleans up its act, new plastics will consume twenty per cent of all oil production within thirty-five years, up from an estimated five per cent today. Plastics production is expected to double in the next twenty years, and almost quadruple by 2050, yet just five per cent of plastics are recycled effectively, forty per cent ends up in landfill and a third in fragile ecosystems such as the world's oceans. At least eight million tonnes of plastics leak into the ocean, which is equivalent to dumping one garbage truck into the ocean every minute. A carelessly discarded plastic bag can break down in the sea, especially in warmer waters, but the process releases toxic chemicals which may be digested by fish and end up in the human food chain. Research released a year ago found there were more than five trillion pieces of plastic floating in the seas, many just five millimetres across. Larger items can be a threat to sea life, such as turtles and seals, which swallow them and are in danger of choking.

Scientists have also found countless tiny fragments that drift to the bottom of oceans, carpeting the seabed. The environmental and health impact of this is unknown, but it's certain that it will not help the oceans. Plastics are workhorse materials with unbeaten properties. However, they are also the ultimate single-use material, because after use they are discarded and often end up in sewers or the ocean. We must rethink the use of plastics, provide a global economy in which plastics never become waste, and can be turned into valuable feedstock for recycling plants. Unfortunately, the plastics recycling industry is reeling from the recent plunge in the price of oil; at thirty dollars a barrel, it's far more expensive to recover plastics and recycle them than to use virgin crude. Solving the problem will not be easy, especially as industry is pressured to produce more, to meet growing demand from emerging markets. Bioplastics are currently more expensive to make than the petro alternative, and recycling systems are inefficient.

Our vision is for a new plastics economy, in which the industry, governments and citizens work together to ensure that plastics never become waste, and so cut the leakage into our stressed natural systems. The plastic problem is dire, but it is surely not unsolvable. It is said that all that is necessary for evil to triumph is for good men to do nothing, so I call on all you good people to save our oceans.

Professor Watercloset finished his speech, then returned to the table where Dr. Zee Garbo sat. She raised her glass to him and said:

"Great speech. Congratulations, Peter." They chatted amicably as they ate dinner, yet there was only one thought on Peter's mind.

"Your room or mine," Zee Garbo said, seductively, and Peter jumped up so rapidly that he knocked over the wine bottle. They were in fact soulmates and kindred spirits, so for Professor Watercloset and Doctor Garbo no trip would be complete without a visit to the local sewage plant. There had been local reports of a brown ooze emitting a strange green mist, so they drove out the following morning and smelt the familiar whiff of sewage, as they approached the Holdenhurst Treatment Works. This is an open sewage plant, so in summer it hums a bit. Additionally, there's less rainfall to move the sewage along the drains, so it hangs around longer and smells.

To counter the smell problem, the plant had recently spent £2m, and Peter had to admit, as he entered the plant, that the smell had improved since his last visit. Yet, in periods with little rainfall, the smell persisted at Holdenhurst – not as bad as the 1858 Great Stink in London, but the locals complained bitterly about the rotten eggs smell.

Some folk have suggested encasing the Holdenhurst Treatment Works in an aircraft hangar arrangement, but there are three excellent reasons why this is unlikely to happen. Firstly, the cost would be an exorbitant £20m. Then, there is the danger aspect: the gases which dissipate harmlessly into the air could build up. And, the sheer size of the place would threaten the environment.

A modern treatment process is extremely eco-friendly, and so is the Holdenhurst site, and covering it up would decimate the deer who reside in the copse there, as well as destroying foxes and badgers who live in the grounds. The manager explained all this as he took them through the plant, and promised, the smell would dissipate when the new overland pipeline was complete, from Boscombe Chine Gardens to Fisherman's Walk, near Montague Road.

The overland pipe would allow for repairs to be carried out to Bournemouth coastal interceptor sewer; 18 metres below ground it takes the flow to Holdenhurst - this would considerably reduce the smells at the sewerage plant. The plant manager explained all this in a really witty manner, he was a bit of an amateur comedian and sewage plants don't receive many visitors, so the manager took full advantage. Peter and Zee were finding it difficult to hide their disdain, to them sewage was a serious business, not the butt of tasteless jokes.

It may seem strange to some readers, but Peter and Zee did not share the Luddite views of romantic poets like Ginsberg, who reject industrial blight and worship nature in its original form. "Artificial worse-than-dirt-industrial-modern," Allen Ginsberg may have thought, but for Peter and Zee there was beauty in the sewage plant, the stark utilitarian looks appealed to them. Art is beautiful but engineering has purpose, engineers don't just sit back and watch, they make things happen using innovation and creativity.

The grime was no man's grime but death and human locomotives,
all that dress of dust, that veil of darkened railroad skin, that smog of cheek,
    that eyelid of black mis'ry, that sooty hand or phallus or protuberance of
    artificial worse-than-dirt—industrial—modern—all that civilization spotting
    your crazy golden crown— **Sunflower Sutra** - **Allen Ginsberg**

NO JOB IS FINISHED TILL
THE PAPERWORK IS DONE

SCOTLAND

Sewer was blocked by large Pooh

Last updated 17 Feb 2014 00:03 GMT

A WINNIE THE POOH TEDDY BEAR
BLOCKING THE SEWER WAS FOUND
DUMPED IN EAST KILBRIDE MANHOLE

THE TURD BURGLAR NO 1 IN TURD GAME

Peter and Zee then retired to the manager's office for tea, where Peter intended to ask the manager about the reports of a strange green slime at the plant, but the manager was more into sewer humor.

Peter tried to raise the subject of fatbergs and Brown Blobs, but could see by posters on the wall that the manager was a sewer joke fanatic, he now had a captive audience so he launched into his act.

"Someone broke into the police station and stole the toilets. The cops are searching, but so far they have nothing to go on," he laughed.

"Do you know why *Star Trek* is like toilet paper? They both go past Uranus and capture Klingons." The manager was a riot so, Peter and Zee hurriedly finished their tea and excused themselves; the toilet humour wasn't to their taste, and there were some non-sewer sights they still wished to see.

With more than £100m of investment ploughed into Bournemouth in recent years, the resort has become the Miami of Britain, upmarket hotels and a multi-million-pound entertainment complex. Yet, Bournemouth has lost none of the charm of the traditional British seaside holiday: pretty beach huts line the seafront, while locals and tourists alike soak up the sunshine and atmosphere. Whether swimming in the sea or eating delicious fried fish 'n' chips, while watching a colourful world roll by, there is something in Bournemouth for everybody.

From Scarborough to Blackpool and Weymouth to Bournemouth, the U.K. has a proud tradition of popular seaside holiday resorts, and Bournemouth is among the finest. It's long and generous beach – the most photographed in the U.K. – is only part of the draw. There are two historic piers to explore, Bournemouth Pier has a zip-wire running from pier to shore, and an indoor climbing centre. Boscombe Pier is less adventurous, offering a charming musical trail featuring giant chimes and mini-golf, on the final hole edible golf balls drop into the sea to feed fish. Yet you may have guessed by now, Peter and Zee were not be seen at any of these spots. As mentioned before they were utilitarian, not in the hazy philosophical sense, but in the simple practical sense. Although they both loved nature and respected the environment, they acknowledged the need for industry, provided it was responsibly conducted.

Bournemouth Reformed Plastics Company was not a normal tourist haunt but for Peter and Zee it was fascinating, plastic waste had been the focus of their trip, so turning recycled plastic into valuable products was a must see. Outdoor furniture, gates, fencing, signage, and much more. Made from weather-resistant, maintenance-free 100% HDPE plastic, never needing replacement. But, what really interested Peter and Zee was a finding in the recycling laboratory, where they were studying types of fungus in a research project, when one of the fungi made a bid for freedom – this really piqued Peter's interest.

This was not a Brown Blob only a fungus, but what excited the researchers, was in its escape bid the fungus ate its way through the plastic sponge sealing it in, the fungus then assimilated the sponge like any other food. The researchers were now working to develop the fungus strain to make it a more efficient digester, that could potentially help get rid of plastic waste, as a researcher explained.

"You put in plastic, the fungi eat the plastic, the fungi make more fungi and then from that you make biomaterials... for food, or feed stocks for animals, or antibiotics." Peter and Zee noted the breakthrough with interest, it was an exciting development, then they turned their attention to the "touristy" side of Bournemouth. – and there was plenty to see.

Peter wanted to visit Bournemouth A.F.C.'s Vitality Stadium, while Zee wished to see the Russell-Cotes Art Gallery, where the main hall had an exquisite collection of high-Victorian and pre-Raphaelite art. They finished their dual visits in Bournemouth, then began the long drive back to Whitechapel, as they drove Peter casually asked:

"You fancy a bit of narrowboating? Once more, he surprised Zee; Peter was a real outdoors man, with an affinity for watersports.

Why not? Dr. Zee Garbo thought. They were both freelancers with no formal schedules, and from a narrowboat they could study the sewer outfalls into the Thames River, which may prove interesting? And, they really did, by nearly killing the two fatberg fighters? Thus far in the story it has all been theory, how the fatberg has been excreting slime, that could turn into a dangerous Brown Blob. Soon they would be face to face with this spawn of the fatberg, an exceedingly unpleasant experience.

Thames **Narrowboat** HOLIDAYS

The canal tells you stories
The canal sings you songs
They hang in that space
Between memory and water
Ian McMillan

The Narrowboat

China is the pioneer of canal building, for their Grand Canal was built in the tenth century. The pound lock still used in British canals today is said to have been invented by Ch'iao Wei-Yo in the year A.D. 983. Yet, early Chinese canals were mostly extensions to natural rivers, while almost a millennium earlier, around A.D. 50, Roman engineers in Britain built the Fossdyke, connecting Lincoln to the River Trent – this was built for both drainage and navigation.

They also built the nearby Caer (or Car) Dyke, extending almost 40 miles to the south of Lincolnshire. It is believed that this provided a supply route for transporting heavy goods between Cambridge and York. Britain went on to became the first country with a nationwide network of transport canals. They were served by narrowboats designed to carry as much cargo as possible, so they were long and narrow with flat bottoms – thus, the well-known narrowboat came into existence. When road and rail systems took over, canal transport fell into disuse, but the canals provided great locations and widespread attractions for a narrowboat holiday trade, and naturally outdoors man Professor Peter Watercloset became a fanatic narrowboat aficionado. By the end of the eighteenth century, the canal transport boom was over. Most British canals were completed by 1815, because then the smart money moved into railway transport.

At first, the canals and railways coexisted; the railways concentrated on passengers and light goods, with the canals moving bulky and heavy goods. By the middle of the nineteenth century, the railways had been efficiently organized into an integrated national network. Such stern competition forced canal tolls down, sending the companies into a decline from which they would never really emerge. After years of neglect and damage caused by World War 11, both Britain's canal and railway systems were nationalized by the government in 1947. The 1950s and 1960s saw a resurgence in the use of British canals, mainly for holiday leisure purposes, and the Inland Waterways Association was formed to promote the rescue of canals. Today, most commercial traffic is restricted to just a few navigations; the rest of the canal system is awash with private pleasure boats.

Yet, there remained a problem. The canals had gradually fallen into disrepair and had to be refurbished, so a famous band of volunteers came to the rescue, Peter was among them. Today, there are more boats using the canals of Britain than during its commercial heyday, so repairing the canals became a priority, to accommodate the many pleasure boats.

T.V. presenter and historian Sir Tony Robinson is backing a campaign, calling on people to bring back to life thousands of miles of derelict historic canals, which helped make Britain the world's first industrial nation. As part of the campaign, an online map was published, which inspired people to unearth more of their local history and help save the canals which shaped where they live. The map enables people to find their nearest lost canals, explore their history and get involved with local groups restoring the canals. Over 200 miles of canals have been restored since the turn of the millennium, and a new report by the University of Northampton highlights economic and social benefits. The University report shows how historic canals can once again bring prosperity to communities, boost the local property prices and help people to lead active and healthy lifestyles. Sir Tony Robinson is working alongside the Inland Waterways Association, in an effort to get more people behind the local restoration efforts to refurbish canals.

So, as is his wont, Sir Tony launched a cunning plan. Professor Peter Watercloset was a resident of Whitechapel, and London has myriad canals, so Peter had been involved for decades in the canal cleaning project. At the height of the industrial revolution, Britain boasted over 5,000 miles of waterway, helping to transport goods and raw materials across the country. They were the envy of the world, and helped to establish Britain as an industrial powerhouse. Over time, with growth of road and rail systems, canal networks fell into decline and would be lost, but for the intervention of a gathering of dedicated mid-1900s volunteers. Professor Peter Watercloset was determined to involve Dr. Zee Garbo in the canal cleaning project, so as an introduction they would do some canal boating, this was part of his cunning plan. The unsuspecting Doctor Zee Garbo was destined to become a waterway cleaning lady, thanks to the Machiavellian machinations of her scheming lover, Professor Peter Watercloset.

Yet in truth it was really great fun, Peter soon got the nickname the "Rubbish Paddler," for his use of a surfboard to get close to the litter on the water. Now he hoped to introduce his new love to his hobby, as his apprentice, Zee was looking forward to it. Their aim was to recycle or upcycle the waste material found, head of this visionary band of dedicated waterway litter pickers is Sir Tony Robinson, whose cunning plan is cleaning up the canals of Britain.

cunning Plan

"The waterway network is part of the fabric of our nation, but it's easy to forget that not so very long ago some of our most popular canals were almost lost forever. The fact that we can still enjoy them now is thanks largely to the vision, dedication and sheer hard work of volunteers in the 60s and 70s. These inspiring men and women just wouldn't take no for an answer, and worked on the basis that nothing was impossible. We need to recapture that spirit within our communities, to support today's volunteers in saving waterways." **Sir Tony Robinson**

Although the cruising narrowboats of today are built to the same design as the early transporters, they are very different inside, for they use the cargo space to provide all the comforts of home. They have hot and cold running water and central heating. The kitchen or galley is usually fully equipped with a fridge and stove, along with microwave cooker and a full range of utensils. The saloon areas are spacious and comfortable, while the lounge area usually has a T.V./D.V.D., as well as a radio and C.D. player – truly a well-equipped and comfy home away from home. Narrowboats only travel at about 3 or 4 miles per hour, so you can take in all the marvellous scenery at a leisurely pace, though there is some work to do. Narrowboating holidays are suitable for almost everyone, but the boats do require two fit adults to be on board: one to handle the boat while the other operates the locks. So, the first task that Professor Peter undertook was to acquaint Zee Garbo with steering a narrowboat, which Zee soon picked up, for she was an accomplished lady. The canals meander

165

their way through miles and miles of unspoilt countryside, as well as passing pretty villages and vibrant cities, and Zeeloved every moment.

"The countryside looks different from the water, with something new around each bend," Zee enthused to Peter, as she steered the boat, which was true. Because travelling at 3 m.p.h., everything passed at a relaxed pace, you had time to absorb the scenery.

"Travelling from Birmingham to London used to take twelve days," Peter remarked. That was when canals were the "motorways" of the eighteenth century; now, they were tranquil corridors, providing a leisurely way of travelling.

"You picked up the steering quickly. Turned yourself into a real helmswoman," Peter congratulated. Zee was doing well; although steering was quite simple, there were some tricky bits to remember. Most of the cruising canal narrowboats normally have tiller steering: pushing to the right will make the boat go left and vice versa. The big secret of narrowboating is taking your time.

Plan your manoeuvres well in advance and remember two things: the boat will take a few seconds to respond, and your boat will pivot from the centre point of its length. This means that you need to keep a watch out for both the front and the back of your narrowboat, or you may run into a nasty accident. A boat is not like a car; if you line up the front of the boat only, then try to turn into a narrow lock, you will run the risk of hitting the bank or wall with the back of your boat. Peter made sure that the first lock they approached had a lock-keeper on duty, so that Peter could remain in the boat to guide Zee into the lock.

"That's it, Zee. Not too much helm, now."

It actually proved unnecessary, for his love had done some sailing back in Poland. She soon picked up helming and was completely in control of the boat. At the next lock, Peter left the boat to operate the lock, and Zee steered the boat neatly in. They had become an expert narrowboat team. After a few locks, Zee decided to change places and operate the lock by herself, while Peter helmed the boat. It was not really much of a problem, because the efficient lock mechanisms could easily be operated by a woman. Then, as cursed luck would have it, Professor Peter Watercloset bumped the narrowboat as he entered the lock. Dr. Zee Garbo was merciless on him, a regular Captain Bligh she was.

"Too much helm, Peter? I've told you a hundred times to watch the back of the boat!" Peter Watercloset chuckled and took the banter good-naturedly; they declared a nautical truce and both became skilled narrowboat skippers. Peter's mishap was not that serious – it had just been a slight bump on the boat's fenders – so no damage had been done. They motored on, taking turns helming or operating locks, which are amazing feats of engineering. Canals are flat, but the landscape rises or dips, so their voyage was on canals of different levels, all separated by locks. A lock is a chamber which you take your boat into, to either go up or down, then you need to empty or fill the chamber accordingly, so that the narrowboat is on the same level as the water in front.

Going up, you open the gate and take the boat into the lock, then you close the gate behind the boat; using your windlass, you open the sluice gate and allow the water to flow from the top pound into the lock. The boat will then rise as the lock fills with water, when the water level inside the lock is the same as the water level ahead, you then open the top gates and take the boat out. You must remember to close both the sluice gate and the lock gate behind you!

This is vitally important because, if you forget, you could create a tsunami and damage the canal rather badly. A boater with a bad memory once caused over £3m in damage to the Shropshire Union Canal, by foolishly leaving lock doors open. Going down a level is just the opposite, you open the lock gate and take the boat into the lock, remembering to close the gate behind the boat. Then, open the sluice gate with your windlass and allow the water to drain out the lock; the boat lowers as the locks water level drops.

When the water level inside the lock is the same as the water level ahead in the canal, open the bottom gates and take the boat out. Water will always flow downhill, so when the lock gate is closed against the pressure of the water, the gate will not open until the water level is equal on both sides. This immense pressure keeps lock gates waterproof, so remember to close the sluice gate and the lock gate.

"Breech the windlass and balance the beam, me hearties. Paddle gears and edge the cill," Captain Zee (née Bligh) ordered, imperially.

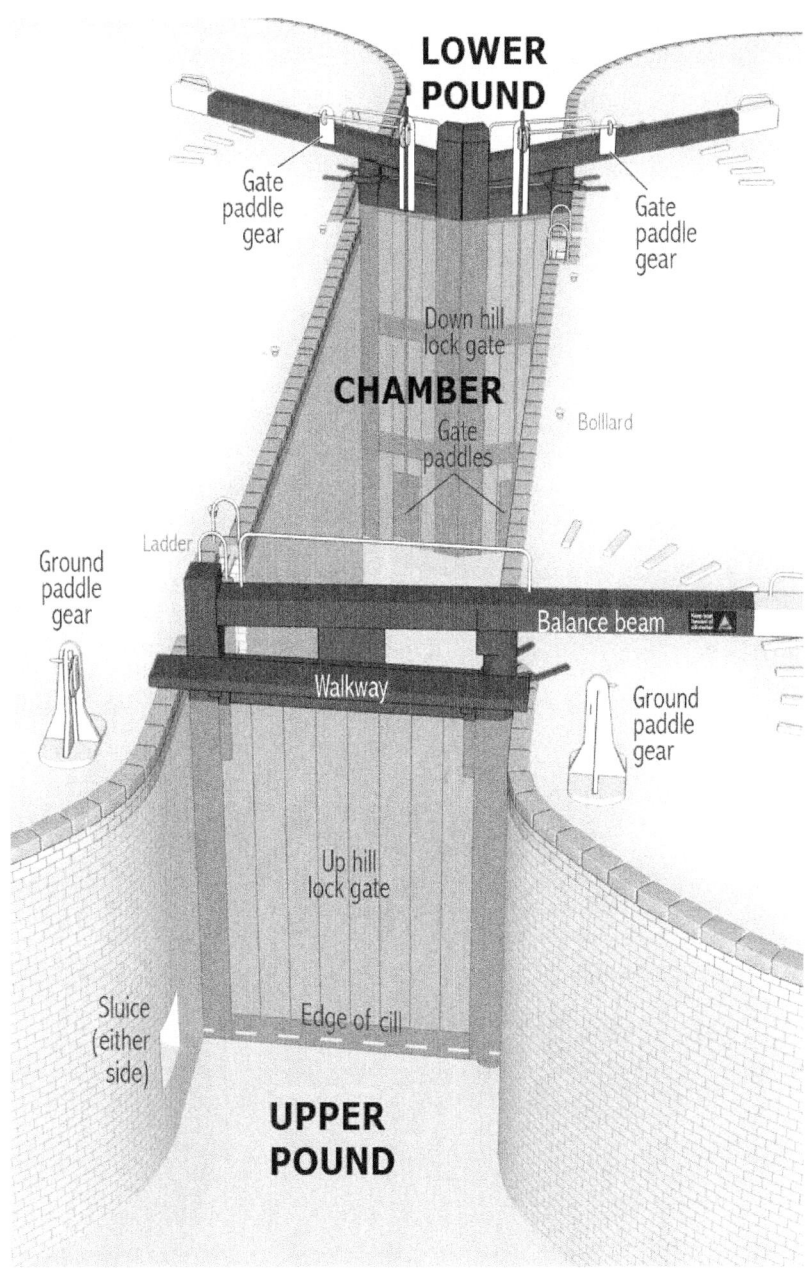

LOWER
POUND

Gate
paddle
gear

Gate
paddle
gear

Down hill
lock gate

CHAMBER

Gate
paddles

Bolllard

Ground
paddle
gear

Ladder

Balance beam

Ground
paddle
gear

Walkway

Up hill
lock gate

Sluice
(either
side)

Edge of cill

UPPER
POUND

171

- THE POUND: this is the stretch of water between two locks, where the levels now vary.

- THE CHAMBER: the main feature of a lock is the watertight enclosure, which can be sealed off from the pounds at either end, by gates.

- GATE PADDLE GEARS: a guillotine mechanism above the gates allowing gate paddle doors to be lifted (opened) or lowered (closed). They allow water to enter or leave.

- GROUND PADDLE GEARS: as above, but they operate sluice paddle doors. Situated on either side of the lock, they connect to the chamber via a sluice tunnel, which allows water to enter or leave the chamber.

- EDGE OF CILL: this is a ledge inside the lock on which the gates sit. They are watertight doors which seal off the chamber from the pounds. Each end of the chamber is equipped with a gate.

- BALANCE BEAM: a long arm projecting from the gate over the towpath. As well as providing leverage to open and close the heavy gate, the beam also balances the weight of the gate in its socket, and so allows the gate to swing more freely.

- THE WINDLASS: also known as the lock handle or iron, this is a spanner-like tool which is kept in the boat, used for opening and closing locks.

Onward they motored, for Peter's destination was a west London suburb quaintly named Little Venice, which for the last 30 years had been the venue for a festival hosted by Inland Waterways Association. Around 100 decorated canal boats cram into Little Venice to compete for "Best Decorated Boat", or perhaps the "Best Dressed Boater". This free event attracts boaters from all over; some travel for many miles, work through numerous locks and take several weeks, just to take part. In 2011, the canals bloomed into a riot of colour in Browning's Pool, because that year's theme was "Canals in Bloom."

Boaters had produced eye-catching floating displays which wowed the crowds, the theme of blooming flowers for decorating the boats gave endless possibilities for the competitors' creative talents, and the 2011 cavalcade was a floating flower shop. The festival is not just for boaters, but also for tourists and interested locals. Thousands of spectators come to soak up the atmosphere around Little Venice, to watch the boat parades while sampling the food and drink on offer. Visitors have no need to go hungry or thirsty, with Greek dishes, Indian street food, crepes, traditional fish and chips, wraps, ice creams and, of course, a real ale bar, all available on site. Traders, community groups and charities set out their stalls to provide cheese, fudge, sausages, cakes, hand-made cards and crafted toys. Zee Garbo was entranced at the glittering display before her: clothing, jewelry, plants, accessories, creams and lotions. There were exotic items not normally available in traditional stores – truly a shoppers' paradise.

"Thank you for bringing me, Peter," Dr. Zee Garbo enthused, as they walked amongst the stalls. She had heard of Little Venice before, but had not realized it was so beautiful. This neighbourhood of London is around the junction of the Paddington Arm of the Grand Union Canal and the Regent's Canal; to the south is Paddington Basin and famous Hyde Park.

Many buildings are Regency-white-painted, stucco terraced townhouses, and taller blocks in the same style, set amongst the canals – it is truly picturesque. Little Venice is one of London's prime residential areas and contains shops, restaurants, theatres and pubs. Canalside venues include Canal Café Theatre, Puppet Theatre Barge, Waterside Canal Café, and Cafe La Ville. In the north, where Little Venice blends into Maida Vale, are historic, grade-II listed pubs like Warwick Castle, Warrington and Prince Alfred. Peter and Zee moored their narrowboat and, as well as watching the canal festival, spent time exploring the area. The origin of the quaint name "Little Venice" is sometimes attributed to the celebrated poet Robert Browning, who lived at Beauchamp Lodge, in 1862–87. This was disputed by Lord Kinross, in 1966, who asserted Lord Byron (1788–1824) humorously compared the locale to Venice. Some famous people lived there; Katherine Mansfield stayed as a music student at Beauchamp Lodge, during 1908-9, while Sigmund Freud lived briefly in what is now the Colonnade Hotel.

Situated on Warrington Crescent the Colonnade was originally a pair of houses dating from 1863. It is particularly ornate, with pretty mouldings and a continuous first-floor balustrade. Mathematical genius Alan Turing, who broke the German Enigma code during World War II, was born in 1912 in a maternity home situated right in Warrington Crescent – though Alan Turing never broke the code of who named Little Venice. The name was eventually applied as an electoral ward of City of Westminster, and the Inland Waterways Association has hosted a

"Canalway Cavalcade" there since 1983. Some famous people have attended this event, as you can see from the adjacent picture, see if you can recognise them? The fatberg fighters you already know but the other two are nearly as famous, both of them generous contributors to restoration of canals and rehabilitation of wildlife, seen by the little rescued duck in the front characters hand, good friend of Sir Tony Robinson.

Then came the serious side of their narrowboat adventure, because removing the giant fatberg from the Boris Johnson Tunnel had resulted in 400,000 tonnes of sewage flooding the Thames. More than 100,000 fish died on just one day, in June 2011. Peter and Zee motored their narrowboat to a sewer outfall near Whitechapel, and beheld a shocking sight, which brought tears to their eyes. Gasping for breath and nibbling on floating faeces, fish twitched feebly then tilted pathetically on their sides and stopped moving. The rotting smell flared the nostrils, as dead fish piled up on the riverbank.

"The Boris Johnson Tunnel is inadequate," Doctor Zee snapped. It was a really sore point with her, because Boris Johnson had promised that no more than 20 million tons of raw sewage would be dumped into the Thames River annually, not this awful carnage!

The tunnel vision of Mayor Johnson was the problem; because Professor Peter Watercloset had repeatedly warned, the proposed new tunnel was too narrow. Built in 2010, the Boris Johnson Tunnel quickly resulted in the formation of a deadly fatberg. According to London Water figures, over 62 million tonnes of sewage were dumped into the river in 2011 – a large increase from the 55 million in 2010.

The sewage system was bursting at the seams, which is why Professor Peter Watercloset and Dr. Zee Garbo, were pressuring the myopic Boris Johnson into building a new mammoth super-sewer. The sewers built by Joseph Bazalgette between 1831 and 1866 were visionary structures, built to accommodate a population of 4 million, at a time when only 2 million people lived in London. Today's population of 8.6 million is much more than planned; it has exploded from 7.4 million people in 2004, and in the next 20 years the Office for National Statistics predicts London's populace will grow beyond 10.5 million. Another sewerland visionary was needed, that man was Professor Peter Watercloset.

Peter persisted doggedly in his attempts to raise public awareness for a new super-sewer. Not only would this solve London's sewage problem, but Peter's vision included establishing acres of new public space, by creating seven paved platforms over the Thames River. The proposed platform on Victoria Embankment, joined Northumberland and Regent Street sewer overflows. Like at Blackfriars Bridge Foreshore, where platforms will be built to link to the main tunnel. These spaces will be for public use, a fine example of public service mixed with public use.

The new sewer was urgently needed, for Mayor Johnson had not considered the impact of climate change, extreme rainfall was now seven times more likely according to Metrological Office scientists. In 2010, London Water warned that 7,000 basements in Hammersmith and Fulham, Kensington and Chelsea were at risk of being flooded with sewage. Yet the London mayor was infuriated when the European Commission sent a warning letter to the U.K., saying the terrible condition of the Thames River violated the E.U.'s strict *Urban Waste Water Treatment Directive.*

This was a law created to prevent pollution.

After putting up a fight in the European Court of Justice, on 18th October 2012 Mayor Johnson would be ordered to clean the Thames or face multi-million-pound fines. Such obstinacy typified the crass attitude of Boris, instead of backing the super-sewer proposal of Professor Watercloset, the mayor railed against the interfering E.U., and suggested Britain should pull out of the European Union.

The super sewer proposed by Professor Watercloset carried a price tag of £4.2bn ($6.4bn), which terrified the mayor yet he waxed eloquently about his pet project, the mythical "Garden Bridge" reserved solely for wealthy friends. Which on forthcoming page 336, will be shown as a profligate extravagance. Peter had anchored the narrowboat near the outflow pipe of the Boris Johnson Tunnel, which had flooded the Thames with sewage, for he wanted to draw samples from the river to record the devastation. Night had fallen and it was too dark to motor on, so they decided to moor the narrowboat, and spend the night next to the sewer outfall.

"It really smells here," Zee sniffed the air, which was filled with the rank stench of rotten fish and sewage. Boris Johnson had returned the Great Stink to the Thames River, so Peter riposted wittily:

"Perhaps the smell comes from the rotting Thomas Wildey, hanging on the gibbet," Peter chuckled and Zee was perplexed.

"Who was Thomas Wildey?" Zee asked in some puzzlement, for she was unfamiliar with the legends of the English canals and rivers, so Peter explained the myth to her.

"Thomas Wildey murdered a mother and daughter, for which he was hanged. His body was placed in a gibbet and rotted for months, so a mist and smell in the area is said to be caused by Wildey."

"Fascinating. Please tell me more," Doctor Zee grinned, for she enjoyed ghost stories. So, Peter complied, for he knew many stories. The atmosphere was perfect for ghost stories, the night was inky black and there was mist over the river. The stench of death lay thick in the air, as Peter sat in the cockpit telling ghost stories, there were plenty about the waterways and soon another one would be added?

"Next to the River Tyne, heading up toward Bardon Mill, a woman wearing a blue dress pushes a pram. This phantom woman walks at speed along the bank of the river, past the spot where the body of a woman and baby were found, pre-twentieth century." Peter informed, then he paused and mused.

"These stories are perhaps related to a legend popular in Scotland, one story recounts that an Old Spinning Lady, sits on the bank of a stream, endlessly spinning her little wheel. While, near Barton on River Isle, floating high enough so that her feet remain dry, Lady Isabel passes over the water. Also near Barton is the "Beautiful Face in the Lake", accidentally killed by her father, because she ran away with a knight. Her spirit haunts the water and is said to bless any who see her face."

HUMBER ESTUARY LIGHTS

BABY IN PRAM

MAN ON GIBBET

KING OTTER

SPINNING LADY

CANAL SPIRIT

184

"There she is, I see Lady Isabel, I'm blessed," Zee joked, pointing out the cockpit.

Peter ominously warned his love: "Don't you joke, Zee, or the "Canal Spirit" will grab you and hold you underwater to drown."

"What can I do?" Zee cried in mock terror.

"You must capture a king otter," Peter laughed. "This large water mammal if caught, will grant a single wish in return for its freedom."

There were many legends and Peter knew quite a few, for he had been narrowboating for many years. The ghost of Peg O'Neill is said to haunt the Ribble River, demanding an animal sacrificed to the river every seven years; a man once tried to cross the river before he made the sacrifice and he promptly drowned. Yet, lucky are people who witness the ghostly "Bishop's Barge" sailing up the Brundall River! The Barge is covered with fine cloth and silk and contains 28 rowers; the bishop blesses the sick as he passes – but he had not heard of Covid 19.

Long into the inky night, Peter and Zee talked of watery ghosts, like the eerie Humber Estuary green lights, which forecasting the drowning of a fisherman.

"Am I going nuts, or are those green lights?" Zee asked and Peter thought she was joking, then he saw what looked like static electricity at the sewer outfall, where the narrowboat's stern was anchored. Peter decided to check it out, he clambered along the cabin walkway. Suddenly, the boat lurched, and Peter was in the water.

"PETER, ARE YOU ALRIGHT?!" Zee screamed, but he was a tough old nut and, grasping the rails, he scrambled into the cockpit.

"Start the engine, Zee!" Peter gasped, as he went for the anchor. Something huge had grasped the stern of the boat, and was pulling it down into the water. Then came a terrible stink in the air, completely smothering the dead fish smell; something quite different. The smell was putrid beyond belief – a stink which seemed situated in the stench of selfishness, the heart and core of modern liberalism.

186

Professor Peter was suddenly terribly afraid, something truly evil had emerged from the sewer outfall of the Boris Johnson Tunnel.

"THE FATBERG IS ALIVE!" Zee screamed.

"Give the engine full throttle, Zee!" Peter panted, as he struggled with the anchor. They stared fearfully at the stern, but the inky night revealed only the eerie, flashing green lights.

"IT'S PULLING US DOWN!" Peter shouted, for by now the stern of the boat was underwater. Peter grabbed the tiller and pulled it hard over. Driven by the engine, the boat slewed sideways then, with a splash, the stern rose and the bows settled in the water – for the Brown Blob had lost its grip!

"WE'RE FREE!" Zee shouted, and kept the engine on full revs as they motored away from the sewer monster. Glancing back, all they could see were flashing green lights.

"I'm not leaving this here," Zee said, determinedly. She was mad as a hellcat. "We're going caving!" So, that's exactly what they did.

The Secret Sewer

It's interesting that, not long after Peter and Zee went caving in an old flint mine in Whitechapel, a mining disaster flooded the news; the 2011 Chilean mining accident riveted the attention of the world. A cave-in at San Jose gold mine trapped 33 men 2,300ft underground, and they were only rescued after 69 days. The state-owned mining company Codelco took over rescue efforts from the mine's owners, exploratory boreholes were drilled and, seventeen days after the accident, a note was found taped to a drill bit pulled to the surface:

"Jimmy Savile se esconde aquí abajo." ("Jimmy Savile is hiding down here.") The Chilean Mining Ministry, the NASA space agency and British Broadminded Television threw themselves into rescuing Jimmy Savile. On 9th October 2011 the miners were winched to the surface one at a time, in a purpose-built rescue capsule, as an estimated one

billion folks worldwide carefully watched. Yet, despite all the spectators, Jimmy Savile was not spotted, and the mystery of that strange Spanish note has never been solved, for only Harry Hack really knows and he's still not telling.

"A fatberg killed Savile," Harry insists to this day, which may well be possible, considering Peter and Zee's narrow escape in the canal? They reported the incident to police, but the desk sergeant just stared at them, tiredly; there were many strange stories emanating from the canal. So, they motored back to their boat-hire basin, where they got more attention, due to burn marks on the narrowboat's stern?

They'd approach the fatberg from another angle, enter through the back door as it were, and prove their theory conclusively. Dr. Zee was an experienced caver. She had explored nearly all the caves of the Polish Tatra Mountains; with a total length of 134km, they were popular with the world cavers. So, Zee organized the protective gear.

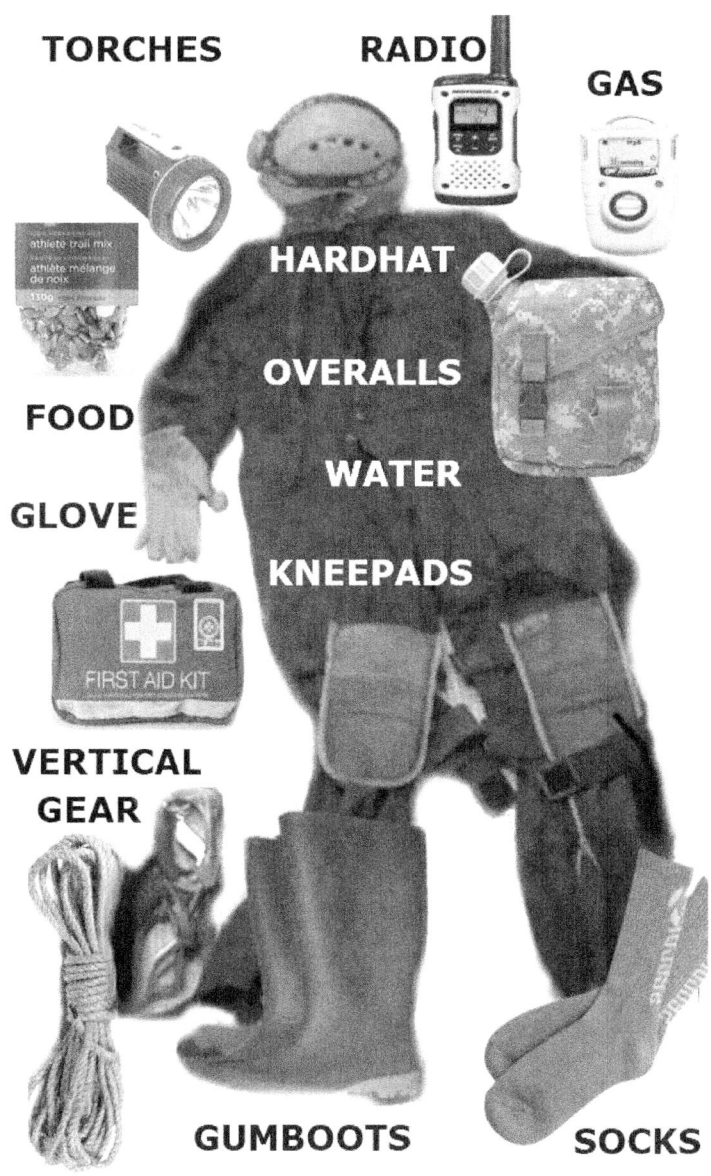

TORCHES RADIO GAS

HARDHAT

OVERALLS

FOOD

WATER

GLOVE

KNEEPADS

VERTICAL
GEAR

GUMBOOTS SOCKS

They were exploring a largely dry cave system, so they wore cotton one-piece "Long Johns," under a protective oversuit. They carried the latest L.E.D. lighting, which offered superior duration and brightness, and is considerably lighter than miners' lead-acid lamps. They had protective kneepads and elbow pads, neoprene gloves were worn as protection against the cold, and Wellington boots have good grip and great water resistance.

While helmets are used to protect the cavers against occasional falling rocks, they find much more use in protecting the cavers' heads from bumps and scrapes, as the caver moves through low or awkward passages. You might find this overly excessive for traversing through the Whitechapel Caves, where guides conducted tours for tourists, but our two scientists intended going where tourists never go. In fact, even the Whitechapel guides never dared to enter that locked door, where depraved evil lurked?

"The fatberg dared to attack our narrowboat. Let's see what that evil entity is made of."

After the vicious attack Zee had immediately vowed to approach the fatberg from another angle, she was an experienced caver so she knew how to do this. Doctor Zee Garbo was angry, the fatberg had made a determined enemy, so the two lovers prepared for war. Peter Watercloset and lovely Dr. Zee Garbo had fallen in love, so they probed each other's minds, wanting to know each other.

"Where on Earth did you get the outlandish name Watercloset?" Zee asked impishly.

"I'm proud to say that I was born with the name, it's fairly uncommon: only two families in Britain," Peter smiled. Watercloset was indeed an unusual surname, imagine going to school with such a name, yet Peter had never thought of changing it.

"Like in the Johnny Cash song, I grew up quick and I grew up mean, my fist got hard and my wits got keen," Peter parodied wittily, and Dr. Zee Garbo laughed delightedly as she recalled the wise words of *A Boy Named Sue.* Peter passed it off lightly, but his boyhood had not been easy; he had to fight hard to survive.

"What about you? Where did Doctor Zee Garbo come from?" Peter asked, he grinned while thinking of the film *Doctor Zhivago,* directed by David Lean and based on the 1957 Boris Pasternak novel. Zee caught the grin and replied at once:

"I'm the secret daughter of Greta Garbo," Peter was about to laugh but he saw she was serious, which absolutely flabbergasted him, so he pressed his love for more answers.

"Who was your father?" Peter asked.

"Well, that is the question. Around the time I was born, my mother Greta Garbo had many affairs: conductor Leopold Stokowski was one, also writer Erich Maria Remarque," Zee paused for a moment, then continued. "I think my father was the photographer Cecil Beaton, because he described an affair with Greta Garbo in 1948; I was born in 1949."

Professor Peter Watercloset was staggered. The daughter of Greta Garbo? It utterly floored him.

"What was your mother like?" Peter had to ask. The screen goddess Greta Garbo was a noted recluse; not much known about her.

"I never met my mother or my father. They paid for me to be brought up by nuns in Poland," Zee said, in a matter-of-fact way. "The Polish nuns educated me and later arranged my university entrance."

Then, Dr. Zee dismissed the subject, her mother Greta Garbo had lived into her nineties dying in 1990, but Zee had never contacted her.

"Forget the chit-chat, Peter. We must figure out how to use the Whitechapel Caves, to get into the secret sewer under B.B.T. Studios."

The famous caves under Whitechapel had over ten miles of dark and mysterious passageways. Hewn from soft chalk, the caves were mined by hand and were interconnected with the sewers. Excavated for the use of flint and lime, the caves were mined right up to the 1830s, then used as an ammunition depot in World War One. The caves were divided into Saxon, Druid and Roman technology; recently discovered intertwining passageways gave an insight into British history, but Peter and Zee intended to look farther?

The Whitechapel Caves have also been used as suitably spooky cavern locations, for such television programs as *Doctor Who* and *Randall and Hopkirk*, and as such they are visited by film buffs and history fans. They continue to capture the interest of all ages, and are a major London tourist attraction for anyone interested in geology.

Dr. Zee was more interested in biology, for the caves ran under Ripper Street, which was the location of most Jack the Ripper killings. But, far more importantly, it was also the current London address of British Broadminded Television, which was serviced by manholes emitting a mysterious green mist. Dr. Zee Garbo was determined to find the source of that mist, and she hoped to use the Whitechapel Caves to do so. Finally, her painstaking research at the London Water Board showed the way. "We now have a map!" Zee exulted. It had taken much ferreting, but she had found it.

Whitechapel has many underground networks – tube trains, electricity, water – but there was another key one: this was the complex network of pipes carrying London's waste and also surface runoff water, ending up at Crossness or Beckton. In typical Victorian style, the industrial nature of the facility didn't stop the creation of carefully tiled tunnels and storage chambers, but finding maps of this hidden network was difficult. Likely for security reasons, the authorities do not publish maps, and it took some really hard pressing before the London Water Board agreed to release some old maps to Dr. Zee. One of them, dated 1880, was exactly what she was looking for, because it showed a series of disused sewers right under the B.B.T. building. Could they be the source of the mysterious green mist?

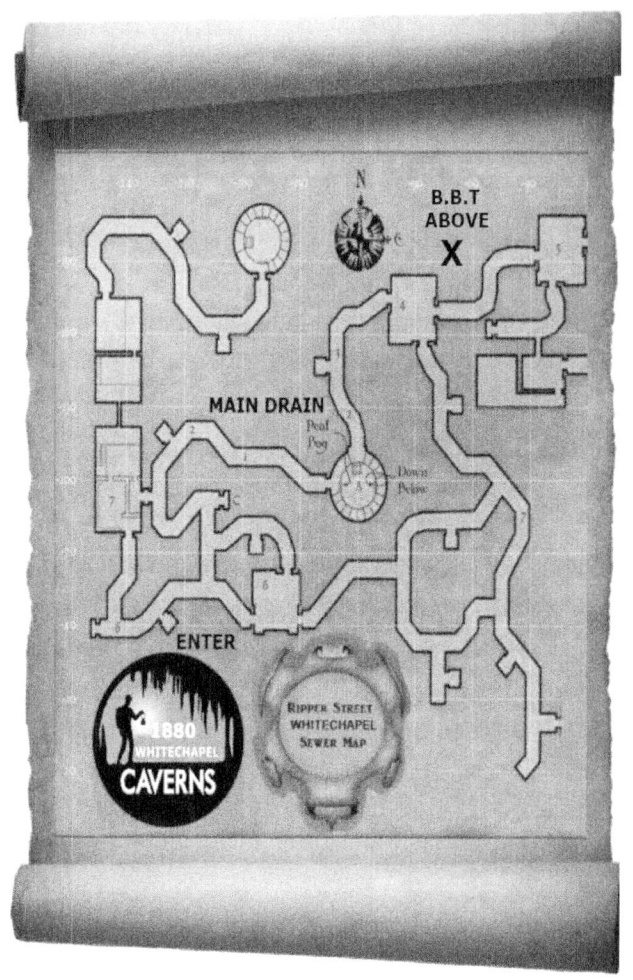

Zee and Peter were now properly equipped for their visit to the Whitechapel Caves. The old 1880 map described them as "caverns", and placed them next to the abandoned sewer. They had to take great care, because sewer gas contains methane gas (CH4), so there is a risk of explosion hazard or even fatal asphyxiation. Sewer gases also contain the rotten egg smelling, deadly hydrogen sulphide (H2S).

So, besides their protective clothing, they also had a G.A.S. Sniffer (standing for "gas analyzer sulfide); the combustible gas analyzer was set at its most sensitive setting. The instrument would respond to a widespread range of volatile organics, but also give an instantaneous indicator of a substance present at the time of the test, so at the first hint of gas they would get out, pronto.

Dr. Zee Garbo had authorization from the London Water Board, to enter the abandoned sewer under British Broadminded Television, so the guides at the Whitechapel Caves were courteous and helpful. That was until they approached the bolted door, which connected the caves with the secret sewer, then the guide unbolted the door and left in a hurry (they were taking no chances) Dr. Zee Garbo stepped through the door and activated the G.A.S. Sniffer. There was a faint reading, but nothing dangerous, so Peter and Zee entered the sewer. They were intent on tracing the source of the entity which attacked their narrowboat – an evil which came into existence because of the narrow tunnel vision of stubborn London mayor Boris Johnson. Resulting in the formation of a fatberg, caused by people flushing cooking oil and plastic wet wipes down the loo. Moves were now afoot to mark products to indicate which were *"Fine to Flush"* – certification which should also include Boris.

They studied the map then moved forward, the murky tunnels cast shadows which played tricks with the imagination; there was a Jack the Ripper behind every corner! Yet the police linked only five killings to Jack the Ripper: they were Mary Ann Nichols, Annie Chapman, Elizabeth Stride, Katherine Eddowes and Mary Jane Kelly. Named the "Canonical Five", to keep the list accurate, their murders from the 31st August to 9th November 1888 are the most likely to be linked. The murders were never solved, and legends around them became a combination of genuine research, pseudohistory and folklore. The term "Ripperology" was coined to describe analysis of Ripper cases. Yet, Jack was a novice compared to Peter Dinsdale, who killed 26 children, while the Yorkshire Ripper Peter Sutcliffe slew 13, the West family snuffed out 12. The acid bath murderer John George Haig dissolved 15. Yet, these figures cannot compare to the many who died of Covid-19, thanks to the tunnel vision of Mayor Boris Johnson, who in 2019 would spew mass slaughter.

The carnage of Covid-19 was yet to come, though. Right now, our heroes reflected on folk tales of London sewers. Like the canal legends, there were many horror stories about London's sewers. There was a city-wide panic back in the 1860s, following the death of a well-known politician, when it was rumoured that a band of thugs were garroting people and disappearing into the sewers. Then, news stories around the turn of the century, claimed verifiable archaeological discoveries of hidden subterranean habitats, when large human remains were found in the city's sewers. Yet, no story was more chilling than gossip that London sewers are full of giant pigs, which will one day run free from their foetid dwelling and run riot in the city.

"Black Swine in the Whitechapel Sewers" is one terrifying Victorian urban legend which proves intractably resilient, because someone came up with the story that a sow had somehow got into the sewer, littered some offspring and fed them on edible rubbish washed into the sewer – which gave Peter an idea.

"BLACK SWINE! RUN FOR YOUR LIFE!" Peter screamed hysterically, sneaking up behind Zee Garbo – love makes you childish.

"YOU SWINE!" she screamed pretending to hit him. Then Zee said, darkly: "Take care, Professor Watercloset. Did you know that Jack the Ripper was a woman?" Peter laughed at this patent absurdity. "That's patent nonsense Zee. Jill the Ripper doesn't quite have the same ominous ring to it." Yet, was it possible there was some truth in the theory? As they walked on, Zee Garbo elaborated on the theory. A series of notes signed *"Jack the Ripper"* led the police to believe that the killer was a man. But, was it possible that the police had got it wrong, woman are just as capable as killing as are men? For, police detective Frederick Abberline had recorded a witness claiming a woman leaving a murder scene, while wearing the dead prostitute's clothes. London historian John Morris has stated the case for a female killer in his 2012 book *Hand of a Woman*; putting doctor's wife Lizzie Williams in the frame.

"Jack the Ripper was a Polish barber," Peter riposted to the enraged Zee Garbo, who protested hotly, for she was Polish. Yet, there was evidence for it: Jack the Ripper had been recently revealed as 23-year-old Polish barber Aaron Kosminski, after tests taken from a bloodstained shawl revealed two sets of D.N.A. traces, of both Kosminski and the Ripper victim Catherine Eddowes.

Yet, Zee Garbo would soon prove to be eerily prescient about a female Ripper, when scarlet harlot Buxom Boris ripped into the people of Britain and caused horrifying slaughter. Interesting indeed, but scary talk in the dark sewer.

They pressed on, and the passage narrowed until it was crawling room only. Finally, they came to the broad chamber directly under British Broadminded Television.

"We've arrived," Dr. Zee grinned.

"Thank heavens," Peter panted.

Dr. Zee Garbo had found what she sought: the

source of the mysterious green mist Evil Neville and the Old Farts had identified. The curious, brownish sludge which produced the mist lay in the crosscut directly below them, so Peter bravely volunteered to climb down, and collect a sample for Doctor Zee Garbo to study.

"Is this green mist dangerous?" Peter asked, as his boots sunk into the brown sludge, and the green mist rose up around him.

"The G.A.S. Sniffer registers negative," Zee assured him. There was a faint rotten egg smell, but not too bad, as if the Brown Blob had not yet fully developed. Zee handed down a sample bag, and Peter dug in with a shovel, into the stinky, sticky mess. It was heavy going for the sewage was really sludgy, to say nothing of the smell, they both had nose plugs but Peter removed his to breathe better.

It's really rank," Peter gasped, he was used to the sewage smell, but this was different.

"This is curious stuff," Peter remarked, as he filled the sample bag. It was almost as if the brown substance shrank away from the shovel, but perhaps it just had a plasticity which seemed to resist. Then, Professor Peter screamed at the top of his voice.

"IT MOVED! I swear, it moved!"

He struggled to get out of the crosscut, but the Brown Blob pulled him back; bubbling green tentacles seemed to encircle his boots.

Zee grabbed his hands and pulled. Peter kicked hard and struggled out of his Wellington boots, which were held fast by the green mist, now solidifying into clingy tentacles. Then, they both bolted for their lives, the barefoot professor rivalling Usain Bolt. For, now a new danger presented itself – something deeply feared by Professor Peter Watercloset. His worst nightmare had come terrifyingly true, like something out a horror movie.

"BATS!" cried the petrified professor, for he possessed an atavistic fear of bats. Holding Zee's hand, he hotfooted it barefoot for the entrance, the sample bag clutched firmly in his other hand. Peter really didn't mind the rats scurrying around his feet, for they were kind of cute, but he was scared stiff of bats. Perhaps it was the vampire legend which instilled the fear, for Hallowe'en had become popular in Britain, and vampires were the favourite outfits. The glow in the dark fangs, fake red blood which chills your bones, and trademark plastic bats hanging from your shoulder. Bats have been part of our ecosystem for fifty million years, while modern-day concepts of human vampires have only been around since the 1800s, yet most people know more about vampires than they do about bats? There are only three species of bat which drink blood, and over a thousand others which consume fruit and insects, so the bat is one of nature's prime pest controllers. Yet the *Dracula* novel, published by Bram Stoker in 1897, has cemented the link forever between bats and vampires, which was perhaps the source of fear for Professor Peter Watercloset.

Bats are not normally found in sewers, but abutting the sewer were the Whitechapel Caves, which the bats could use as an ingress. The movement of two humans may have disturbed them.

Flying around the sewer in a panic creates a chaotic amount of noise, so the bats simply ignored their personal navigation systems; their echolocators were on, but the bats weren't listening, and this caused them to bump into the running Peter Watercloset. This would result in him developing strange, flu-like symptoms: coughing, sore throat and fever, plus a loss of smell? So, in line with lessons learnt at *Exercise Cygnus*, Dr. Zee put Peter into lockdown, isolated in his room until his system wiped out the virus. Blood tests indicated Peter was not infected by SARS, but a new unknown strain of coronavirus.

Because Peter's was a primary infection, Dr. Zee wondered if his blood could produce a vaccine. He was closely monitored by Dr. Zee, but Peter was a strong man; he recovered in a few days and no trace of the virus remained. Still, Dr. Zee kept a blood sample for a possible vaccine. Bats can pass on zoonotic viruses, but Peter's case was unusual, because a primary infection from bats is rare; another animal is usually an intermediate host between bats and humans. A bat's strong immune system prevents it dying from infections, so they carry and pass on the virus to other animals, who infect humans. Could blood from a primary bat infection be used to develop a vaccine, Zee wondered? This would have to wait, for the fatberg took centre stage again. Harry Hack had turned the B.B.T fatberg autopsy into a musical comedy called *Flushing Fatbergs!* The stinking mass would even be animated, and Harry planned to release stink bombs in the theatre.

Peter and Zee weren't into self-aggrandizement, but the resultant publicity would encourage London Water to assist them, and also educate the public about the proper use of toilets. That the only things which should be flushed down the toilet are the "three *p*s": *p*ee, *p*oo and *p*aper of a toilet roll variety; anything else goes into rubbish bins. London Water examined all wet wipes and introduced the *Fit to Flush* standard, the Whitechapel Fatberg was a handy publicity vehicle, as it was a global celebrity. The newspapers reeked of it and a slice of the fatberg was displayed in London Museum, which the excited curator described as: *"One of our most fascinating and disgusting objects."*

So, London Water allocated a laboratory to Dr. Zee Garbo, and she began to analyze the smelly Brown Blob sample Peter had brought back from the sewer. Her tests indicated that neither the Brown Blob nor its green slime displayed any key characteristics of life, like the ability to grow and reproduce, or use energy then excrete waste. It was incredibly frustrating. Dr. Zee had no proof the fatberg was developing a deadly life form. Also nagging at her was the advent of a bat coronavirus in Peter's blood, although there was no link it was worrying, what did the future hold for Britain? A deadly disease and the rise of the fatberg, because the fatberg fighter's boffin Dr. Zee failed to prove that the fatberg was producing a life form

"But, the nasty thing moves," Evil Neville exclaimed, and Peter backed him up, because he was sure it had grabbed him in the sewer.

"Yes, sometimes, movement is listed as a characteristic of life," Dr. Zee mused. Then she continued, pensively: "Yet many living things, such as trees, coral and barnacles, are incapable of movement yet they are classified as being alive."

"How do you classify the Brown Blob, Doctor?" Evil Neville asked curiously, he had become an enthusiastic member of the fatberg fighters' team, but Dr. Zee hesitated before she answered him. Was it a virus which is a special organism, capable of reproducing within host cells, existing independently of its host? Unfortunately, it was impossible to state with certainty that the Brown Blob was alive, it appeared to move and change position but could it reproduce? What of sensitivity, could it detect or sense stimuli and respond to them, and could it grow in size by increasing the number of its cells. Was it capable of respiration, by creating chemical reactions?

?

So, they were stumped, with nothing concrete to show authorities. Harry Hack of B.B.T. had no interest in helping, and the Whitechapel counter-terror police, would be reluctant to arrest a lump of sewage.

"We must find a way to alert the authorities," Peter fretted, worriedly, convinced that the fatberg would spawn a life form. Then something happened that shook both Peter and Zee, who were both blithely unaware of it, so it hit like a bolt from a blueblood.

"There's only one thing for it: I'll have to take up my seat in the House of Lords." Evil Neville offered.

HOUSE OF LORDS

The Right Honourable the Lords Spiritual and
Temporal of the United Kingdom of Great Britain
and Northern Ireland

House of Lords

The British House of Lords, also known as the House of Peers, is the upper house of Parliament, which is unlike the elected House of Commons, in that all members of the House of Lords are appointed. Membership of the Lords is drawn from the peerage, who are chosen by the current monarch on advice of the prime minister and the House of Lords Appointments Commission. The House of Lords scrutinizes bills which have been approved by the House of Commons, and while it is unable to prevent a bill passing into law, except in certain limited circumstances, it can delay bills and force the Commons to amend their decisions.

The United Kingdom government was defeated 48 times by the lords during the parliamentary session of 2010-12, so they are a pretty influential group of old farts. The House of Lords is the only upper house of any bicameral parliament which is larger than its lower house; the House of Commons has a defined 650-seat membership while there are currently 790 sitting lords. Very few of these are female, since most hereditary peerages can only be inherited by men, but this is gradually changing, as can be seen below.

The first women in the House of Lords took up their seats only in 1958, forty years after women were granted the right to stand as MP's in the House of Commons. These women were life peers appointed by government, while women hereditary peers were able to sit in the Lords from 1963, the Lords were nearly as misogynist as B.B.T.

In 2015, the first Church of England female bishops sat in the House of Lords. The same year that Michelle Georgina Mone, the Baroness of Mayfair took up her seat, bringing a bit of needed glamour to the House. The beautiful baroness is more partial to lace lingerie than lordly scarlet and ermine robes, topped by an England or Springbok rugby cap, which has become the fashion in the Lords.

Baroness Mone is a canny Scots entrepreneur. In 2010 she was awarded an O.B.E. for her contribution to business, for Michelle Mone is co-founder of the lingerie company Ultimo. Also the inventor of black shell support bras, now she is hoping to stiffen the Lords, for the House has lost considerable clout in the power struggle between elected government and the appointed lords. The Lords membership once included all hereditary peers, other than those in the peerage of Ireland, until the House of Lords Act of 1999, which decreased the membership from 1,330 in October 1999 to 669 in March 2000.

Fortunately, the 1999 Act also allowed the right to

membership of 92 hereditary Scottish peers. So, as a result of this lordly loophole, Evil Neville became a member of the House of Lords, when the recent death of his elder brother made him Laird of Loch Ness. A supreme court replaced the House of Lords in 2009, as the final court of appeal, but the Lords still carried plenty of clout. Which Lord Neville would use in 2019, to curb the power-crazy Boris Johnson, who became Tory leader and attempted to establish a dictatorship? It was Lord Neville and fellow lords who stopped Prime Minister Johnson from forcing a ruinous no-deal Brexit on Britain, proving how valued were the lords.

"I never knew you were part of the Scottish peerage," Peter observed, and Lord Neville opened up about himself.

"My elder brother was a typical haughty Scottish laird, whose 20,000-acre estate was strictly no tourists, but friends-only hunting and fishing. Now, with my brother gone, I'm the Laird of Loch Ness," Evil Neville informed rather glumly, for he preferred motorbikes.

"I imagine you were the black sheep," Peter smiled.

Neville grinned, naughtily. "Aye, that I was; no interest at all in hunting or fishing. All I wanted to do was canyon jumping on my Norton Atlas, which my brother disliked, as he thought it would attract the tourists." The reluctant Lord confessed to his friend, they chatted amiably as they relaxed on the hard wooden benches of Ryanair's first class. They were flying to Dublin for the pivotal Six Nations game between Ireland and England, despite the fact that Evil Neville was a Scottish laird, he was also an avid England rugby supporter. The reasons for this will be revealed later, though they were pretty obvious.

They landed at Dublin Airport and made their way to the adjacent taxi rank, Peter Watercloset slowed his pace, for Lord Evil Neville walked with a cane. Then they were off to the Aviva Stadium. With a capacity for 51,700 spectators, it was built in 2007, on the site of the revered old Lansdowne Road stadium.

Aviva Stadium was now home to all Irish rugby and Republic-only football, strange country Ireland Evil Neville and Peter Watercloset were both fanatic England rugby fans – Peter because he was a born 'n' bred loyal Englishman, and Evil Neville because his home nation Scotland wasn't that good at rugby. In a desperate attempt to lift Scottish rugby, the Royal Bank of Scotland sponsored the 2011 championship, so it was called R.B.S. Six Nations, but once more Scotland battled it out with Italy to avoid the "Wooden Spoon", which was given to the side who comes last. Italy lost to Scotland, but had the great honour of beating France, and Andrea Masi became the first Italian to win Player of the Championship. So, you can see why Evil Neville had given up supporting Scotland, and became a fanatic England fan. He was again disappointed, as Ireland destroyed the England rugby team in Dublin. England would become champions after France beat Wales , but the Dublin defeat rankled Evil Neville, because it robbed England of the Grand Slam.

Brian O'Driscoll Jonny Wilkinson

The Brian Blessed voice boomed disappointment from the stands, as three Jonathan Sexton penalties gave Ireland an early 9-0 lead, which they extended as the rampant Irish scythed over. Ireland led England

17-3 at half-time, and Evil Neville foamed at the mouth. Ireland's captain Brian O'Driscoll broke the scoring record with a 25th try, England legend Jonny Wilkinson came on, but to no avail. The result was a crushing let-down for England, who were chasing a first Grand Slam since 2003, when the now England team manager Martin Johnson captained them to a 42-6 win in Dublin.

"England got it very wrong," Martin Johnson admitted in the pub afterward, and Lord Neville thought back to those glory days of 2003, when England have won the Rugby World Cup. Beating Australia 20-17 in a game which entered the history books, as one of the country's great moments of sporting triumph. The final, in Sydney, was won just 26 seconds from the end of the match, with a breathtaking drop goal by Newcastle fly-half and youngest member of the squad, Jonny Wilkinson. It was the first time a Northern Hemisphere side won the world title, the nation rejoiced for England invented rugby, now they'd won its highest honor.

SYDNEY

CORBRIDGE

JOY IN OZ . . . Jonny Wilkinson celebrates at the final whistle.   JOY AT HOME . . . mum Philippa can't hide her delight.

THAT'S MY BOY!

Mum does the shopping as Jonny wins World Cup

FULL REPORTS — Pages 3, 4, 5, 32, 33 & 58 - 64

NEWCASTLE ......3 | MIDDLESBROUGH ..0 | CREWE ALEX 3
MAN CITY ....0 | LIVERPOOL ....0 | SUNDERLAND......0

Lord Neville was an England mascot; a genuine Scottish laird supporting England was a rarity. He could not attend all the rugby games because of his damaged knees, but fiery Evil Neville was there for important matches, in his specially reserved, tartan-covered seat.

"Well, I suppose they are a young side," he remarked to Peter on the flight back to London, because ten of the England side were 25 or under. Evil Neville comforted himself with this, as he pondered another mission, he must convince the House of Lords of the danger of the fatberg. Both the fatberg fighters thought deeply on this, as they ate a delicious Ryanair first-class dinner of packaged peanuts and stale potato crisps, washed down by muddy Irish tap water. They landed at Heathrow Airport and Peter rushed off to consult with Zee, for he had decided to start a fatberg petition, it was a last desperate resort. How else could they get their message across, but setting up a petition was not as easy as it seemed.

The largest petition in British history would come about in 2019, when 6 million people signed for Brexit Referendum 2, and marched in the biggest protest since the Iraq War. After the false Brexit promises of devious Boris Johnson imploded, and his European Union exit proved problematic, so Boris threatened a no-deal Brexit. Then he lied to the Queen and misled Parliament, curiously, Boris is still not in prison?

That lay ahead; now it was 2011, and a fatberg threatened London. Lord Neville stirred the sleepyheads at the House of Lords, but the old fogeys would take ages to act. So, Professor Watercloset decided to start a petition, and Doctor Zee Garbo supported him.

"I can't do it as I'm not a British citizen," she pointed out. So, it was up to Peter, but good Dr. Zee would assist gathering signatures.

Yet, they soon discovered that creating a new petition, then getting enough signatures to have it seen and debated, can be a challenging process. Once you create a petition, you get five people to support it, the Petitions Committee checks your text and it gets published, unless it's rejected for being offensive or illegal. After 10,000 signatures the petition gets a response from government; after 100,000 it's considered for Parliament debate. Only 10 make it that far, from 30,000 petitions submitted yearly. Peter and Zee were battling to get 100 signatures, so getting even 1,000 seemed impossible. Like Harry Hack of B.B.T., the newspapers scoffed at a threat from the fatberg, and without media publicity their online campaign faltered, so they were reduced to a door-to-door effort.

"It's useless, Peter. I'm exhausted," Zee conceded.

They gave up after 150 signings, it was excruciatingly hard work. Peter and Zee were worn out. The worry over the fatberg, combined with their petition efforts, had taken its toll, so they decided on a weekend break at the Loch Ness Estate of Evil Neville. Situated right on the shores of world-famous Loch Ness, with its own private beach and commanding some of the most spectacular views in Scotland, the Loch Ness Lodge was the perfect place for a relaxing weekend break. Evil Neville would not accompany them, for he was at work in the House of Lords, convincing them of the fatberg threat, so two old family retainers ran the Loch Ness estate. Errol Neville was the black sheep of the Neville clan, his parents were killed in an auto accident when he was young, so he'd been brought up by an elder brother.

The elder Neville brother was a stern Scots patriarch, who strongly disapproved of his younger brother's passion for stunts on motorbikes. So, young Errol Neville left the clan while in his teens, and started the "Hills Angels" motorcycle club in Glasgow, where he picked up the name "Evil" Neville. After he became famous as a canyon-jumping stunt rider, the brothers had briefly reunited, but then fallen out again over Evil Neville's passion for England rugby. So, after his brother's death, Neville left two family retainers to run the estate as a tourist venue, and the Laird of Loch Ness only visited occasionally.

Peter and Zee returned refreshed from their weekend Loch Ness break. Their petition had come to naught in the House of Commons, so they urged Lord Evil Neville to redouble his efforts in the influential House of Lords, it was their last hope.

"Why not propose the passage of a bill?" Peter suggested, a bill would highlight the danger of fatbergs and force the authorities to act.

So, Evil Neville started the lengthy process. The First Reading is the first stage of a bill's long passage through the House of Lords. This is normally pretty swift, because there is no debate, just the reading out of the bill by the member of the lord in charge of it. Once formally introduced, the bill is printed and then comes up for the Second Reading. This can take some time, for members of the Lords debate the main principles and purpose of the bill, and flag up any concerns or specific areas where they think amendments are needed.

Then, the bill goes to the tedious Committee Stage, where discussion of amendments takes place, starting two weeks after the Second Reading. The Committee Stage can go on for many months. If the bill has been amended, it's reprinted with all the agreed amendments, then it moves to the Report Stage – to celebrate this achievement it's smoked salmon and Pimm's No. 1 in Bishops' Bar.

The Report Stage gives the Lords another opportunity to examine and make further changes, followed by caviar and Champagne in the Peers' Dining Room. After the Report Stage, the bill is reprinted to include amendments, and thankfully moves onto a final Third Reading.

Then comes partying in the bar – not the "Bar of the House", for that is not a pub but a railing, marking a boundary where visitors may not pass. The seven restaurants in the House are pretty cheap, because their deficit is filled by public money, amounting to £1,348,673 in 2011. So, thanks to the amount of time spent in restaurants, bills usually take about six months to wind their way through the legislative process in the House of Lords, although some can take much longer.

We've not yet mentioned that, before introducing any legislative proposal, the Legislation Office chief clerk will spend a long time developing the idea, before drafting the law. If the bill started in the Lords, it then goes to the Commons, where the process starts again. So, you can see that it's a lengthy affair. Passing a Fatberg Bill would take too long so the canny Laird of Loch Ness decided to approach the Doorkeepers – the oil which runs the machinery of the House of Lords.

"They are the key," Lord Evil chuckled. The House of Lords has 24 doorkeepers in the department of the stern Black Rod – he is the principal doorkeeper, and his doorkeepers work in teams, who are each managed by a senior doorkeeper. Their sworn responsibilities include maintaining security in and around the chamber, providing a reception facility at the Peers' Entrance, and managing members of the public wishing to view the Lords proceedings. They also provide a message and letterboard service for the peers, and are trained in first aid and security. But, more importantly, the doorkeepers attend committees of the House. So, the canny Lord Neville sought the advice of an influential Committee Office clerk, who organized inquiries and drafted reports, as well as carrying out research and providing information to members. The main duties of the clerks were to quickly respond orally or in writing to requests from members, and to prepare briefing papers on subjects of public and parliamentary concern. The clerks work in all the different offices of the House and they play a key role, Lord Evil Neville told the fatberg fighters.

"I've invited the chief clerk and a few lords to Loch Ness Lodge." Peter and Zee were also invited, a great chance to present their case.

Hunting in Scotland takes place from August to the end of October, the unpredictable Scottish weather was behaving, so Peter was keen to shoot a red deer in a traditional walk-and-stalk Scottish hunt. Coincidently, or perhaps conveniently, the chief clerk invited by Lord Neville was also an avid hunter. So, Neville dispatched the two to the Highlands, accompanied by a stalker and sage advice.

"This clerk is influential. Warn him of the fatberg," Neville whispered in Peter's ear, who didn't need a second invitation.

Red deer are the largest wild deer in Britain, and one of the native species; the majority are found in the Scottish Highlands. This was not the cruel comedy of English fox hunting, where riders and baying hounds pursue a tiny, terrified fox; this was true hunting, which took some skill. Hunting on hill ground is where Scotland's red deer stalking traditions lie, and it relied on the experience of the stalker. First, a strategic approach to a suitable shooting range, then selection of an appropriate cull animal, while remaining unseen. Placing an accurate shot for a fast kill, then carrying your quarry home in the Land Rover, in company of the satisfied stalker, is a great experience.

While Peter was hunting the chief clerk, the beautiful Zee Garbo was fishing for lords, while angling the bountiful Loch Ness for brown trout, ferox trout, sea trout and the mighty Atlantic salmon – you never know what you will catch in Loch Ness! Zee was an expert fisherwoman, she soon snagged the two old lords who accompanied her, and a few trout as well. If you have never felt the kick of the Atlantic salmon on your line, or heard the roar of the red stag across the Highlands, then you are missing out on an awesome hunting experience, which was almost as satisfying as bagging a chief clerk, or bringing down a brace of lords. So, all in all, the weekend retreat had been a really worthwhile endeavour.

"We've really bagged the dilly old farts," Evil Neville snickered, for all the talk at Loch Ness Lodge was about the threat of fatbergs. On their return to London, Lord Neville immediately asked the lords to establish a *Select Committee for Fatberg Threat,* and the weary lords were not inclined to argue, for a great scandal had befallen. The press had a field day when information emerged from the House of Lords, that there was considerable hanky-panky going on, the Lords desperately needed something to distract the press – fighting fatbergs was the answer.

The cynical press described the House of Lords as ermine-clad peers, swilling Champagne and swanning around Your Lordships' House at the taxpayer's expense; tired old farts with snouts in the trough, greedily pocketing £300 a day for just pitching up. The newspapers alleged that there were 29 peers, who claimed a total of £750,000 in expenses, without ever speaking in a debate. In 2009-10, only 388 – or 47% - of peers attended over 68 days. Just 31 had an official leave of absence, while 300 or so were AWOL.

Some armies shoot AWOL deserters, but not the Lords. In 2011, the House sat for just 6.5 hours a day, for which the lords each got the equivalent of £46.15 per hour, not a penny of it subject to tax. It was a good time to approach the lords on the fatberg issue, for they were reeling in shock from newspaper allegations regarding expenses. Then came a shocking leaked video of the deputy speaker snorting cocaine off a prostitute's breast, while ranting, drunkenly:

"Those in the House who live in the capital claim 'free money' for coming into Westminster, and doing 'f*** all work'." The lords were desperate for some good press, and the fatberg threat might bring that. So, the fatberg fighters moved stealthily in, because the lords also do some excellent work. Though the press revelations about the House of Lords were truly shocking news, history also records that a *Select Committee for Fatberg Threat* saved Britain, as Labour lords led by Lord Neville would one day save Britain from batty Boris.

"The egregious Internal Market Bill places Britain in the wrong and damages the U.K.'s reputation as a defender of the rule of law. When the history of these troubled months comes to be written, it will not be kind to the current prime minister and his cabinet."

Lord Stevenson of Balmacara.

In October 2020 the Lords would block the damaging *Internal Market Bill,* intended by devious Prime Minister Johnson to force Britain into a harmful no-deal Brexit, Lord Stevenson described it best above: So, despite their faults, it's wise to retain the House of Lords. It's the lords who analyze and then amend the sometimes-insane laws pushed through by MP's in the House of Commons. The average age of Lords members might be 69, but it's also true that they debated all night on the *Committee for Fatberg Threat,* so they must be retained.

The House of Lords have between them a priceless pool of experience and expertise, and their great strength is that they are not career politicians; fewer than 200 lords are former MP's. Remember that if the House of Lords were entirely elected, it would be packed with venal politicians, eager to rubber-stamp every bill their Commons M.P. buddies put forward. They would also demand more money. In 2011, M.P. salaries equated to £532 every day Parliament sat, while the lords managed on just £300. Like any government organisation the House of Lords must be subjected to scrutiny, and occasional reform, but it should never be elected. The revising, scrutinizing and delaying powers of the Lords are all valuable instruments for ensuring legislation is well drafted, effective and representative. Given the political turmoil of recent years, the British people do not have the stamina for more elections, nor do they have the wish to multiply their political class. A nominated House of Lords allows people to be brought into the political arena, who are not necessarily politicians by nature. They can however bring skills from other arenas in which they have been successful: business; sport; science; technology; entertainment.

And lastly, it must be taken into account, that although the myopic House of Commons ignored the fatberg warning, as did the press and British Broadminded Television. The sager House of Lords passed a Bill warning of the fatberg, which called on an organization named MAMBA, to look into the fatberg threat. Thankfully the wise House of Lords had acted, MAMBA now awaited a visit from the fatberg fighters, the fight against the fatberg was at last moving ahead.

COUNTER-TERRORIST FIREARMS OFFICER

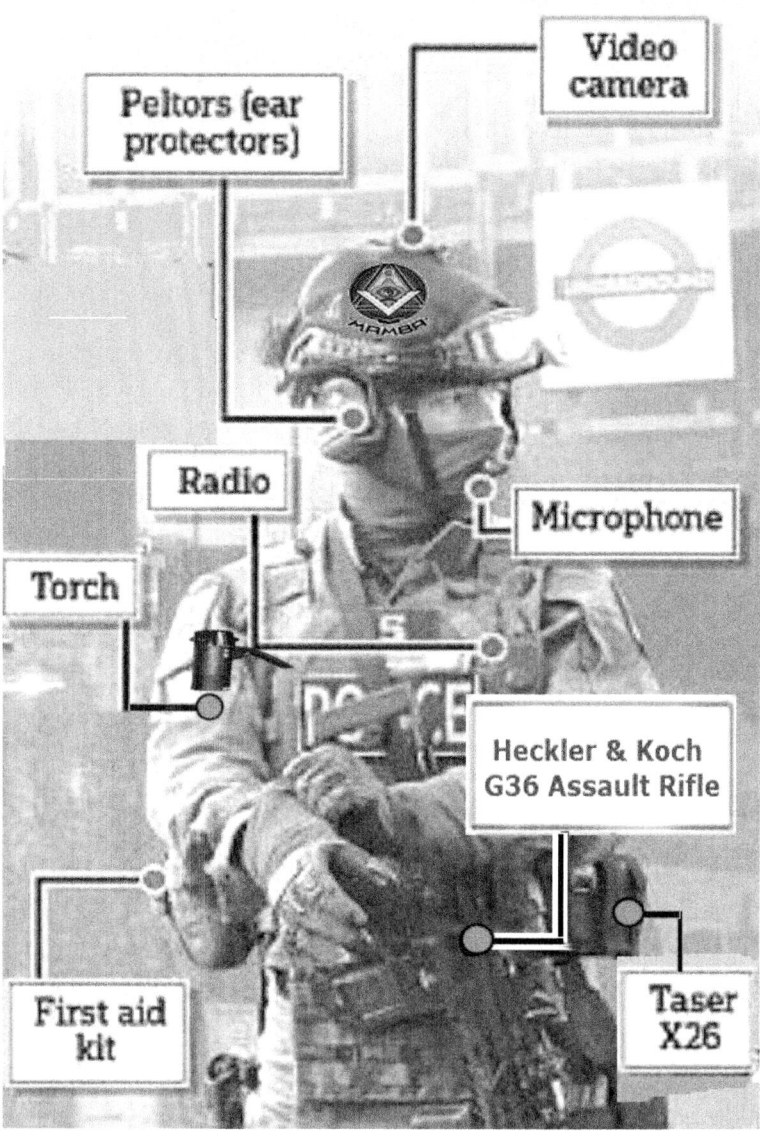

Peltors (ear protectors)

Video camera

Radio

Microphone

Torch

Heckler & Koch G36 Assault Rifle

First aid kit

Taser X26

The Faceless Man

Clad in their grey Kevlar body armor, they carry state-of-the-art weapons, including sniper and automatic assault rifles, handguns and submachine guns. These first one thousand London counter-terror specialists are capable of racing to the scene of any potential incident, on board specially adapted Honda scooters which, like the mobility scooters of Evil Neville, were pretty special units. The Honda Gilera GP800 is a V-twin-engine 850cc machine, which has become known as the world's fastest scooter.

Suzuki kicked off the maxiscooter craze in 1999, with its mighty Burgman 400, then Yamaha followed that with a 500 T-Max in 2000, but the Honda Gilera eclipsed them all. With armed officers riding pillion, the first thousand counter-terror specialists can cut through the heavy London traffic on these scooters, which are capable of reaching top speeds of 125m.p.h. They also carry state-of-the art support gear, including battering rams and heavy-duty cutting equipment. They are the tough new breed of super cops, on duty 24/7, to keep London safe from terror attacks. But they'd never pursue a Brown Blob without evidence; that is the code of the London Bobby, these heavily armed MAMBA policemen are descendants of the 1829 first thousand London Bobbies. Who were issued with a wooden truncheon, carried in a long pocket in their coat tail, a pair of handcuffs and a wooden rattle to raise the alarm, later replaced by a whistle.

Sir Robert Peel
1788-1850

In Britain today, all policemen are commonly referred to as "Bobbies" (originally, they were known as "Peelers", in homage to farsighted Sir Robert Peel, 1788-1850). Today, it's hard to believe that nineteenth-century London did not yet have a professional police force; only the Bow Street Runners, founded in 1749 by author and magistrate Henry Fielding. The Runners originally numbered only six men, backed by privately funded police called "thief-takers", who worked for rewards offered but malicious arrests were commonplace.

So, in 1829, Home Secretary Sir Robert Peel passed the Metropolitan Police Act, which provided for permanently appointed and paid constables to protect the capital of London. Dressed in blue tailcoats and top hats, the first thousand began to patrol London on 29th September 1829; the Bow Street Runners were phased out and the Peelers were chosen from the best candidates – many policemen today would fail the test.

The uniform was carefully selected to make the Peelers look more like citizens than the redcoat soldiers. They must be in their twenties and at least 5'7" tall, with no criminal record. Victorian police worked a seven-day week, with five days unpaid holiday a year, pay was £1 per week and they were not allowed to drink. Not much in today's terms, but back then any job was a gift from Heaven. Then, as now, all policemen are controlled by civilian authorities. Before any military unit goes into action on U.K. soil, authorization must be given by a civilian committee, held in special conference rooms within Whitehall. Referred to as COBRA, this committee is headed by the prime minister. They analyze the level of threat and decide how to respond, before issuing orders how to react. Each U.K. police constabulary maintains a specialist firearms capability, with tactical team members trained to Authorized Firearms Officer standard; A.F.O officers carry out law enforcement operations outside the capability of unarmed constables

These heavily-armed armed units are the first thousand trained marksmen deployed onto the streets of London. At a lower level than COBRA there exists another unit, called Metropolitan Association Monitoring Behavioural Attitudes (MAMBA). They are not located in Whitehall, but rather conveniently right in Whitechapel. So, the select committee at the House of Lords contacted MAMBA, and suggested they meet with Professor Peter Watercloset.

Arrangements were made and the three fatberg fighters duly presented themselves at MAMBA.

"Now we'll see some action," Zee hoped.

The Metropolitan Association Monitoring Behavioral Attitudes (MAMBA) had many functions. Originally established to monitor any terror threats around the capital London, as is the liberal penchant it soon turned into an Orwellian "Big Brother". With the enthusiastic assistance of British Broadminded Television, MAMBA became the "Thought Police" of the George Orwell novel *1984*, and B.B.T. were of course the nosey parker "Telescreen" described in the novel. So, it was naturally with some trepidation that the three fatberg fighters approached the imposing MAMBA building.

"They certainly seem to be watchful," Zee observed, as she glanced at the posters of eyes decorating the lobby, where the stern Rosa Klebb receptionist indicated they wait.

"They're a real bunch of nosey parkers," Evil Neville muttered. He hated any form of authority, and he'd heard some nasty rumours about MAMBA, and how they poked their nose in.

"Let's hope they're prepared to listen to us, and take action," Professor Peter Watercloset said, worriedly. He was convinced that the Brown Blob spawned by the fatberg presented a deadly threat.

MAMBA is not to be confused with the grossly inefficient COBRA of the U.K. government (this is an acronym formed from "Cabinet Office Briefing Room A", though "Clowns Ordering Bar Room Alcohol" is more like it, for drinking and high-jinks transpire).

MAMBA appeared to be not like that, they were shown into a boardroom, where a heavily guarded Faceless Man addressed them. The Faceless Man was the most simpatico listener that any of the three visitors had ever encountered in their lives; he listened carefully to them, and answered every question politely and at some length.

"Certainly, Professor, I can see why the green slime of the fatberg worries you…

"You have done remarkable work, Doctor; I must

applaud you for your efforts…

"Of course, we'll move immediately on this, Lord Neville – you have my word on that…"

The Faceless Man smoothly assured them, they were almost hypnotized by the silky flow of his words, and were greatly comforted as he ushered them out. It was only when they reached the lobby that they realized The Faceless Man had not actually made any firm commitment; they could not remember one solid promise – or even what he looked like? It was George Orwell *doublespeak* at its best, solemn promises in vague terms, which were never kept.

"What did he actually say?" Peter queried.

"He actually said nothing," Evil Neville spat.

"I don't even remember what he looked like," Zee confessed, it was remarkable.

They paused in the lobby as they realized they'd been duped, they had been imbued with confidence that a plan had been formed, when it had all been nothing but silky-smooth talk.

"Another Boris that one," Evil Neville rasped.

METROPOLITAN ASSOCIATION

MONITORING BEHAVIOURAL ATTITUDES

"I'm going back, to face Faceless man!" Evil Neville muttered angrily, but the canny Dr. Zee had a much better idea.

"I'd love to see that," she whispered, pointing to a sign which read *"Laboratory"*. First, though, they would have to slip their escort. They were accompanied by an armed guard, which was very strange.

"Just want to pop into the loo," Zee addressed him sweetly.

"You can see yourself out," the guard said and walked away.

The way was now clear, so they entered the laboratory.

Shock can be a bizarre thing. In that moment of disbelief everything becomes blurred, then sharpens into clear focus. Reality seems to narrow to a single point, time stretches and distorts, then comes rushing into focus and things seem larger than life. That's the way they felt when they first laid eyes on the Baby Brown Blob! It was unbelievable, that the focus of their fears was housed right here, inside the MAMBA building where they had come for help!

They approached the clear container rather gingerly, though it seemed to be adequately secured. Above it was what appeared to be a life-sustaining system, gauges and tubes pumping some liquid.

"They're keeping this thing alive," Dr. Zee marvelled, as she watched the strange green mist circulate through the clear pipes above the container, her interest as a scientist was piqued.

Peter was shocked. "So, our fears were correct? The fatberg host has spawned a life form. But is it dangerous, will it attack?" It was a valid question, was MAMBA playing with fire?

"It attacked us on the narrowboat," Zee shuddered.

"We'll soon see about that," Evil Neville spat, and reached up for the main isolator. It cautioned not to switch off, but before Peter or Zee could intervene, he pulled the switch.

"That will sort Baby Fatberg out," Evil grinned.

The result was instantaneous – but it was the three of them who were sorted out, as they were hit by a toxic green mist.

"GET OUT!" Peter screamed but it was far too late.

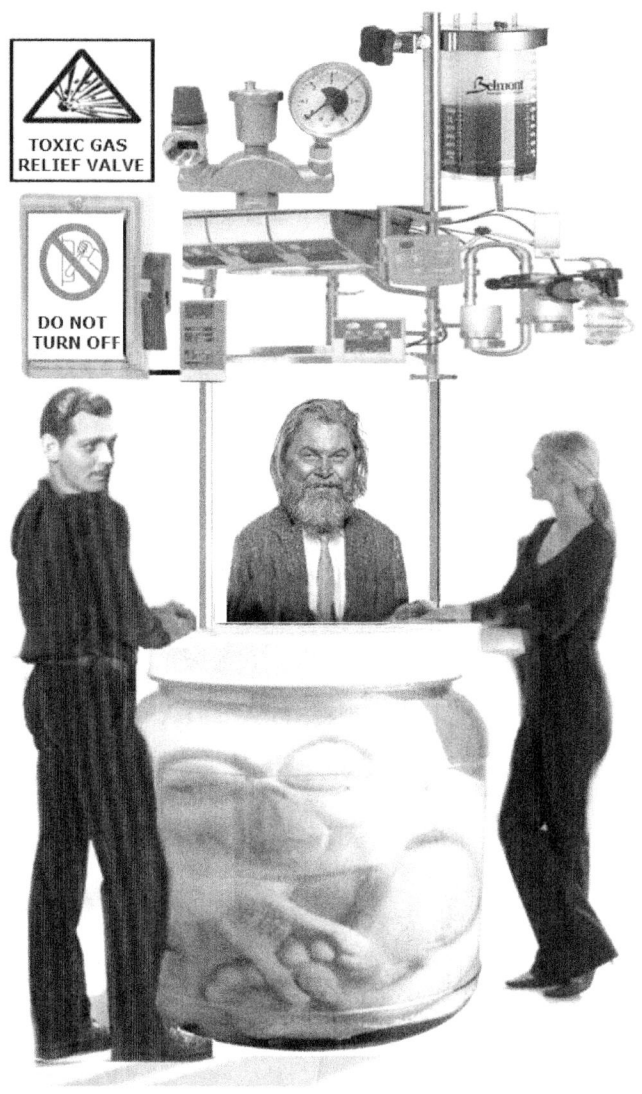

Tell a Scotsman not to do something and it's guaranteed he will! The *"Do Not Turn Off"* sign was like a red flag to a wild bull, though it was unfortunate

Evil Neville had not noticed the other sign: adjacent to the bronze relief valve was an ominous notice warning of toxic gas.

It was unwise to play with this machine, because the relief valve began releasing a toxic green mist. The stink was rank beyond belief: a nose-burning, throat-clogging miasma; the same smell Peter and Zee had encountered at the narrowboat attack. As it drifted across the laboratory, they rushed for the door. But their knees buckled and they fell; half-conscious to the floor. Fortunately for them, gas alarms were screeching, then security men came rushing in with gas masks.

They were escorted to the lobby, where a doctor examined them and ruled them fit to go home. Accompanied by a scooter escort, a Kevlar-clad guard drove them back in Peter's car. As he drove, they glanced at his handgun, and even wild Evil Neville kept silent.

It was a curious business. They wondered why the Metropolitan Association Monitoring Behavioural

Attitudes (MAMBA) kept such a well-armed security force. And why was there an Illuminati Eye displayed in the MAMBA building? No info was forthcoming.

Peter and Zee made telephone calls and sent emails. They were answered with the utmost British politeness, with no info forthcoming of any substance. A secret government department in Whitechapel was conducting dangerous experiments with Brown Blobs, but nobody was talking. It was a highly dangerous business for they were playing with fire, what if the Baby Brown Blob broke free and grew, the narrowboat incident showed how vicious it could be. Were there others down there in sewerland, then began Peter's nightmares; he had been reading the books of George Orwell. Perhaps it was frustration or maybe the noxious green mist – possibly the novels he was reading – causing Peter Watercloset to have nightmares and awake screaming. So would you if you had those dreams, but it was part of a learning curve, Pater would soon stumble on a Gematria.

"I must press on," he muttered.

In the dream, he could not recall how they'd captured him; all he remembered was a cell with Illuminati Eyes on the walls. Flat on his back he was unable to move a muscle, every inch of him held captive by leather straps binding him to a table. Peter's eyes darted wildly around the cell; on every wall were giant posters, with an unnerving movable eye in the centre. It was eerily hypnotic, having all those eyes zoning on you, as though they were alive. The eyes were cleverly contrived with a hidden mechanism, moving them to scarily track you, while a bold caption warned that you were being watched.

Peter tore his attention from the posters, for an interrogator was approaching: it was The Faceless Man from MAMBA. The man with no face greeted him politely, as ever, but the interrogation which followed was brutal. The Faceless Man looked down at Peter and smiled, sadly. Underneath his hand was a strange machine, with a control knob and figures marking the faces of two dials.

"This is the Truth Machine," The Faceless Man informed Peter, who knew something terrible was coming

"Shall I give you a demonstration?" The Faceless Man said. Then, without any warning except a slight twist from his hand on the knob of the Truth Machine, waves of excruciating agony washed over Peter Watercloset. It was frightening, for he could not see how it was happening, but the effect was devastating,

"STOP! I BEG YOU!" Peter cried.

"Do you now comprehend, Professor, the awesome power of MAMBA?" The Faceless Man said, ominously. He then added, menacingly: "Remember, throughout our little chat, that I have power to inflict great pain on you. If you prevaricate in any way or fall below your usual level of intelligence, you will instantly cry out in agony. Do you understand that?"

"YES! YES! I UNDERSTAND!" Peter screeched fearfully, and The Faceless Man's manner immediately became less severe.

He took a pace or two up and down, then paused. When he spoke, his voice was gentle and patient, as though he wished to impart knowledge. The man had the air of a neoliberal: anxious to explain and persuade; to elucidate the trusted liberal virtues of selfishness.

"I am taking trouble with you, Professor, because you are worth trouble. You have been asking awkward questions – this is why we decided to bring you in for a little chat. You know perfectly well what your problem is: you are suffering from a rare form of amnesia, rendering you unable to remember real events." The Faceless Man paused again and studied Peter, to see if his words had sunk in.

"You have convinced yourself that you remember events which never occurred."

"What events are you referring to?" Peter asked guardingly, afraid of the Truth Machine, but still the man twirled the controller again, and Peter writhed in agony screeching in pain.

"That was not wise of you," Faceless Man said, ruefully. "You know well what I am referring to. You have been telling people that the Metropolitan Association Monitoring Behavioural Attitudes has been experimenting with a Baby Brown Blob," he sighed.

"I was badly mistaken," Peter babbled, wildly. "We obviously misinterpreted what we thought we saw." Thankfully, Faceless Man moved away from the terrible Truth Machine. Then Peter steeled himself, for the man approached again to resume his interrogation.

"British Broadminded Television have a slogan dealing with free speech," the man intoned, gravely. "Repeat, if you please…" Everybody in London was familiar with this B.B.T. slogan; it was the London liberal mantra.

"Who controls the past controls the future; who controls the present controls the past," the by now groggy Peter Watercloset repeated obediently, for he had been expertly brainwashed. The first tactic was to isolate the victim away from friends or family, so that the victim only has the manipulator to converse with, to get their information from. Then the victim is broken down, so their manipulator can start rebuilding them, in whatever image they desire. A person can only be brainwashed, if their manipulator is in a superior position to them, which the Faceless Man certainly was.

"Is it your opinion, Professor," The Faceless Man asked, "that the past has real existence? Consider all the rumours concerning the abuse of children at B.B.T., for example: it's patently obvious that this never happened." But Peter could not let that pass, so he summoned his manhood. "There are too many rumours, so there must be some truth in it," Professor Peter Watercloset replied, bravely but foolishly?

The Faceless Man eyed him sadly, then he twisted the knob of the Truth Machine entirely to its zenith. The agony was so great that, at that moment, there was what seemed like an eruption – though Peter was not certain there was any noise, just a hollow sensation of excruciating agony. Although he had been flat on his back when the eruption occurred, Peter had the curious feeling that he had been knocked there, space and time no longer had any meaning.

The Faceless Man had become like a teacher now, correcting an errant but stubborn student, patient but persevering in his mission.

"Do you honestly imagine the venerable Sir Jimmy Savile ever abused any child?" he asked gently.

Now, his student replied dutifully: "Sir Jimmy was a great man. raising millions for charity, he never abused children." Peter drooled like a lobotomized looney; the Truth Machine had fried his brain.

"Look at you sing now, Professor," The Faceless Man cackled jeeringly, because his foe had broken down completely.

"YOU DID IT!" sobbed the professor. "You reduced me to this zombie state – you and your neoliberal Truth Machine," he wailed.

"You reduced yourself to it," The Faceless Man spat coldly. "Your do-goody obsession with helping others, your pitiful deficiency of liberal self-centeredness brought you to this." Then he snickered, for something amused him. "Yet, look at you now: you've betrayed everyone and everything," he sneered spitefully.

But, a flicker of pride flared in the broken man.

"I HAVE NOT BETRAYED ZEE GARBO!" Peter shouted, his love for Zee was his last vestige of manhood – he still had that!

"YOUR LOVE WILL NOT SAVE YOU!!" Peter's confession of love had touched a nerve, and

The Faceless Man suddenly showed raw emotion: his blurry face seemed to redden and his body twitched, spasmodically. Was this insolence from a supposedly broken man a last, futile act of defiance? A pathetic thrust at lost dignity? Or was Professor Watercloset still his own man?

"We will see about that, Professor," The Faceless Man snarled.

A door then opened, and in strutted Harry Hack of B.B.T. He was pushing a portable television. Harry also carried a surgical head clamp, which he fitted to Peter.

"The worst thing in the world, Peter," Harry Hack revealed, as he worked, "varies from individual to individual." He adjusted the clips in the clamp to Peter's eyes. With head clamped fast and his eyes held open with clips, Peter could not tear his eyes away from the screen.

Those who have watched the pompous B.B.T interview program *Hurt Talk* will know what agony Peter Watercloset was undergoing: hour after hour of neoliberal claptrap. Peter watched appalled, as Harry Hack attacked artists while promoting the controllers. Ream after ream of fascist *Hurt Talk* propaganda unfolded before his aching eyes. But, with his head clamped and eyes clipped open, there was no turning away, no escape from the horror.

Flashing before Peter's eyes were publishers who noted that Wordsworth died 200 years ago, so lyrical poetry was no longer acceptable; only obscure blank verse was accepted. Know-it-all reviewers decided what poets must write; publishers or newspaper editors supplied the liberal ethic, writers merely ground out the words.

It's now called "cancel culture", where editors are fired for running controversial pieces, books are withdrawn for inauthenticity and journalists are barred from certain topics. New musicians are launched by talent shows and artists by competitions; liberal judges produce art and talented artists are slaves, like the mythical Gulliver of Jonathan Swift, the artist are tied down and controlled by intellectual pygmies.

Vampires and schoolboy wizards were on the decline, so the liberal controllers now promoted hard porn, for when editors control literature it enters sewerland. The corrupt media who direct British art and literature will enter history, as felons who hacked telephones and bribed corrupt cops, yet allowed their good chum Jimmy Savile to rape little children right under their noses. The impact of liberalism on British writing was horrific: books were either about celebrities or written by celebrities; nothing original was emerging and book sales plummeted. The quote of Albert Einstein below encapsulated it: we are not talking here of charitable, classical liberalism, but selfish, modern neoliberalism. Boris Johnson liberalism, which was enriching elite friends and ignoring the needy, while censoring dissent – they were the people B.B.T. eulogized.

"The intuitive mind is a sacred gift and the rational mind a faithful servant. We have created a society that honours the servant and has forgotten the gift." Albert Einstein.

273

A full day of watching *Hurt Talk* programs hurt Peter awfully, Harry Hack wiped Peter's teary eyes and applied eyedrops, while Faceless Man waited patiently, for there was only one way that Professor Peter Watercloset could possibly save himself.

Peter had to interpose another human between himself and that torturous television. The Faceless Man and Harry Hack both smiled cynically, for there was just one person in the whole world whom Peter could possibly interpose, and he was shouting, over and over:

"DO IT TO ZEE GARBO! NOT TO ME!
Dr. Zee Garbo awoke suddenly to the sound of hysterical screaming, because Peter had been reading Orwell's *1984,* and was having a nightmare.

"You've wet your pajamas; we'll have to change the bedsheets," Zee said sulkily, it had happened before, she wished Peter would stop reading Orwell.

"I must press on Zee," Peter babbled, recently he'd stumbled upon a Gematria, and was using the works of Orwell to interpret it

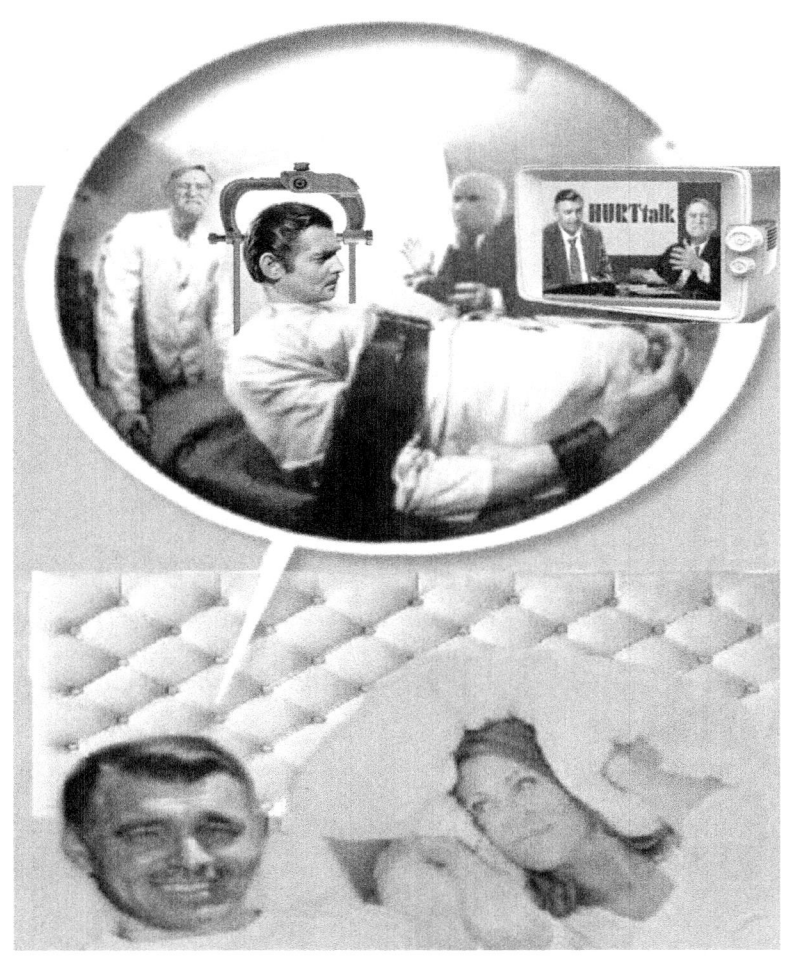

GEORGE ORWELL

25th Jun 1903 – 21st Jan 1950.

Covid-19 Prophecy

Professor Peter Watercloset continued to have literary nightmares, all based on the novels of the great writer George Orwell, because Peter was a fanatic fan of his works. Born in India in 1903, Orwell died at University College Hospital London in 1950, just 47 years of age.

Was Orwell sending messages of a threat to London? Why was the eerie green mist seen mainly around Ripper Street sewer manholes, where British Broadminded Television was located? Right above the blocked Boris Johnson Tunnel, where the Baby Brown Blob seen in MAMBA laboratory spawned? Why was no further information forthcoming, why were the press not interested in reporting it?

Like cagey B.B.T. Television, MAMBA had a strict censorship code; both were ideal role models for the books of George Orwell. Who described himself *"socialist by allegiance liberal by temperament?"*

CHINA BAT = 666
C🦇VID

George Orwell attacked both systems vigorously in novels and essays; he was especially scathing of Tory-type neoliberalism. Professor Watercloset began studying ancient Gematria to interpret his weird nightmares, filled with indecipherable portents. Riddles like the one above began to flood his sleep, what could a Chinese bat have to do with Covid, how did it lead to the number 666? Commonly called the Devils Number, as it's in the *Book of Revelations,* how could it possibly tie into a Gematria?

Peter Watercloset sought the answer in George Orwell books, for Orwell highlighted the two Big Fails of Tory type twentieth-century liberalism: a breakdown in middle-class liberals connecting with the working class; and the poverty gap created by liberalism's individual rights ethic. If variances existed between rich and poor, which are deeply embedded in liberal structures, then rich and poor will always be fundamentally divided.

In *The Road to Wigan Pier* (1937), Orwell mocked the liberals' smug assumption that they were attuned to the lower classes. Thoughts of George Orwell flooded Peter's fevered mind, as he tried to sleep and not disturb his partner Zee, yet there were many nights that Peter awoke screaming.

Gematria images were embedded in his dreams, and it had become a driving imperative to unearth the code, to unravel what these dreams meant? Some scholars say 666 was written in Hebrew, where numbers can mean words; translating the Hebrew spelling of 666 spells Neron Kesar, or Nero Caesar, who was infamous for his persecution of Christians.

So, these scholars naturally assume that the Apostle John, who authored *The Book of Revelations*, was referring to the sadistic Emperor Nero. There are other explanations, the image overleaf was self-explanatory, Boris the clown would introduce Brexit. But there were other images in Peter's dreams, some of them truly terrifying, like a seven-headed beast?

Note the two familiar faces entwined, bearing the mark 666 like in *Revelations*, what on earth could be the meaning of these chilling images.

NOTE - Double number 6 (as in 6-12-18), place against alphabet, then add numbers to reveal 666.

A local prophet called the Bard of Aylesbury had unearthed the Gematria on the previous page, 666 meaning that if you don't heed the Gematria, then evil will surely follow. Professor Watercloset had inherited it and he unraveled the interpretation below, then he compared it to works of George Orwell to discern a deeper meaning. Lord Neville and Doctor Garbo were fascinated by Peter's work, and also began using the Gematria, to find answers in their own lives. Zee even forgave Peter the occasional wet bed, such is the lot of a hard-working prophet.

THE TORY = 666

THE LIBERALS = 666

MARK OF BEAST = 666

COMPUTER = 666

DIGITAL I.D. CHIP = 666

SATAN SPEECH = 666

SATAN'S SEAL = 666

SATAN CULT = 666

BOOK OF THE DEAD = 666

Gematria come from Assyro-Babylonian-Greek alphanumeric codes, later adopted by Jewish scribes, who assigned numerical value to letters in the belief phrases will appear. Like this 666 Gematria, **The Tory** and his minions **The Liberals**, will force you to wear the **Mark of Beast**, using a **Computer** to monitor your **Digital I.D. Chip**. **Satan Speech** propaganda binds you in **Satan's Seal**, producing a generation of lost children called **Satan Cult,** spawn of failed social systems noted in **Book of the Dead**.

BIG BORIS
IS WATCHING

Professor Peter placed the writing of George Orwell in italics and the Gematria in bold, to see how it compared alongside the book *1984;* it was scary how similar the two were. **The Tory** is *Big Brother* in the picture, who watches to ensure **The Liberals** force you to bear the **Mark of Beast**. In his great novel, George Orwell writes: *"At this moment the entire group of people broke into a deep, slow, rhythmic chant of 'B-B! B-B!' — over and over again, very slowly, with a long pause between the first 'B' and second."* This was rather similar to B.B.T., and also reminiscent to chants of "Boris! Boris!", portending that either *Big Brother* or **The Tory** will come to dominate U.K. society, ably assisted by **The Liberals**, who control the media in Britain. The hero in *1984* is Winston Smith, who has a sinister device installed in his flat to track: *"Any sound that Winston made, above the level of a very low whisper, would be picked up by it."* That device today is the **Computer,** operating in nearly every home in Britain, to find out what the nation thinks?

Should you dare to refuse to wear the **Mark of Beast**, you will soon be sniffed out by **The Tory,** who will instruct their minions **The Liberals**, and you may quickly find a computer virus blocking your system. In the novel *1984* the *Thought Police* of the ruling party, keep track of everyone via their intrusive *Telescreens,* but in the Gematria **The Tory** are *Big Brother* and the *Thought Police* are B.B.T journalists like Harry Hack. Who don't need a telescreen to monitor you; they can easily do this through your so-called "personal" **Computer**, which is not as personal as you may think? Think about this, you buy a book on football and your **Computer** is flooded with adverts for games. You check out airfares for a holiday and, before you know it, your "private" **Facebook Site** is plastered with advertisements for hotels. Because of "cookies", which are unique snippets websites place on your computer, recognizing you every time you log in. It allows websites to record login details and other information, to save you entering them over again.

F – 36
A – 6
C – 18
E – 30

B – 12
O – 90
O – 90
K – 66

S – 114
I – 54
T – 120
E – 30

= 666

GEORGE ORWELL 1984

Mark Zuckerberg Born 1984

Now, imagine how simple it is for **The Tory** to monitor your **Facebook Site** post and find out if you are wearing the **Mark of Beast.** The law allows employers to monitor employees' use of the internet, so employers use information on social websites to conduct sneaky background checks on employees, it's dead simple for a force as powerful as **The Liberals** to check up on you. Remember that every post placed on your **Facebook Site** is monitored by **The Tory,** so building your profile is simple, using that tool called a **Computer**. Do you think it's a coincidence that **Facebook Site** adds up to 666, or that Facebook founder Mark Zuckerberg was born in 1984? It's frightening I know, but it's vital you are fully aware, so you can better protect yourself against invasion of privacy by **The Tory**. You can fight back by password protecting all your devices, it can be a nuisance but it's worth it, Big Brother Boris is constantly watching. Remember to always sign out of your accounts, this significantly reduces the opportunity for snooping, change your Facebook

287

settings to ensure the default privacy setting isn't set to public. Also, always clear all your browser history after using the Webb, not just the porn.

DIGITAL I.D. CHIP = 666

The Tory don't only gain information from social sites; the Gematria also includes a **Digital I.D. Chip**, which is contained on credit cards which everybody uses. Merchants, of course, use data on purchases for stocktaking and planning the future, but they can easily monitor individual customers, too. In Britain today there is an unholy trinity of media/business/banks; the big credit associations all have credit fraud detection units, and they cooperate with the trinity by supplying them with "metadata", which includes card or account numbers and how much is spent by customers?

The liberal press can get the names of individual account holders from banks issuing these credit cards, so you had better believe that **The Liberals** watch you closely. Business is controlled through this media/business/banks trinity, and cartels of banks can legally refuse to do business with targeted enemies of **The Tory**, supposedly because of "suspicious activities" which are not revealed. If political or business opponents annoy **The Tory**, the pound plummets due to investor concerns – it's manipulation from the trinity creating panic. In his book *1984* Orwell writes that handwriting is obsolete and you dictate *Newspeak* into the *Speak-Write*. This new language of *Newspeak* is the official language of party official documents, and it basically means shortening everything you write. For example, the *Ministry of Peace* is called *"Minipax"*, while the *Ministry of Love* is *"Miniluv"*. Written in 1949, the Orwell novel exactly describes modern social networking, where the words are abbreviated: *"b4"* (before); *"bc"* (because); *"brb"* (be right back), etc. Texting and *Twitter* have crunched our language to the bare minimum. Then there is the *1984* journalist's language of *Doublethink,* which means the exact opposite of what's being said. The novel by George Orwell explains it as *"The power of holding two contradictory beliefs in one's mind simultaneously, and accepting both,"* – an exact description of garbage spewed by liberal hacks such as Harry Hack.

Nowadays in British liberal publishing, **Satan Speech** is also widely expressed in pornography. *1984* describes Winston's lover Julia as earning her living working for *Pornosec*, cleverly nicknamed

"Muck House", which churns out cheap pornography for the drunk, randy proles; the Julia of today would of course have written the novel *Fifty Shades of Grey* and made a fortune. In the *1984* novel *Big Brother* brainwashes everyone. The Gematria describes this as people having **Satan's Seal** – the modern neoliberal media use *1984* type *"hate weeks"* to achieve their ends. George Orwell writes of the telescreens' sound during the campaigns, designed to ramp up hysteria against a new target: *"It was a noise that set one's teeth on edge and bristled the hair at the back of one's neck. The Hate had started."* Exactly how the liberal media control society by picking targets and ramping up the hysteria. Both British newspapers and B.B.T. television savaged Sir Cliff Richard, but sacred Sir Jimmy Savile was strictly off-limits. Then came the shocking *News of the World* hacking scandal: investigations conducted from 2005 to 2007 showed myriad celebrity phone hacking, then a 2011 report exposed phone hacking of murdered schoolgirl Milly Dowler, plus message-deleting which destroyed vital

evidence. Relatives of deceased British soldiers and 2005 victims of London bombings were also hacked, leading to the resignations of media mogul Rupert Murdoch and chief executive Rebekah Brooks. So, their old pal and university chum of Boris Johnson, Tory prime minister David Cameron, established the Leveson Media Inquiry. Needless to say, activities of **The Liberals** impacted on British youth, as Evil Neville had discovered crime was rife among youth gangs, where a **Satan Cult** was being formed. Young people became unmanageable, because of silly liberal laws forbidding parents or teachers from properly disciplining unruly children. In 1984, Orwell notes: *"It was almost normal for people over thirty to be frightened of their own children."* The children in *1984* are encouraged to *"Report deviant parents. Neighbours are ordered to spy and report to Big Brother any aberrant behaviour among their friends."* Does this not resemble the daily dirt you see splashed across the newspapers, who utilize unnamed "informed sources" to dig the dirt on political

293

enemies? The neoliberals feed off a **Satan Cult** they created, and obsession with social control is their hallmark. Could neoliberalism be the great deceiver called "Antichrist", claiming to be the new Messiah who brings justice for all, but creating wealth for the few and poverty for the many? Was the Brown Blob part of the **Satan Cult**, and why did it seem attracted to British Broadminded Television? Most of its activity was underneath B.B.T. Headquarters, what on earth did that indicate? "Why?" pondered the fatberg fighters, the picture below provides an answer. Prime Minister Boris Johnson would develop a childish crush on American President Donald Trump, who promised marvelous trade deals if Boris disobeyed the Gematria and entered the *Book of the Dead,* by attempting to forge a no deal Brexit.

THIS BOOK CELEBRATES THE DEATHS OF LIBERALISM AND
SOCIALISM THE TWIN BIG LIES OF THE TWENTIETH CENTURY

BOOK OF THE DEAD = 666

Book of the Dead celebrates the deaths of all failed philosophies, and pays tribute to George Orwell for pointing out the paucity of socialism and liberalism. Since time immemorial, philosophers sought to succeed where both these philosophies fail, to introduce a social system that eradicates the rich/poor divide. In ancient Greece Aristotle offered justification for private property, while Plato suggested a man may neither take what is another's nor be deprived of his own, which the neoliberals heartily applaud. But they're not keen on Aristotle's state distributive justice, which the socialists rather favour, while their grasping commie friends' side with the fanatic Socrates, who wanted separate families abolished and property shared. Yet, Aristotle argued that common ownership generated conflict, for men display greater care for what is their own, so his distributive justice was not redistribution of existing wealth; it was rather the distribution of state resources, because Aristotle did not consider the equalization of possessions would eliminate injustice.

Some 300 years later, a wise man born in a humble stable stated: *The poor shall always be with ye*, it remains true 2000 years later. Despite the clownish attempts of Karlo Marx, founder of the Marx Brothers funny family, the rich/poor divide remains embedded. So, perhaps in his desperation to be comical, Karlo turned to the Bible: *From each according to his ability to each according to his need.* This Marxist maxim was nicked from *Acts 4: 32-37,* but Karlo neglected to mention that it was intended to establish the fledgling Christian movement, not as a general injunction for all of mankind. Karlo the Clown should rather have quoted Apostle Paul? "*If there be first a willing mind, it is accepted according to a man hath, and not according to that he hath not. For I mean not that other men be eased, and ye burdened: but by an equality, that now at this time your abundance be a supply for their want, that their abundance also may be a supply for your want.*" Apostle Paul, 2 Corinthians 8: 12-14.

KARLO

Das Kapital,
THE
MARX
BROTHERS
SILVER SCREEN COLLECTION

JEZZO

LENNO

STALO

Karlo the Clown should rather have plagiarized Apostle Paul, who recognized that givers, not takers, must decide on what to give. Giving must not be charity, but assistance, so the takers can lift themselves, then reimburse the givers. That verse by Apostle Paul should be read by every politician, for Marxism has not succeeded anywhere in the world, while the neoliberal mantra of *my country only* is unchristian and unworkable. Yet, using this, Donald Trump won American 2016 elections, and Boris Johnson gained the xenophobic Brexit referendum vote, propelling ambitious Boris to centre stage.

666 doubled when the Conservative Party, known as **The Tory,** united with **The Liberals** in 2010 to form a unity government. Prompting the losing Labour Party to implode into full-blown Marxism, by grooming the Marxist monomaniac Commie Corbyn, for the Labour Party leadership. **The Tory** of the Gematria smiled smugly, **The Liberals** known as Liberal Democrats, tore themselves apart in the ill-fated coalition. While Mayor Boris Johnson prepared meticulously for the 2016 Brexit Referendum, by inciting xenophobic Tory members to favour leaving the E.U., as this would provide a platform for his campaign to become prime minister.

This terrified Professor Peter Watercloset; the venal London mayor running the country was a prospect too ghastly to contemplate. So, Peter approached his good friend Lord Evil Neville, to halt the horror show from the House of Lords. Peter Watercloset introduced Evil Neville to the Gematria, and together they arrived at a chilling deduction, which boded ill for Britain. Do the 666 math yourself on **Devil Fatberg** and **A U.K. Brexit,** and you'll unveil two UK perils. Britain was nearing an abyss, monomaniac Commie Corbyn panted for a Marxist Britain, and power-hungry Boris Johnson thirsted to be king. Given the Marxist threat, Boris would win an election handsomely, and a **No Hard No Deal** Brexit would become a reality. What was the right path, selfish neoliberalism of Boris Johnson or impractical Marxism of Commie Corbyn, could there be a balance? Some say liberal individualism's roots can be traced to Christianity; God's relationship with people is on a one-to-one basis, so it's with individuals and not groups. Yet, that negates the selfless charity of Christianity, and the perfect gift of giving postulated by Apostle Paul? Maybe the West should look outside their own culture to Africa, is the Holy Mountain a Christian society based on a social/liberal balance?

"Then the lion shall lay down with the lamb, and the bear shall eat grass like the ox, and the child shall play on the hole of the asp, and nothing shall hurt nor destroy in all My Holy Mountain!"

Towards the Mountain
An Autobiography by the author of Cry, the Beloved Country
Alan Paton

There is a word in South Africa - Ubuntu - that describes his greatest gift: his recognition that we are all bound together in ways that can be invisible to the eye; that there is a oneness to humanity; that we achieve ourselves by sharing ourselves with others, and caring for those around us.

— Barack Obama —

Speaking at the Nelson Mandela Memorial
10th December 2013

"No Man is an island. If a clod be washed away by the sea, Europe is the less, as well as if a promontory were, or of a manor of thine own."

John Donne got it precisely correct in his poem: which was a passionate argument for a united Europe, yet Boris Johnson continued to pursue his Brexit ambitions. On long, talkative nights Lord Neville and Professor Peter Watercloset, attempted to thwart the London mayor. While Dr. Zee Garbo continued to work on an antidote to the fatberg, from a sample she had obtained from MAMBA.

"I've got it, Peter!" Dr. Zee Garbo exalted; her lovely eyes wide with excitement. "The Baby Brown Blob has developed into an early life phase, but I've discovered how to defeat the chemical Asterix and kill it." Peter waited eagerly for Zee to elaborate.

"The answer is to use a stronger counter chemical named Obelix, to counter the building block of Asterix. This inhibits proliferation of hepatic stellate cells," she finished, excitedly, and Peter at once asked: "Is the Obelix chemical freely available?"

"It's a type of plant-derived cytokinin," Dr. Zee replied, "which can reduce apoptosis of cells. Obelix inhibits proliferation of H.S.C.s." Dr. Zee then went on to explain: "So, the good news is that Obelix is mass-produced to treat liver fibrosis. I've already looked into ordering mass stocks of Obelix," she grinned triumphantly at them.

"The trick really, was to identify which stellate cell to attack, but I had help there." Zee informed shyly, for the Gematria now helped her to make decisions.

An Asterix = 666

China Bat Covid = 666

The mysterious Gematria China bat threat remained, but at least the **Devil Fatberg** danger had abated. So, Doctor Zee Garbo met with Metropolitan Association Monitoring Behavioral Attitudes, who were really helpful this time. As the Baby Brown Blob they were studying, had burst out its bottle and escaped down a toilet, government was pretty miffed with MAMBA. The Faceless Man eagerly promised them his full support, and this time he was deadly serious, so he called meetings where scientists and faceless bureaucrats met. Thanks to the studies of Professor Watercloset, the Gematria had provided Dr. Zee with the answer. **An Asterix = 666** was the key. The old sewers under the B.B.T. building were identified as the main threat, yet the question was how to distribute the Obelix chemical; the MAMBA Honda scooters were too big for Abbey Mills' narrow corridors. So, Evil Neville volunteered the Old Farts mobility scooters, but snakes can be really lethargic, and so it was with dawdling MAMBA. The 2010 Tory/Liberal government had imposed a period of austerity, on everything except MP salaries and perks, it was hard times for the proles in Britain. Lack of funding had slowed MAMBA to a snail's pace, they missed important deadlines and made lame excuses, and seemed to slither on forever. Then, a scientific finding in California shook the snake awake!

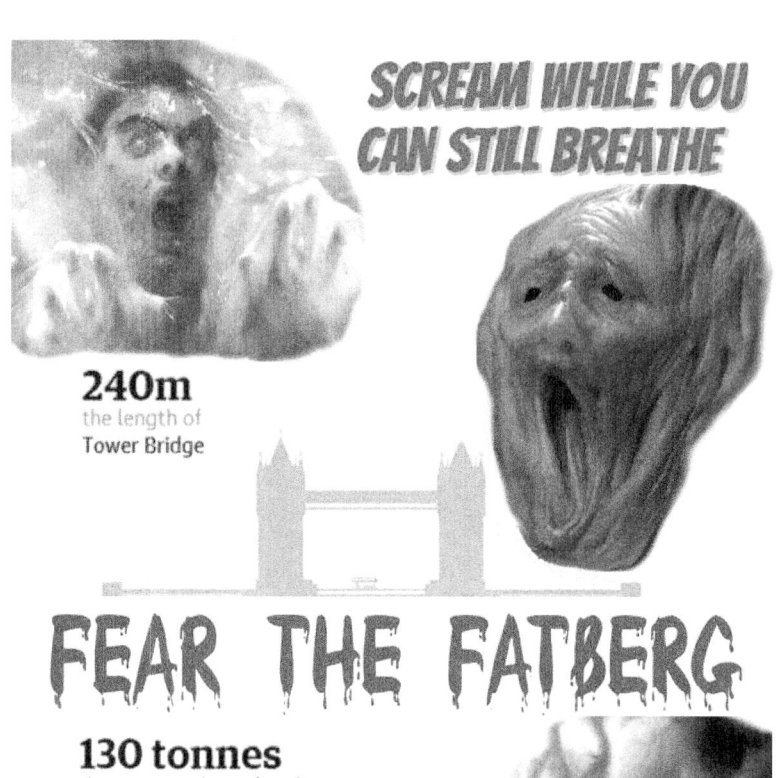

SCREAM WHILE YOU CAN STILL BREATHE

240m
the length of
Tower Bridge

FEAR THE FATBERG

130 tonnes
the estimated **weight** of
the congealed mass of fat
which is the weight of ...

two
Airbus A318 aircraft ...

... or ...

19
African elephants

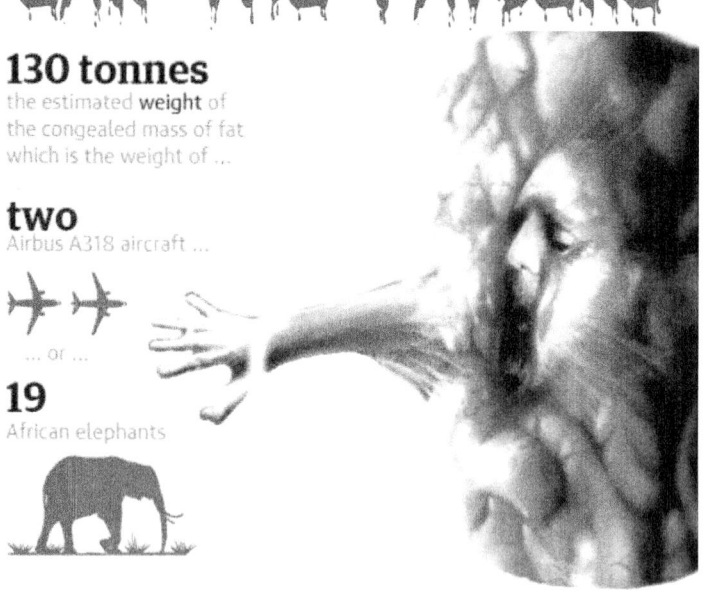

Fighting Fatberg

Professor Peter Watercloset was frantic, for California University had produced electricity-eating, living cells – "electric bacteria" – which used energy in its purest form. Rather similar to the *Frankenstein* monster – which was brought to life by galvanic energy, for all life is nothing more than a flow of electrons – our cells break down sugars and electrons flow through them, which pass on to electron-hungry oxygen. Life is clever, for it figures out how to suck electrons out of what we eat. Science was long aware of basic cell types which consume pure energy sources to survive, but none as weird as the new electric bacteria. Unlike any other living entity, they eat and survive on naked electricity, in the shape of electrons harvested from rocks. There are other reports about a phenomenon called "electric fog"; one report comes from an airline pilot and another from a tugboat captain – both therefore reliable – and both emanate around London?

There is a common thread to the reports: both claimed that a "cloud" or "fog" had electric or magnetic effects on the environment. Overleaf is an interesting report from the British steamer *Mohican,* taken from a news report of 1904. Every man of the crew vouched for the account by Captain Urquhart; a lookout reported seeing lightning and then a *"strange grey cloud"*, so it seems that lightning can conduct static electricity through heavy fog.

"For that length of time the vessel was enshrouded in a strange metallic vapour, which glowed like phosphorous. The entire vessel looked as if it were afire and the sailors flitted about the deck like glowing phantoms. The cloud had a strange magnetic effect on the vessel, for the needle of the compass revolved with the speed of an electric motor, and the sailors were unable to raise pieces of steel from the magnetized decks." -

Log of Captain Urquhart.

The log of Captain Urquhart describing a *metallic vapour*, is eerily similar to a recount by narrowboat Captain Watercloset? Now, let's try to tie the different accounts together, and surmise what could happen if the conditions were exactly right - if heavy fog and excessive lightning occurred at the same time? Californian biologists grew electric bacteria on battery electrodes inserted in slime, so what would happen if a massive lightning storm, sent static electricity flashing through a Whitechapel fog into the sewers? Would this galvanize the green slime excreted by the fatberg, into a fearful *Frankenstein*, living Brown Blob monster? Which would leave its dank dwelling to slither out of sewer manholes, and stalk the foggy streets of Whitechapel with malevolent intent - or perhaps even attack the narrowboat of Professor Watercloset? Was it not possible that the fog itself, which abounded in Whitechapel, could be the carrier of static electricity into the sewers - through the old William Crimp stink pipes which still existed? Scary though it sounds, it's scientifically possible.

"*Fog everywhere. Fog up the river, where it flows among green aits and meadows; fog down the river, where it rolls defiled among the tiers of shipping, and the waterside pollutions of a great and dirty city. Fog on Essex marshes, fog on Kentish heights. Fog creeping into the cabooses of collier-*

brigs; fog lying out on the yards and hovering in the rigging of great ships; fog drooping on the gunwales of barges and small boats."

Charles Dickens, *Bleak House.*

It was the most intense lightning storm ever seen in London. The air crackled with static electricity and people reported their hair being haloed wildly around their head. The conditions were ripe for an "electric fog", because the lightning had charged the air. Then, the fog rolled in, but not just an ordinary fog. The conditions that cause London fogs are fairly unique, sometimes those conditions conspire, to create an extraordinarily heavy fog.

"A real Dickens of a fog," it's described in London. Fogs like this great pea-souper described by Charles Dickens no longer occur in London, though it took another disaster like the 1858 Great Stink for London to act. The 1952 "Great Killer Fog" lasted for five days and killed an estimated 4,000 people. So, a *Clean Air Act* was passed in 1956, forcing Londoners to burn smokeless fuel or switch to gas or electricity, for power sources had become cheaper as industries grew. The British tradition of home and hearth was ending; the patriotic wartime exhortation of *"keep the home fires burning"* could now get you a hefty fine, as open fires were forbidden by law. The 1956 Act took a long time to become effective, but it did finally work; the bizarre Sam Bartram incident would never occur again. Once again, it's best to have another writer describe the event, after all Sam Bartram was there hidden in the fog, so it's best to let him tell of *The Vanishing Goalkeeper.* These anecdotes of fog are amusing, they also serve the purpose of conveying what London fogs are really like, for very soon a Dickens fog will be the central focus of the story.

"Fog down the river, where it rolls defiled among the tiers of shipping, Chance people on the bridges peeping over the parapets into a nether sky of fog, with fog all round them, as if they were up in a balloon and hanging in the misty clouds."

THE VANISHING GOALKEEPER

"Soon after the kick-off the fog began to thicken rapidly at the far end. The referee stopped the game and then, as visibility became clearer, restarted it. We were on top at this time, and I saw fewer and fewer figures as we attacked steadily. I paced up and down my goal-line, happy in the knowledge that Chelsea were being pinned in their own half. The boys must be giving the Pensioners the hammer, I thought smugly, as I stamped my feet for warmth. Quite obviously, however, we were not getting the ball into the net, for no players were coming back to line up, as they would have done following a goal. Time passed, and I made several advances toward the edge of the penalty area, peering through the murk, which was getting thicker every minute. Still I could see nothing; the Chelsea defence was clearly being run off its feet. After a long time a figure loomed out of the

curtain of fog in front of me. It was a policeman, and he gaped at me incredulously.

'What on Earth are you doing here?' he gasped. 'The game was stopped a quarter of an hour ago.' And when I groped my way to the dressing-room, the rest of the Charlton team, already out of the bath and in their civvies, were convulsed with laughter."

Report by Sam Bartram.

"Peasoupers" were a thing of the past in London. However, as another song says, there can still be a "Foggy Day in London Town". The British capital is particularly liable to natural winter fogs, because it's surrounded by low hills with marshland on its outskirts, and the wide Thames River running through the city. So, the geographical location of London encourages a meteorological temperature inversion, as warm air traps cold air beneath it for days on end, then carbon-laden smoke from power station and factory chimneys are unable to rise and seep into a fog

- turning the air into varying shades of yellow, brown or black. This is beautifully captured by the impressionist artist Claude Monet in his paintings of London fogs, which if you look carefully - clearly show carbon in the fog conducting electricity, that spawned life on such a Monet-foggy London night.

As Professor Watercloset predicated it must come, the fatberg spawned it, and a massive electrical storm imbued it with a pulse of life. Although caused by laws of physics, it was also a classic case of Karmic Law, that the first fatal fatberg attack was witnessed by doubting journalist Harry Hack. Carried out by an offspring spawned by the giant fatberg, although much smaller, the Brown Blob was a natural-born killer – as Harry Hack would bear terrified witness to.

British Broadminded Television is situated in Whitechapel, in old Abbey Mills pumphouse, the Byzantine building design shrouded by fog creates a scary atmosphere. Harry Hack shivered as he left the building, the chilly winter fog wrapped around him like a damp cloak; it made things seem grotesque and spookier than they actually were. Fog shrouded the vehicles in the car park into a cloud of invisibility. It was late at night, so there were no people about, but Harry cheered up as he spotted the camper van of Sir Jimmy Savile, who used the vehicle to coach young girls for his show. Harry Hack was about to approach the vehicle to say hello, when he heard a loud clang, Swinging around, he noticed the open manhole, with its cover lying next to it. Crackling static issued from the manhole, which mingled with the fog and created an eerie scenario. The air was electric, as though something bizarre was about to happen. Harry Hack peered through greenish fog, at the Brown Blob emerging from the manhole. Harry was sure his eyes were deceiving him, but the smell was very real. The stink was rank beyond belief – a nose-burning, throat-gagging miasma, it drifted across the car park like some grim portent. A stink situated in a stench of selfishness, self-centered conceit and arrogant pride, the heart and core of modern neoliberalism.

318

Harry was too shocked to even gag as, rooted to the spot in horror, he watched the fatberg emerge from the opened manhole, then amazingly spread itself out into a massive Brown Blob. It seemed the fatberg was capable of shape-shifting, also able to move freely, for it slithered stealthily across the car park, toward the parked camper van of deviant Jimmy Savile. The cry in the throat of Harry Hack never sounded, words were shriveled by the terrible smell, so there was no warning as the fatberg spread over the camper van Paedophile 1.

Just an awful momentary sight of terrified Sir Jimmy screaming at a window, thankfully he appeared to be alone, there was no young girl. For the entire van was enveloped, the fatberg seemed to burp then, slid back into the open manhole, Sir Jimmy and his camper had vanished. A late worker from B.B.T found Harry Hack dazed and babbling incoherently in the car park. He was taken to London Hospital, then later transferred to their Arkham Psychiatric Facility.

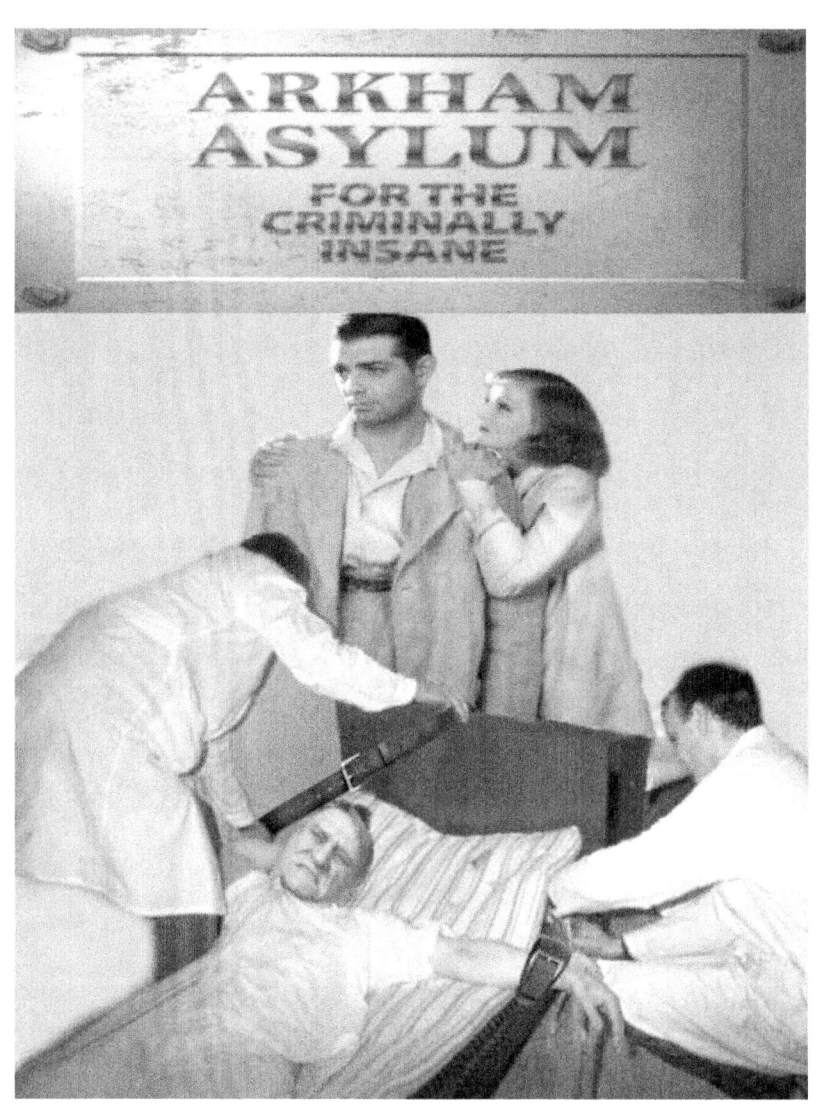

320

Professor Peter and Dr. Zee Garbo visited the writhing and screaming journalist, but Harry Hack was still not out of his shock, they visited a week later but now he was comatose. It took another week before he began to talk, but it was just wild babble.

"Sir Jimmy was not killed by a fatberg. He died peacefully in his sleep last week, aged eighty-four," Peter Watercloset reasoned with Harry.

"I tell you, the fatberg got him. I saw it, man; it was terrible!" Harry Hack babbled and writhed under his restraints, the shrinks had him strapped down in case he tried to hurt himself. The hack was sadly deluded for Sir Jimmy Savile's funeral has taken place at Leeds Cathedral, hundreds of fans gathered in the city center to pay their respects, as the former DJ's gold coffin made his final journey through the city.

"Sir Jimmy had a grand state funeral," Zee Garbo assured Harry. She'd not attended, but seen it on British Broadminded Television: young girls throwing things at the coffin, while Prince Charles showered praise in a statement released by Clarence House:

"The Prince of Wales and Duchess of Cornwall are sad to hear of the death of Sir Jimmy Savile, their thoughts are with his family." **Clarence House**

After the royal statement Rolf Harris took the microphone, he was visibly distraught.

"Jimmy was a wonderful man. His public face is well known, but we knew him more, as an uncle to the children," Rolf sniffed.

"He was a very good friend to all of us. Uncle Jimmy will be missed by the kiddies," the singer Gary Glitter sobbed, brokenly.

"We are all going to be worse off without Sir Jimmy around," the publicist Max Clifford predicted, gloomily. And he was dead right, for arrest warrants were being prepared.

The funeral of Sir Jimmy Savile was held on 9th November 2011, just weeks after miners were pulled out of the Chilean mine, where Jimmy Savile was alleged to be hiding – a coincidence? Did B.B.T. stuff another body into that gold coffin? Was Savile's funeral staged and was Prince Charles involved? Or, was Sir Jimmy swallowed by the fatberg? It worried Peter and Zee, because Harry Hack stuck to his story, which backed their theory of fatbergs spawning deadly life. So, the two scientists acted. They asked London Water to assist MAMBA to pour Obelix chemicals into sewers, under B.B.T. Headquarters, where the threat was. The T.V. station was shaken by Sir Jimmy mysteriously vanishing; they suspected he'd fled to Chile, to avoid the *Operation Yewtree* probe. So, B.B.T. staged a cover-up state funeral and agreed to assist with distributing Obelix, hoping it would divert attention from possible paedophile revelations.

20-gallon plastic drums of Obelix chemicals were stacked outside the Ripper Street headquarters of British Broadminded Television. The Obelix would be distributed by MAMBA, into sewers under the building, where Baby Blob and the giant fatberg were found. Dr. Zee surmised that other breeder host fatbergs were spawning Brown Blobs in the Boris Johnson Tunnel, which was rather telling.

"Why is the spawning around B.B.T.?" Professor Peter pondered.

Doctor Zee noted: "Sir Jimmy was killed in

B.B.T. car park." The story of Harry Hack now made perfect sense, but why at British Broadminded Television, why did the fatberg congregate there?

"Because the bloody Brown Blobs feed on pure evil!" Evil Neville put in.

Peter and Zee felt cold shivers. Did Brown Blobs increase in power by consuming evil? Were the fatbergs intent on becoming *prime evil?* Did the blob attack their narrowboat because it sensed a threat to its fatberg host? Could it be planning to consume more paedophiles? What of the other molesters who abounded at B.B.T.; would the spawn of the fatberg gain strength by eating them all?

The thought galvanized Professor Peter Watercloset into action, so he marshalled the Old Farts Club, who'd been brought in to help with distributing the Obelix chemical drums. The maneuverable mobility scooters were ideal vehicles to travel the narrow corridors of Abbey Mills, which the MAMBA Honda scooters could not negotiate. 20-gallon Obelix drums were strapped to the front of the scooters and the Old Farts were primed for combat. They were truly the best of the British, and would be recorded so by history.

"We have nothing to offer but blood, sweat and tears. Also, a full drum of Obelix, you foul fatberg!" Evil Neville   roared.

"Now, this is not the end. It is not even the beginning of the end. But it is, perhaps, the end of the beginning."   Winston Churchill

Maps were given to the Old Farts to deliver Obelix chemicals on mobility scooters, to inaccessible sewer drains inside the B.B.T. building. The old Abbey Mills pump station, which now served as British Broadminded Television Head Office, always had a nauseating rotten egg smell wafting from sewers under the building. This emanated from the sewer inspection chambers built of brick, the main chamber at Abbey Mills was a Victorian work of art, with cobbled and stepped courses of brick and no mortar used above channel pipe levels.

The MAMBA scientists had conducted a drain camera inspection survey, to find any concealed chambers or traps, then they used a sonar drain tracer to locate it at ground level. The outside sewer drains could be handled by London Water and MAMBA, and the inside ones by the Old Farts Club, where the modern Boris Johnson Tunnel still ran to Beckton. The advice of Professor Watercloset had been ignored, and now the narrow tunnel vision of Mayor Johnson had created a fatberg which spawned a Brown Blob. The awful consequence of which now manifested in a terrifying spectacle, as panic-stricken people fled the B.B.T. building, pushing and screaming hysterically.

THE BLOB IS IN THE BUILDING

FREEDOM FROM FATBERGS

The bawling Brian Blessed voice boomed out, and Lord Neville never wavered. At that moment he was a truly a Great Britisher. His mobility scooter advanced and the rushing crowd parted, right behind Evil Neville came his five brave riders, primed and ready for battle. Evil Neville knew the Brown Blob came from the main inspection chamber, so he headed in that direction down the corridor. Then, his shocked eyes beheld the fearsome Brown Blob.

Wreathed in flashing static electricity of iridescent green, writhing and pulsing as it slithered remorselessly forward, it filled the corridor, and the stink was putrid beyond belief – a smell situated in the stench of selfishness, the heart and core of modern neoliberalism. Is that why the malevolent Brown Blob was so inexorably drawn to British Broadminded Television? It moved onward in a series of waves; the front reached forward with greenish tentacles, while the back seemed to crest, filling the width of the corridor. It now manifested that the Brown Blob had the ability to alter its size to suit surroundings; any bigger and it would be stuck in the narrow corridor, yet the vicious blob that consumed the camper of Jimmy Savile must have been massive. The Brown Blob was also highly corrosive, it had absorbed a metallic van.

The swirling, green mist caught chokingly at the throat, so the Old Farts hurriedly attached the gas masks MAMBA had fortuitously provided. It was the Old Farts versus the fatberg – or, rather, its odious offspring the Brown Blob – which moved forward eager for the battle. Lord Evil Neville was ready for it, on his specially prepared mobility scooter, which could manage the tightest turns and navigate the smallest of spaces. Evil Neville opened the faucet on the Obelix drum and moved forward, the chemical flowed down the corridor and the Brown Blob shrunk back, the smell of the Obelix chemical appeared as odious to the Brown Blob as its own smell to humans?

Then, Lord Neville ducked nimbly into a side passage and Scooter Two advanced. They were like Polish fighter pilots, jousting in the skies of honour. More Obelix flowed and the Brown Blob began to retreat. The last four scooters put it into full flight; it backed up, shivering in craven fear, slid down the stairwell to the basement, then slithered down the brick drain to its fatberg host.

"Had it not been for the magnificent material contributed by the Polish squadrons, and their unsurpassed gallantry, I hesitate to say that the outcome of the Battle of Britain would have been the same."

Air Chief Sir Hugh Dowding.

Polish pilots had fought valiantly in the Battle of Britain, while a Polish chemist had triumphed in the Battle of Boris, with a lot of help from her friends of course. In those dank B.B.T. corridors the magnificent wartime speeches of Winston Churchill now seemed to echo. Mayor Boris Johnson enjoyed likening himself to Churchill, who made many speeches supporting the European Union, yet the xenophobic mayor wanted to withdraw from European allies? *Out of his mind; stupefying ignorance; unfit to be president."* The new Winston Churchill once lambasted Donald Trump, but then it changed into a Lewis Carroll *Boris in Sewerland* fantasy, starring Tweedle Don and Tweedle Dum. As Boris envisaged lucrative trade deals with America after winning the Brexit Referendum, this would only last until the Trump defeat in 2020 elections, Boris lacked the foresight to see that far. Right now, he accepted Trump's advice that a no-deal Brexit would benefit Britain, whose current major trading partner was the European Union; half of U.K. exports and imports are in the E.U. A no-deal Brexit would be disastrous for Britain, though hugely advantageous for Trump's America, but Boris would not let that stand in the way of his political ambitions. Even the lives of his own countrymen would be sacrificed, on the altar of Boris Johnson aggrandizement, that lay ahead when Covid-19 would hit Britain.

"If you don't get what you want, then walk away," Trump urged Prime Minister Theresa May who was struggling to pass a Brexit deal, for a no-deal Brexit meant using World Trade Organization rules. Yet, no country relied solely on W.T.O. rules; they all had other trade deals, one of the best was the U.K.-E.U. pact.   That's why the *B.B.C.* and *Guardian* newspaper, found Boris never mentioned a no-deal Brexit in the 2016 referendum, a "substantial USA deal" to soften a no-deal Brexit was Donald Trump's idea. But the Irish backstop clause in the Theresa May deal backed a *Good Friday Agreement* on open borders, which Boris wanted dropped to retain support of Irish Unionists. As guarantor to the *Good Friday Agreement,* and One Ireland nationalist backer, America would then block any new U.S.-U.K. deal.

Additionally, the E.U.-Canada deal took seven years, a U.S.-U.K. trade deal could take ten years, leaving Britain trapped in a high-tariff trade limbo desperate for any deal. Greedy America was already insisting that U.S. firms like Google, Facebook and

Amazon be exempt from E.U. levies on internet-based firms. Before the end of this book, Boris would betray the Unionists and sell Northern Ireland like slaves to the E.U., in hope of a U.S. trade deal, banking everything on a Trump re-election in 2020. The blocked Boris Johnson Tunnel was another example of Boris tunnel vision, built because London had no funds for broad sewage tunnels. Yet, Mayor Boris Johnson had waxed lyrical over what he gushingly called his Thames Tiara Bridge.

Launched as a privately sponsored gift, Garden Bridge soon turned into a "Bridge Over Troubled Waters," by wolfing up £60m of public cash - plus the promise of an extra £3.5m every year. For what would be a corporate events space and not a public crossing. Built just 200 metres from an existing peasant bridge, the Garden Bridge was for registered guests only; a neoliberal monument to robbing the poor to advance the rich. Another crass example was the £60m Emirates Airline Cable Car, that attracted just four regular users, London Transport fell to a £1bn deficit.

The cable car was sold, the famous "Boris Bikes" were phased out, the controversial "Battler" water cannons failed to quench the 2011 riots. While London burned, from Tottenham to Peckham, Mayor Johnson ducked off on holiday to Canada. The £2m water cannons were sold as scrap for just £30,000, bringing cannons to a knife fight was silly.

Thames Tideway Tunnel

Creating a cleaner, healthier Thames River.

Tunnel vision is a form of situational unawareness, as it narrows focus and you miss things, while some see only a yoke around the neck others see opportunity. Compare Boris Johnson to the new

London Mayor Sadiq Khan, who won the election for Labour in 2016, a positive change was quickly noticed, for here was a new broad vision. Against the advice of sewage expert Professor Watercloset, the myopic former mayor built the narrow Boris Johnson Tunnel, which proved inadequate and was soon blocked by a fatberg. Mayor Johnson returned the Thames River to the Great Stink because, like most cities, London is largely concreted over, so rainwater can flood sewers. To prevent sewage backing up into people's homes, the excess is flushed into the Thames River via a network of 50 overflow pipes, you recall the near narrowboat disaster at one of these outfalls?

Yet, change was now coming, due to the "broad tunnel" vision of Peter Watercloset and Zee Garbo, backed by the visionary new London mayor Sadiq Khan. Born in Tooting, South London, to a working-class British Pakistani family, Khan bears a love for the people of London that the elitist Mayor Boris Johnson never evinced. Khan was a councillor for the London Borough of Wandsworth from 1994 to 2006, before being elected as MP for Totting at the 2005 election, standing down in 2016 when he became Mayor of London.

At last, the voice of Professor Peter Watercloset was being heard. Under the visionary new mayor Sadiq Khan a gigantic £5 billion super-sewer is being built, wide enough to fit three double-decker buses, at 90 metres deep it will run for 20 miles under the Thames. The Thames Tideway Tunnel is the biggest British water project ever conducted, narrow-minded Boris Johnson seethed in envy, while Londoners prayed that Sadiq Khan would be reelected in 2021?

Boris Johnson boasts that crime in London fell by 20% during his tenure as London mayor, but crime in the whole of England and Wales fell by 26%, while the London homicide rate had been falling since 2003. Boris just happened to be mayor at a time of falling crime, outside of his zip-wire stunts and sexual escapades involving corruption, there was nothing remarkable about his mayorship.

342

Fishing for Deals

After becoming the foreign secretary in 2016, Boris Johnson began fishing in earnest for an American trade deal to back a no-deal Brexit, while beleaguered Prime Minister Theresa May struggled to pass her Brexit deal through parliament. Blocked at every turn by Boris and his cohorts, who wanted Theresa May out the way, and also knew well that leaving the E.U. was stupid so a reasonable deal was not possible.

Boris fished for his no-deal Brexit in shark-infested waters, where sailed British and Northern Irish fishermen, who objected to being sold as slaves to the E.U. The Boris bravado of exiting the E.U. in a big bang would soon become a T.S. Eliot whimper, under the reality of national leadership. For the Boris hole card was shaky - namely Donald Trump. You can fool all the people only some of the time; could Trump fool the people again in 2020 elections, the U.K. foreign secretary was playing a perilous game.

343

Boris never know back then, that it would become more perilous, after he became prime minister and Covid-19 hit. Thankfully, the fatberg fighters were there. In 2020, Lord Neville would block Boris's illegal *Internal Market Bill,* which threatened to curtail Brexit talks. Forcing the prime minister into signing a Brexit deal, which avoided the **No Hard No Deal** warned of in the Gematria. Britain sorely needed such guidance, for they would soon be in the position of an amoral, womanizing prime minister negotiating their future.

Boris was sacked in 2004 as Tory vice-chair, for denying an affair with Petronella Wyatt, after her mother revealed the affair did happen. Boris broke his promise to marry Petronella, so she'd had an abortion, another victim of Boris misogyny derived from his Turkish ancestry. Most old Etonians and Oxford alumni do not speak like Boris, his is not a natural persona, but the carefully curated image of a loveable buffoon. British voters fell for it like star-struck besotted teenagers adoring a rock idol.

Boris's coarse language and sassy references to manly infidelities, are scarily similar to the brazen banter used by depraved Jimmy Savile, to cash in on the permissive misogyny of a society brainwashed by B.B.T. liberalism. Boris spouted the benefit of a liberal education, through his flowery Oxford language, Jeremy Corbyn was a "big girl's blouse" while David Cameron was a "girly swot" – the misogynist diminutives echoed Jimmy Savile.

Boris Johnson outraged child sex abuse victims, by jesting that police funding was "spaffed up the wall" investigating historical allegations; this coarse reference to ejaculation brought widespread condemnation, after Boris said in an interview with *L.B.C. Radio*:

"An awful lot of police time is spent looking at historic offences, and all that malarkey." Such sentiment in a land which spawned Jimmy Savile prompted children's charity *N.S.P.C.C.* to respond:

"His remarks were an affront to victims." *SAVE Association*, founded by victims of childhood sexual abuse, suggested hotly:

"Johnson should learn to keep his mouth shut about subjects he knows nothing about. Child sexual abuse is one of those subjects." Yet it must be said that, although injudicious, the coarse remarks of Boris Johnson in no way imply a moral equivalence between degenerate Jimmy Savile and Boris Johnson - or in any way link Boris to Savile's debauched actions. Johnson's victims may well have been childish, but they were all consenting adult women, not the naïve starstruck minors Savile preyed upon.

Boris Johnson never indulged in the criminal degeneracies of Jimmy Savile, but what Boris and Jimmy did share equally was the public's permissive and forgiving attitude toward sexual misbehavior. By assenting to the roguish *droit du seigneur* of Boris the Turk, snobbish Tory members basically approved a medieval custom, of lords of the manor bedding subordinate women. By fostering such fascism, British Broadminded Television lost the right to be called "Our Beeb", an institution belonging and accountable to the people. B.B.T. instead, became synonymous with sybaritic behaviour.

In fact, B.B.T. and Boris became blood brothers, as endorsers of the neoliberal stance of countries like France, where political sexual peccadillos are state secrets. Yet, even leaving aside the moral view on the many infidelities of now Foreign Secretary Boris Johnson, it remains absurd for anyone to imagine, that a man so incapable of controlling his libido or guarding his speech is fit to be trusted with controlling a country. The tainted history of hedonist Boris Johnson makes this proposition truly laughable, yet it would come terrifyingly true. Because, unbelievably, bumbling Boris managed to easily upstage the blundering *Punch 'n' Judy* political parody of awkward Prime Minister Theresa May, and comical commie Jeremy Corbyn.

After Boris Johnson became foreign secretary in 2016, vile Islamophobic messages sprouted on his Facebook page, as anti-Islam Tories flocked to their xenophobic hero. Whose "liberal values" matched the barbarity of Islamic zealots; this insulting poem by Rudyard Kipling was quoted in the Buddhist Shwedagon Pagoda, *"Bloomin' idol made o' mud / Wot they called the Great Gawd Budd."*

Boris used words, not bullets, with the same effect. Whisky exports were endorsed in a Sikh temple which banned alcohol. Africans were "picaninnies with watermelon smiles," Islamic women looked like "bank robbers," while the Burka resembled a "postbox." Was naked Islamophobia that drove Boris to falsely claim, a British mum trained reporters in Iran, ruining any hope of remission of sentence for alleged spying?

"I don't think my comments made a difference," sniffed Foreign Secretary Boris, after wrongly stating that Nazanin Zaghari-Ratcliffe had been in Iran to teach journalism, when in fact she had been on holiday. Yet, four days after Boris made the remarks, they were cited as evidence in an Iranian court, with the threat of doubling her sentence. What made Boris say something so stupid? What type of man separates a mother from her daughter, then denies any wrongdoing, and breezily carries on with no sign of regret?

The British-Iranian mother Nazanin Zaghari-Ratcliffe remains in prison over spying charges, which she strenuously denies. While her British-born, five-year-old daughter Gabriella, who has been living with her grandparents in Tehran while her mother was in jail, was returned to her dad Richard Ratcliffe to start school in the U.K.

Words matter and utterings of Foreign Secretaries, must be made with care. Boris claims his controversial Nazanin Zaghari-Ratcliffe statement "made no difference", yet police reported a fourfold increase in anti-Muslim incidents, from the week before Boris wrote an Islamophobic article to the week after.

In the week following the publication of his *Telegraph* column, in which Boris compared veiled Muslim women to "letterboxes", 38 incidents were reported to police. Of those incidents, 22 involved Muslim women who wore the face veil, but this was just a massive coincidence giggles Boris?

It was no coincidence because, 42% of the street-based incidents where face veils were insulted, directly referenced Boris Johnson and/or the language used in his column. Yet, this was the man the Conservative Party decided to make foreign secretary. Had the Tories gone completely bonkers? Would the next insanity be to make him the prime minister, had madness descended on once Great Britain?

"Unpredictable, gaffe-prone, inconsistent…" was the Foreign Office staff's assessment of their new boss. An increasing public outcry forced Boris to resign as foreign secretary. There were now ominous reports of police probes into his illegal Brexit campaign, and the *Telegraph* had to apologize after Boris wrote this falsehood: *"Polls indicate that a no-deal is closest to the U.K. voters' Brexit idea."* Boris Johnson was stealthily edging toward a disastrous no-deal Brexit, spawned by his pal Trump and the infamous red bus lie, the seedy Trump/Johnson bromance would soon play a major part of this story, unfortunately for Boris a rather sad part.

BORIS BULLDUST BUS

BREXIT BUGGY

"I am satisfied that there is a proper case to issue the summons as requested, for the three offences (of misconduct in a public office)."
District Judge Margot Coleman

The judicial ruling went against Boris Johnson, because he invented the Brexit bus lie, and public officials must not mislead. Yet, the England High Court ducked it; they stated that Parliament was the supreme law, so courts must not interfere. Yet, how would the timid courts react if Boris Johnson interfered by proroguing Parliament, so that he could ratify his no-deal Brexit during the suspension? The Brexit Buggy on the previous page says it all, Batty Boris drove his befuddled buggy onward, forward, backward, sideways… Boris was a master at dodgy driving, which he used in the Brexit campaign.

How a Churchill quote was 'stitched up' to support Brexit

'We have our own dream and our own task. We are with Europe, but not of it. We are linked but not combined. We are interested and associated but not absorbed. If Britain must choose between Europe and the open sea, she must always choose the open sea.'

House of Commons, May 11, 1953

Despite claims by Brexit supporters, Winston Churchill didn't say this in Parliament.

The first part of the 'quote' above was not said in 1953, but written 23 years earlier for America's Saturday Evening Post.

THE SATURDAY EVENING POST

FOUNDED A: D: 1728
PUBLISHED EVERY SATURDAY BY
THE CURTIS PUBLISHING COMPANY

The United States of Europe
By WINSTON CHURCHILL

PHILADELPHIA, FEBRUARY 15, 1930

Churchill yelled the last sentence in a raging row with Charles de Gaulle in 1944.

Graphic by Jon Danzig

Sir Nicholas Soames, who is the grandson of Winston Churchill, launched a scathing attack at this twisting of the war leader's words, in support of the Brexit campaign. He said they had no right to use his grandfather in this way, and suggested Churchill's views would never have aligned with the Brexiteers', because Winston Churchill was a believer in the values of European cooperation. Boris Johnson shockingly responded to this by having the venerable grandson of Winston Churchill deselected as a Tory M.P.

Contrary to the Brexit campaign propaganda, Winston Churchill is recognized as one of the founders of the E.U., and has a building named after him at the European Parliament in Strasbourg. The adjacent poster shows how the Brexit fanatics stitched together two different Churchill quotes, from different times and in diverse contexts, claiming it was said in Parliament in May 1953. While Winston Churchill did write, in 1930, *"We have our own dream and task,"* this did not negate a European Union, but was a desire to retain a United Kingdom and Commonwealth. In 1961, Churchill wrote this: *"Government are right to join the European Economic Community,"* and in 1973 Britain joined the European Union, which was ratified by a 1975 referendum.

Was Boris Johnson behind the 2016 campaign to falsify Churchill's words? Boris had written many books on Churchill, so he was an authority on Churchill speeches. Boris Johnson had blocked every effort of Prime Minister Theresa May to pass a Brexit deal through Parliament, Theresa May finally threw in the towel and Boris became prime minister, now he could impose his no-deal Brexit.

New prime minister Johnson liked to compare himself to the Incredible Hulk, while opposition leader Commie Corbyn was often likened to Mickey Mouse. In the absence of an Action Man like the formidable Sir Keir Starmer, the Incredible Hulk ran wild, while Commie Corbyn wrung his hands and babbled inconsequentially.

357

"The madder Hulk gets; the stronger Hulk gets. No matter how tightly bound, Hulk always escapes!" The prime minister boasted, brazenly alluding to the fact, that British authorities appeared reluctant to act against him. Then, to the horror of the nation, he prorogued Parliament. Royal Assent was obtained by lying to the Queen, that it was necessary to suspend Parliament for five weeks so the P.M. could prepare a *Queen's Speech*. This was an outrageous lie; everybody in Britain knew the real reason for the prorogue was to block Parliament - who supported the Gematria **No Hard No Deal.** The prediction of **A U.K. Brexit** had transpired and **The Tory** had turned out to be *Big Brother Boris*. Now **The Liberals** must be dealt with, or Boris would leave Europe with a no-deal and make England the 51st State of Trump America, Boris had already shown a willingness to dump Ireland and Scotland. Professor Peter Watercloset watched in horror, as the predictions in the Gematria began to come true.

"*FRIENDLY FIRE*
James Michie

The Scotch - what a verminous race!
Canny, pushy, chippy, all over the place,
Battening off us with false bonhomie,
Polluting our stock, undermining our economy.
Down with sandy hair and knobbly knees!
Suppress the tartan dwarves and Wee Frees!
Ban the kilt, the skean-dhu and the sporran
As provocatively, offensively foreign!
It's time Hadrian's Wall was refortified
To pen them in a ghetto on the other side.
I would go further. The nation
Deserves not merely isolation
But comprehensive extermination.
We must not flinch from a solution.
(I await legal prosecution.)"

The James Michie poem was a culmination of two decades of Boris anti-Scottish invective, in 2004 when he was *Spectator Magazine* editor, Boris published the offensive poem. Enraged Scotsmen had quivered in their kilts, and it boiled the Braveheart blood of Evil Neville; he supported England rugby but this went too far! The poem purported to be satirical, but Boris knew that endorsing Scottish genocide would inflame the independence passion, while his catty jibes drove a wedge between the U.K. and the E.U.

Chancellor Angela Merkel had *"served in East Germany's Stasi secret police"*; Emmanuel Macron was *"a jumped-up Napoleon French turd"*, and *"why was Irish leader Leo Varadkar not called Murphy, like the rest?"* Like silly schoolboys the snobbish Tory members giggled, a xenophobic Conservative clique, who wanted Britain to leave the E.U. with a chaotic no-deal Brexit. Both the Chancellor of the Exchequer and the Bank of England Governor, along with every serious economist in Europe, warned that a no-deal Brexit would cause a 2008-type recession.

EasyJet, Microsoft, Goldman Sachs, Barclays Bank, the Deutsche Bank and even Lloyd's of London all threatened to leave in the event of a no-deal. So, Lord Neville turned to his homeland and mustered the troops, Nicola Sturgeon led the Scottish National Party (S.N.P.) and was also the first minister of Scotland, so Nicola petitioned the Edinburgh Scottish Court of Sessions to nullify the illegal Boris prorogation. Rory Stewart was a Tory cabinet minister, but not a Boris fan, Boris the Hulk was facing a Highland uprising!

"Garg'n Uair Dhuisgear!"

("Fierce when roused!")

Rory Stewart has savaged Boris Johnson as an "amoral figure", and "the most accomplished liar in public life". and mocks his affection for mythological figures like Pericles.

""Johnson often compares himself to Pericles, who built the Parthenon, not the Emirates Cable Car."

NewStatesman
The state we're in

Britain should be one of the greatest
democracies on Earth. What went wrong?
By Rory Stewart

"The answer cannot be an adolescent fantasy of being saved by a superhero, but to rather move forward with maturity. The Boris no-deal Brexit is an absence that pretends to be a presence; the negation of a deal masquerading as a deal. It builds on the fantasy of the victim, that you would be better off on your own, if only you could rid yourself of other classes, other groups and other nations. It

fails to recognize that higher tariffs following a no-deal Brexit would lead to inflation and pressure on incomes, an interest rate rise and negative impacts on G.D.P."

"I'm resigning from the Tory Party and leaving the gothic shouting chamber of Westminster. I'm getting away from politics that makes me feel as if Trump never left London."

Last speech of Tory M.P. Rory Stewart.

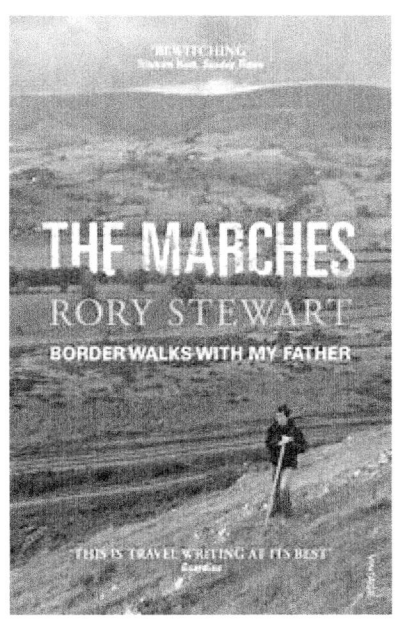

CREAG AN SGAIRBH — CORMORANT ROCK

BORIS THE RIPPER

NO DEAL

BREXIT

THE MAN WHO WOULD BE KING

The Tories were in tatters, twenty MP's had the whip removed by mad whip master Boris. Ten Irish D.U.P. Party MP's, who backed the Tories to form a minority government, withdrew support after Boris bribed the E.U. with an Irish Sea border, placing the whole of Ireland outside the U.K. and as part of the E.U. Boris appeared intent on not only leaving Europe, but breaking up the United Kingdom; as his disdain for Ireland and Scotland showed. The 2019 prorogation of Parliament coincided with a hot summer, and sweating fatberg *MacBoris the Brave* was braced by both Scotland and Ireland. The Scottish National Party (S.N.P.) opposed a no-deal Brexit, and Scottish Tory boss Ruth Davidson resigned in protest.

There are sixty MP's from Scotland in Westminster, and along with the Liberal Democrats they fought against a no-deal Brexit, but the Labour Party, under Commie Corbyn, wilted. Proroguing Parliament was meant to shut out the opposition, as the British heart was torn from Europe, but doughty S.N.P. leader Nicola Sturgeon stood steadfast! While Scotland readied to thwart the no-deal Boris Brexit, the Old Farts drove Brown Blobs to their hideaway, and the Thames Tideway Tunnel of Mayor Sadiq Khan advanced. The foul smell at B.B.T. soon dispersed, as the station realized their role is to serve the public, not the liberal perversions of evil employees. Yet, poor Harry Hack never fully recovered; the fatberg attack broke Harry's liberal spirit, so he retired to Scotland, to do missionary work among the many sex addicts. Like ex-M.P. Alex Salmond, a firm favourite of Scottish juries but still a deeply troubled Scotsman Alec was finished in politics, although he didn't realize it at that time? Professor Watercloset and Dr. Zee Garbo married, then devoted their lives to making sewers safe.

Under instructions from the cacophonous voice of Lord Neville, the London Water Board sluiced Obelix into their sewers, and the whole of the U.K., then the world. The catalytic chemical Asterix was checked and fatbergs no longer spawned vicious Brown Blobs. In fact, the fatbergs were disappearing, as people stopped flushing plastics down toilets. To cut a long story short everyone lived happily ever after, except for fatbergs and Boris Johnson, as well as the coming Covid-19 virus - for antidotes were found for all three.

Peter and Zee honeymooned at the Loch Ness lodge of Evil Neville, where the fatberg fighters plotted against pushy PM Johnson. Who turned into a reincarnation of King Charles I, who prorogued Parliament in 1628; so Boris sought Royal Assent to prorogue, allegedly to ready a *Queen's Speech*?

It was Lord Neville who asked Nicola Sturgeon to petition a Scottish court, to ascertain if Boris lied about his motives to prorogue. Which Nicola Sturgeon did, for she despised Boris Johnson, whose open misogyny and lies to women appalled her Scottish sensibilities!

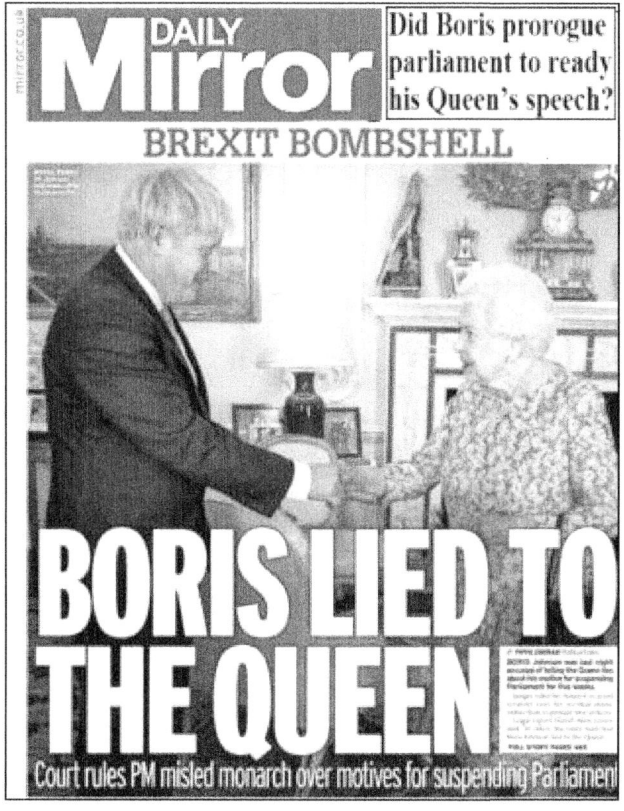

The strategy of Lord Evil Neville had worked superbly, for Nicola Sturgeon awakened a Scottish court, and eleven Supreme Court judges under Lady Hale unanimously backed the Scots. The Queen was incensed at being misled, but at that time of writing Boris and his cohorts were not yet in prison. That could change soon, as more historic Boris lawbreaking was unveiled. American pole-dancer Jennifer Arcuri received £100,000 in public funds intended for English businesses, and granted privileged access to trade missions by London mayor Johnson, with whom Arcuri was having a sexual affair. When would British law make a stand?

Lord Neville then struck Boris another blow, by advising the Scottish National Party and the Liberal Democrats to combine with the Labour opposition, to pass a *Neville Act*. This ordered that if a Brexit deal was not passed before the E.U. Summit on 19th of October 2019, the British prime minister must request Brussels for yet another extension, to avoid a chaotic Hallowe'en no-deal exit from the E.U. If Boris refused, he'd be declared a habitual criminal for his repeated lawbreaking, and detained at the Queen's pleasure – which could be rather lengthy, given his rocky relationship with the Queen

. "I'd rather die in a ditch than extend Brexit!" Prime Minister Boris Johnson screeched, and in desperation he called for a Christmas election. The police hastily staged a Jimmy Savile-style evasion, by shelving the Arcuri affair investigation until after elections. The fascist stance of Boris Johnson won him many fans among the xenophobic electorate, but Commie Corbyn of Labour was ducking elections; polls indicated communism was not favored.

Yet, Nicola Sturgeon backed elections; the Tories would win an election, but there was also a strong likelihood of increased seats for her S.N.P., which could help Nicola Sturgeon prevent a no-deal Brexit. Then more Boris lawbreaking emerged, when the Electoral Commission ruled that Vote Leave broke election law, when the campaign funneled £675,000 through another pro-Brexit group, BeLeave, to duck spending limits.

DEMOCRACY DEMANDS AN INDEPENDENCE REFERENDUM GREENS

2017		2019		2021	
SNP 35	CON 13	SNP 48	CON 6	SNP 64	CON 31
LAB 7	LD 4	LD 4	LAB 1	LAB 22	GRN 8

Smart Alec

2021 seats 0

An explosive *Guardian* article revealed that Boris Johnson knew about it, so by withholding information Boris had again broken the law. The article was dated the 2nd November 2019, the same day that England met South Africa in the Rugby World Cup final. What impact did the news have on England, that their prime minister had again broken the law? Was this why the England team arrived twenty minutes late at the venue? Lord Neville and Professor Watercloset waited patiently in the International Stadium, Yokahama, having flown out to Japan after the Westminster Hallowe'en showdown. The England Rugby Football Union had supplied the tickets, along with the specially reserved tartan-covered seats, for a genuine Scottish laird supporting England rugby was still a rarity. Yet, the *Guardian* article weighed the England rugby team down, Boris preyed on the English mind, and they buckled before a strong Springbok scrum. Who became only the second side after New Zealand, to win the World Cup three times.

Lord Neville was gutted, so they flew back to England to watch the political teams playing. 2019 elections had arrived, so the teams readied themselves. The "red bus lie" and Arcuri affair made the Conservative Party team captain an habitual criminal, fully aware of Vote Leave's illegal overspend. If the UK/EU Brexit deal was not ratified by December 2020, Britain would leave the E.U. with a Boris no-deal Brexit, costing taxpayers £125bn. Small change, actually, when compared to the grandiose manifesto of the Labour Party team captain: this Marxist pal of terrorist groups wanted to renationalize the U.K. economy at a ruinous price of £1trillion. Neither of these charlatans were fit to captain Great Britain, yet given the logistics of British politics, it was unfortunately a choice between the two: hardline Commie Corbyn Marxism, or the hard-Brexit no-deal of Boris, which would have an equally devastating impact on the economy.

It was thus fortunate that cunning Lord Neville had a razor-sharp dirk hidden in his Scottish sporran; the pretender King Boris would come to deeply regret his disdain of Scotland, for the Scottish National Party were due to make an entrance. Led by the fiercely anti-Brexit Nicola Sturgeon, who would demand that Boris scrap his no-deal obsession. A Scottish jury acquitted Alex Salmond of rape, but Nicola Sturgeon described his behaviour as "deeply inappropriate" and severed ties with Alec Salmond, causing him to claim he was the "victim of a witch-hunt". It served the S.N.P. well in 2021 elections; Boris trounced Labour but the top act was the Scottish National Party, their new seats were the highest percentage gain. Boris saw himself as King Charles I, who in 1628 prorogued Parliament. The Scots and Irish voters viewed Boris more as royal antagonist Oliver Cromwell.

The Irish particularly, recall Oliver Cromwell when thinking about Boris, whose turncoat abandonment of Northern Ireland destined the country to become part of a united Ireland and a member of the E.U. The Boris Johnson Irish Sea border is political twaddle, concealing a bribe to the E.U. for resuming negotiations, the duped D.U.P. now realized Northern Ireland had been sold like slaves to the E.U.

The King James 1625 Proclamation started it, the *Penal Laws* of Oliver Cromwell continued the practice, and now Boris Johnson had completed the slavery of Ireland. The English transported 50,000 Irish indentured labourers to their colonies, who were not really indentures; they were political prisoners or people defined as "undesirable." Penal transportation of the Irish hit its height in the seventeenth century, during the 1649-1653 Cromwellian conquest, and savage suppression of Ireland. Thousands of Irish were sent to the Caribbean, "Barbadossed" against their will, as it was called. So, Boris Johnson is more like Cromwell than like King Charles I, because Boris culminated the Irish slave process, by transporting the entire population of Northern Ireland to the E.U.

"We need to remind ourselves that Europe will be our biggest trading partner for several decades and probably beyond. Getting a Brexit deal with Europe should be our primary focus."

Sir Keir Starmer K.C.B., Q.C., M.P.

Fall of the King

Boris Johnson needed to remind himself that King Charles I lost his head for proroguing Parliament, and waiting in the wings was axe-man Sir Keir Starmer, who would shortly hold Boris to account. Modern slave-trader Boris the Butcher is today as hated as Oliver Cromwell in Ireland, the Boris betrayal lost the support of Northern Ireland and roused a raging independence thirst in Scotland, a 1641 Civil War was now a 2019 Brexit War

King Charles yielded in 1646 to the Scots who handed him to Parliament for trial, and the same fate will befall King Boris, who refuses to grant an independence referendum. Because if Boris rammed his hard Brexit through, it would give Nicola Sturgeon a referendum mandate, considering the massive support she received in 2019 elections. The truth is that in Northern Ireland, Catholics will outnumber Protestants by 2021, and they too will then demand an independence referendum. In the 1961 census, 35% of the population was Catholic; in the 2001 census Catholics grew to 44%. When Boris Johnson became PM in 2019, he gave himself the grand title of "Minister for the Union". There has been zero evidence in his handling of Brexit, that he takes this to mean a more inclusive approach. To Boris, the Brexit slogan "take back control," is to rebuild a Westminster-centered UK sovereignty. While wiser Sir Keir Starmer advocates, a policy of pushing more powers out from Westminster, to all the nations of the United Kingdom.

2020 started well for Boris Johnson. Basking in his December election success, the P.M. returned from a celebratory Caribbean holiday with his fiancée. His lifelong dream had been realized; it was party time, with Brexit due to happen, the festivity fireworks planned and celebratory 50p coins minted. The prime minister prepared to take revenge on parliament and the courts, for hampering his attempts to ram through a hard Brexit no-deal.

In the chapter *"Halls of Justice"*, the face of Judge John Deed is used; viewers of the T.V. series may recall his constant fight to keep government separate from the courts. Boris Johnson had won the 2019 election, by blaming MP's and unelected judges for blocking the will of the people; Boris now announced his fascist plans to hamstring British democracy. To centralize power in Whitehall, which Ireland and Scotland were not going to tolerate, "Little Britain" lay just ahead, as the United Kingdom headed for a breakup: 218 years of unity sacrificed on the altar of one man's selfish political ambition!

It's interesting that, just after the 2019 elections, Prince Harry and his wife Meghan emigrated to America, were the Royal Family clearing out before King Boris took over? Naturally, there were other reasons advanced for the desertion of Harry 'n' Megs: the ex-actress herself painted a shocking scenario of abuse and royal racism, worthy of a slot on the T.V. soap *Suits*, which made her famous. Now unveiled on an appalling Oprah Winfrey interview, conducted while grandfather Prince Phillip lay on his deathbed, this clearly showed the scandalized British public that the real problem was not about her ethnicity or her nationality - Meghan Markle simply lacked the class to be a British royal. Piers Morgan quit *Good Morning Britain* when the show received 41,000 hysterical complaints over his calm and reasoned critique of the Oprah Winfrey interview, which in turn evoked a petition of 500,000 names calling for the return of Piers, it appeared that the majority of Britons agreed with Piers Morgan? The popular newscaster was amusedly skeptical of Meghan's suicidal statement on lack of support, for in her bombshell interview she told Oprah:

"I didn't want to be alive anymore." So, Piers questioned, "Who did you go to and what did they say?" Which has not yet received a reply from the whining ex-royals. Then, Piers repeated his doubts: "I wouldn't believe a weather report if Meghan Markle read it. Seventeen different claims by the pair have proved completely untrue, wildly exaggerated or unprovable." Feisty Sharon Osbourne was fired from the quaintly named American T.V. show *The Talk* for defending Piers Morgan.

Then, rather surprisingly, Piers was backed by his long-time arch-rival Jeremy Clarkson, who wrote: "The monarchy has survived countless upheavals, so I'm fairly sure it'll be able to weather the banal musings of a silly little cable T.V. actress." While the acclaimed actress Johanna Lumley noted sensibly:

"The Oprah interview did seem to me a bit one-sided, because everybody knows that the Royal Family can't really answer back." For answering back would only give Meghan the publicity she craved, to promote the book she had written. The 34-page book was based on a poem composed for her husband, she dedicated it to him and her son Archie, calling them:

"The man and boy who make my heart go pump-pump." Yet Meghan's children's book titled *The Bench,* failed to make Amazon's top 200 bestsellers list on its debut, and limped in at a modest No 60 in children's books chart. *The Times's* arts editor Alex O'Connell said: "The story is so lacking in action and jeopardy you wonder if the writing job was delegated to a piece of furniture."

Meghan Markle's literary setback coincided with her sister-in-law, the Duchess of Cambridge's photography book *Hold Still,* making the number two spot on Amazon on its first day of sales. Spearheaded by Kate Middleton who was the National Portrait Gallery patron, the book was a community project, to create a unique collective portrait of the UK during lockdown. People of all ages were invited to submit a photographic portrait, taken in a six-week period and focused on common themes; it was a close study of a nation's behavior under lockdown.

Over 31,000 submissions were received from across the country, with entrants ranging from 4 to 75 years-old, from these a panel of judges selected 100 portraits. Then they assessed the images on the emotions and experiences they conveyed, it was a remarkable exercise, the Duchess of Cambridge had painted the face of a nation. While the Duchess of Sussex had portrayed only her own emotions, perhaps it was this difference in their approaches, that resulted in the differing popularity of the two books?

Meghan Markle was your proverbial *I-Specialist*, and so for that matter was Boris Johnson. While Harry 'n' Megs now hobnobbed with Queen Oprah in America, back home Boris began to neutralize the U.K.'s legal and democratic structures, stripping their power to oppose King Boris. Who laid this out clearly in what he grandly called, "the most radical Queen's Speech in a generation," where Boris made it crystal clear his intention was to use his majority? Not only to impose a no-deal Brexit, but to pass radical reforms.

British democratic institutions would be crippled, and King Boris would become the supreme leader of Little Britain, Commie Corbyn could not stop it for he still ranted on about a communist state. The opposition Labour Party was rudderless, after its fourth election defeat on the trot; Commie Corbyn had failed in his plan to kill another 94 million people. Yet hardline Labour communists clung to power, and a commie candidate was put forward to succeed Commie Corbyn, Tory leader Boris Johnson just giggled for he could not see much threat there.

Then there arose rumors that Sir Keir Starmer might contest the leadership, this worried Boris for Sir Keir was a past head of the Crown Prosecution Services, who believed people must account for their actions. Making it unlikely that unrepentant communists would elect him as Labour leader, communists don't like admitting to minor mistakes, like killing 94 million people. Sir Keir Starmer was a definite no-go, pretender King Boris comforted himself as he prepared for his royal coronation, but Haughty Boris would soon do a Humpty Dumpty.

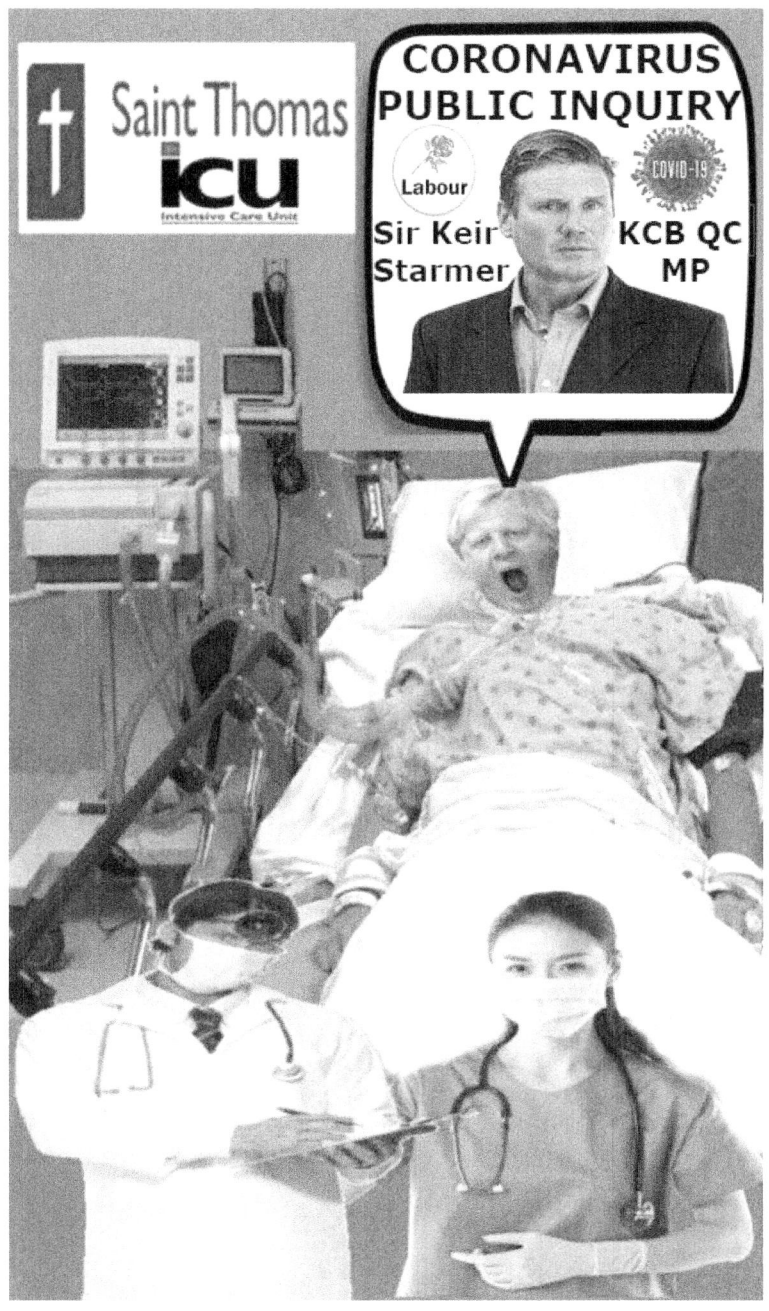

On the 1st April 2020 from his sickbed in the Intensive Care Unit of St. Thomas's Hospital in London, the prime minister of Great Britain Alexander Boris de Pfeffel Johnson, composed a tearful letter of apology which was posted to every citizen in Britain. Because pretender King Boris was now having awful nightmares, that somebody would hold him to account for his initial short-sighted approach to a virulent global pandemic. Bumbling Boris had ignored the warnings of Professor Peter Watercloset and Doctor Zee Garbo, and viewed the deadly Corbynvirus as nothing more than an irritant.

"I was at a hospital the other night, where I think there were a few Corbynvirus patients, and I shook hands with everybody. You will be pleased to know that I continue to shake hands," the prime minister had manfully boasted. Now he was in the Intensive Care Unit and he had passed the virus on to his pregnant mistress. It was his first major test as prime minister, and Boris Johnson failed spectacularly. This man should never have got near Downing Street, he is the worst leader to ever disgrace the P.M. post. Only someone from his privileged background could rise to the top with such a paucity of talent. The **China Bat Covid** warning in the Gematria had kicked in, reports from China stated that bats had passed on a deadly virus, but the prime minister's actions in the run-up to the pandemic raised serious questions about his fitness to hold office. Boris Johnson missed five early COBRA meetings on the impending crisis, because he was concentrating on Brexit – an unforgivable lapse of judgement!

The government was pitifully slow to act on protective equipment for health staff, leaving the N.H.S. ill-prepared to cope with this crisis. Boris Johnson's callous advisers also toyed with the deeply flawed "herd immunity" strategy, before hastily opting for lockdowns – this resulted in lost time which caused 20,000 needless deaths.

"Let pensioners die," Johnson's advisers were alleged to have said, though Downing Street strenuously denied this, *Sunday Times* stuck to their story. How on Earth did this charlatan come to lead Britain? The claims that the prime minister "tends not to work at weekends" give an indication of what went wrong. If Boris Johnson put in more work, he'd perhaps have heeded early warnings by Professor Watercloset and Dr. Zee Garbo, who strongly advised the U.K. government to discard the discredited herd immunity strategy and impose nationwide lockdowns at once. But, Boris Johnson outlined his "take it on the chin" theory of how to tackle the Corbynvirus, on the *This Morning* television show in early March:

"One of the theories is perhaps you could take it on the chin, take it all in one go and allow the disease to move through the population without taking draconian measures." Boris protected the economy to shield himself politically, but rather than challenge him on the outlandish herd immunity strategy, the interviewer nodded meekly and babbled the vital question:

"Are you excited about becoming a father again?" Boris beamed and then warbled on about the wonder of children. At the time, Britain and Belarus were the only European countries not to have shut down their schools, as a true liberal Boris only cared about his own children.

"We've got a fantastic N.H.S. We will give them all the support that they need, we will make sure that they have all preparations, all the kit that they need for us to get through it," the prime minister assured interviewers. But, in fact he didn't, resulting in a shortage of personal protective equipment. Yet, way back Professor Watercloset and Dr. Zee Garbo had warned of a shortage, after they attended Imperial College's *Exercise Cygnus,* which you recall from page 24. How much more warning did Prime Minister Johnson need?

Professor Watercloset and Dr. Zee Garbo were again ignored, but as the death toll mounted, so did the opposition to the freakish herd immunity. People are not cattle, so you cannot treat them as a "herd". The view that you let the Corbynvirus run wild, to kill hundreds of thousands, resembled the medical ethics of Nazi concentration camp experimenters. The only morally acceptable way to achieve national immunity is to produce a vaccine and then inject every citizen.

The clip from *This Morning*, when Boris said, "Take it on the chin," received 2.5 million views on social media in just 36 hours, yet the media were muted. British Broadminded Television loved babbling Boris; he was such fun that people laughed at him, even when he didn't tell jokes. The British media treated it as just another cutesy humorous example of tousle-haired Boris, blurting out something he shouldn't at a time of national crisis. But this was far more serious than the Nazanin Zaghari-Ratcliffe blunder; the B.B.T. was about to learn that clowns running a country could be terribly dangerous. More responsible media sources thought the government's entire top team should go to jail, which actually remains a distinct possibility?

"The whole lot of them belong in prison," an enraged Lord Neville boomed.

"Spot on," Peter and Zee agreed,

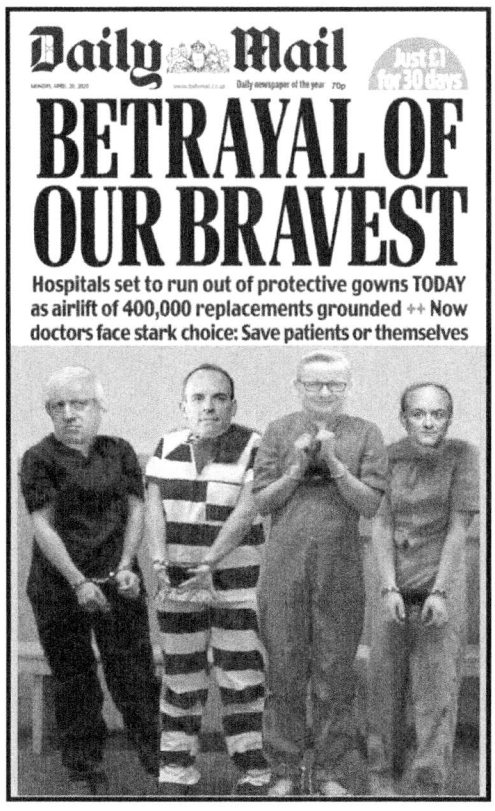

Professor Peter Watercloset and his wife Dr. Zee Garbo were holidaying at the Loch Ness lodge, when the Corbynvirus hit Britain, in early January 2020. They watched appalled as Boris Johnson's government twiddled thumbs, did nothing as thousands died, it was mass murder.

"How can we convince government of the danger?" Dr. Zee lamented, because, like they'd done with the deadly fatberg, the Boris crazy-gang sidelined the Corbynvirus as irrelevant.

"The Johnson administration just sat and watched as the death toll mounted in China in January, and now they've really missed the boat."

"Government were pitifully slow on securing sufficient supplies of tests and personal protective gear," Peter Watercloset added to Zee's comments. They were both top scientists, they knew what they were talking about, while Lord Neville knew the political background.

"The U.K.'s failure to take part in the European Union scheme, to procure equipment to tackle the Corbynvirus, was a sly cover-up, to obscure the foolishness of leaving the E.U.," Lord Evil Neville added, ominously. It was a doltish move by Boris Johnson, for he'd placed Brexit ahead of the Corbynvirus, and this arrogant posture returned to haunt him, when the true Covid-19 horror story emerged. Only now did Doctor Zee Garbo realize the terrible danger of what **China Bat Covid** portended in the Gematria! Covid-19 hit Britain hard and Dr. Zee warned the PM to immediately lock down – but Dr. Garbo and her fellow scientists were ignored!

"The government wouldn't listen; it was only after the P.M. and health minister got sick that they awoke," Dr. Zee lamented later, which was true, because the fact that many Downing Street staff contracted Corbynvirus suggests that people at the top had not been on guard. Warnings grew louder as the death toll rose dramatically, but Boris Johnson's government was still occupied with Brexit. On testing, contact tracing and equipment supply, there was a failure to prepare. Dr. Zee Garbo sobbed when the U.K. missed three chances to be part of an E.U. opportunity to bulk-buy personal protective equipment for health workers. Britain failed to utilize opportunities to get items such as masks, gowns and gloves under an E.U. initiative, while European medical staff received £1.3bn worth of P.P.E. Downing Street later issued a statement saying that the U.K. had been invited to take part in the E.U.

initiative, but officials did not see the email because of a *"communication confusion"*. Then came a low comedy of revelations and denials, backed by threats – it would be hilarious, were it not so tragic.

A permanent Foreign Office secretary had informed the Foreign Affairs Committee that refusing to join the E.U. scheme was a political ploy, to obscure the mammoth stupidity Brexit was now proving to be. The health minister furiously denied this, so the secretary backed down, but the minister compounded the confusion by claiming the U.K. had belatedly joined the European Union scheme – only for E.U. sources to note that the sudden U-turn was too late, so Britain would not benefit from the supplies of P.P.E.

Ministers were then forced to defend the disclosure that millions of pieces of equipment, including respirators and masks, had been shipped from U.K. warehouses to Spain, Italy and Germany. To cover this blunder, the government sourced P.P.E. from Turkey, even though a major argument for supporting Brexit was populous Turkey joining the E.U. – now the U.K. was shipping medical supplies from Turkey! Then came a shocking revelation that 8,000 companies offered P.P.E. within the U.K., but the government only engaged with 1,000 of them, while the aged in care homes dropped like flies, because of a lack of P.P.E. Why did the government act so stupidly, Boris Johnson often likened himself to Winston Churchill, now his Churchill moment had come and he blew it most dramatically?

"He's a national disgrace," the three fatberg fighters agreed. On 7th March 2020, in a show of defiance against lockdowners, both Boris Johnson and his fiancée attended the England vs. Wales rugby match at Twickenham. England had won 33 – 30, yet Lord Neville and Peter Watercloset were furious, because Doctor Zee Garbo had forbidden them from attending the match.

"But Boris is going, why can't we," Peter sniffed.

"Boris is an idiot," Doctor Garbo snapped.

While the fatberg fighters followed sensible isolation rules, King Boris strutted royally around Britain hobnobbing with the peasants, on 13th March Boris was at the Cheltenham Festival attended by 250,000 racegoers. Posing on a horse while waving regally to his subjects, King Boris was at the pinnacle of his career, as he followed up on his historic speech. Which had been made at Greenwich a month before, historically it matched any speech made by Winston Churchill, because Boris mocked the Superman imagery used by Rory Stewart in the *New Statesman*

"We are hearing bizarre autarkic rhetoric that barriers are going up and there is a risk that new diseases such as the Corbynvirus will trigger panic and raise calls for market segregation. That goes beyond what is medically rational, to the point of doing unnecessary economic damage. At this moment, humanity needs some government somewhere, that is willing to make the case for freedom of exchange. Some country ready to take off its Clark Kent spectacles, leap into the phone booth and emerge with its cloak flowing, as the supercharged champion of the right of the populations, to buy and sell freely."

Boris Johnson's *Superman Speech*, 3rd February 2020, Greenwich.

"The answer cannot be an adolescent fantasy of being saved by a superhero, but to rather move forward with maturity."

Rory Stewart *New Statesman* article page 362

Now Britain had its superhero. A true Tory Superman had emerged who was also a super-murderer, unfortunately Superman then ran into Corbynvirus/Kryptonite, and his supercharged rhetoric tamely withered. Now the jovial joker Prime Minister Johnson became the deliverer of grave warnings; talk by his advisers of no lockdowns and herd immunity was banished, and replaced with the daily hangdog bad-news face.

"I must level with you, more families, many more families, are going to lose loved ones before their time." Boris blubbed pitifully on TV. Then, on the 18th March, just days after Downing Street said it was not on the cards, the government announced the closure of all schools. On 20th March, pubs and restaurants were also shut. Boris had belatedly acted, but his delay would cause 20,000 deaths, was there anyone in the world more obtuse than the British prime minister? Or more dangerous, perhaps Donald Trump who would kill more, for he had a larger flock of sheep to slaughter.

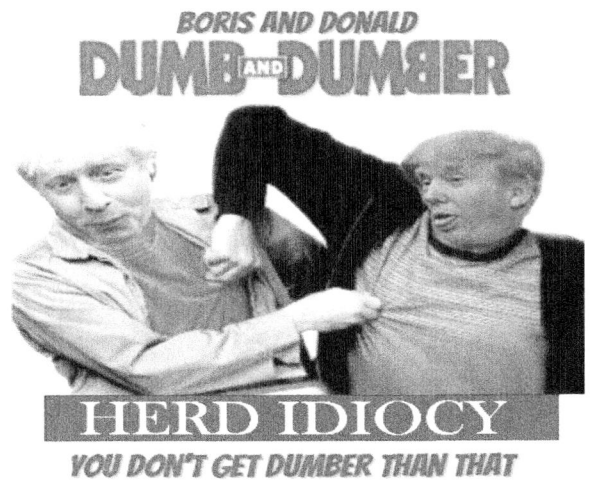

If the U.K. has serious questions to answer, so has the country who saw the worst of the outbreak, for the United States was slowest of all to act. Donald Trump lied for months about the threat posed by Corbynvirus, while offering advice like injecting yourself with disinfectant. Surely, only idiots would vote him back in 2020! The grand Boris plan of dumping the EU in a no-deal, then forming trade deals with Trump America, now looked in serious jeopardy? If you consider that China quickly brought the pandemic under control, but there were now millions of Corbynvirus cases in the U.S., and deaths had hit 230,000. This was the highest total in the world, while Britain, at 46,000, was currently fifth, with the highest total in Europe. By not heeding the advice of scientists like Dr. Zee Garbo and Professor Watercloset, Boris Johnson delivered a fatal blow to Britain. In contrast to Britain's 46,000 deaths, Germany had recorded just over 9,000 – around a fifth of the British total – while Germany's 83 million population is higher than the U.K.'s 67 million. Because Germany did not contemplate pagan herd immunity, it went into lockdown early and conducted extensive tests, precisely as the U.K. failed to.

Check back to page 201 and you'll see, that Boris the Ripper stands supreme in the cruel lexicon of British mass murderers. Dr. Zee Garbo had produced the Obelix chemical as an antidote to Asterix, clearing Brown Blobs from London sewers, now the doctor was frantically trying to find a vaccine for the Corbynvirus. Anyone who has watched a pandemic horror movie knows the key, is to lock down early to throttle the virus, which batty Boris

Johnson ignored so Doctor Zee Garbo must now urgently create a vaccine!

Dedicated Dr. Garbo now returned to her MAMBA laboratory, to try and develop a vaccine to fight the Corbynvirus, for Zee had a theory involving her husband Peter. Who had developed flu-like symptoms after his terrifying encounter with bats in the Whitechapel sewers. Could Peter's blood be the key to developing a vaccine, was that the meaning of the Gematria **China Bat Covid**? It greatly interested Dr. Zee, for Peter contracted a primary zoonotic infection, and you remember that Zee kept a sample of his blood.?

So, the doctor could use the disease-causing virus in a form that will not harm a person – a partial, weakened virus – to prompt the immune system to form antibodies as defenders against disease. Once it is determined how the virus will be modified, vaccines are then created through a three-step process.

An antigen is generated when viruses are grown in primary cells, like in chicken eggs for influenza vaccines, or on continuous cell lines in human cultured cells. The antigen is then isolated from cells used to create it, and the vaccine is made by adding adjuvants, also preservatives and stabilizers. Adjuvants increase immune response of the antigen; stabilizers increase the vaccine's storage life; and preservatives allow for the use of multi-dose vials.

Vaccines then undergo rigorous safety testing, and are continually monitored for safety. But Dr. Zee could shorten this test period, because she had used the blood of Professor Peter Watercloset for her vaccine – a case of primary zoonotic infection from bats, whereas another animal is usually an intermediate host carrying disease between bats and humans.

Dr. Zee Garbo pondered where to apply her virus research. There were offers from Moderna and Pfizer-BioNTech, but after consulting the Gematria she took up a post at Oxford University. This was decided after Peter and herself extensively studied the Gematria and came across **Oxford Vacc.** Dr. Zee headed up the Oxford University project called "Oxford/AsterixZee", named thus because the fatberg Asterix virus was defeated by the Obelix antidote. Her Oxford vaccine was unique as, unlike others, it used a genetically modified virus from Peter's blood to store D.N.A. codes for a CoV-2 spike protein.

Not only was the Oxford option cheaper than Moderna and Pfizer/BioNTech vaccines, it's easier to store and transport, as it doesn't need to be stored at ultra-cold temperatures. But time was now of the essence, for Hong Kong scientists had confirmed a healed patient being reinfected four months after the first infection.

This rubbished the Boris Johnson herd immunity strategy and highlighted the urgency of a vaccine. To placate the vaccine skeptics, it was decided to inject the parliamentary Tory cabinet first - if they survived, then the vaccine was safe; if they didn't, then at least the country was safer. Covid stands for coronavirus disease, but in Britain people tended to call it "Corbynvirus", because this virus spreads like a wildfire and, like communism, it could kill millions. So, Dr. Garbo set about testing her vaccine, while her husband Peter Watercloset attempted to eradicate the communist virus in the Labour Party, by replacing Jeremy Corbyn with Sir Keir Starmer. Lord Neville backed Peter to the hilt, somebody had to brace Boris, before he murdered thousands more.

Throughout this book, the lawbreaking of Boris Johnson has been highlighted, and you'll be bored by the repeating of his many crimes, for they are too numerous to mention again. Time after time, Boris skirted the fringes of the law, and each time he easily skated away, for it appeared the authorities were afraid to act against the landed gentry. What was needed was a fiery and determined opposition leader, with a firm grasp of the principles of law; not a dilly-dally daydreamer communist who vainly imagined he could revive a failed system. Rather the type of man who would ensure the wise Gematria principles, and back pioneers like Doctor Zee Garbo.

I already got vaccinated with the Russian COVID-19 vaccine

And I can tell you not to woяяy! I still dou't seə anч sidə efectoski secundarioski
и меня зовут Лопес Обрадор, и я коррумпирован и лжец и почему я даю

No Hard No Deal was highlighted, when Labour
Lord Neville leaked a Tory report to the media.

Where the Tories admitted that if a second Corbynvirus wave coincided with a no-deal Brexit, the military may be drafted in to airdrop food to the Channel Islands, and the Navy used to stop British fishermen clashing with EU fishing boats. Parts of the U.K. may face power and petrol shortages, with thousands of lorries stranded in Dover, while shortages of medicines caused by port blockages could lead to the spread of animal diseases.

Hospitals may be overwhelmed, town halls go bust and troops drafted onto the streets, if the economic toll caused public disorder. A Tory spokeswoman said the document "reflects a responsible Government ensuring readiness for all eventualities," neglecting to mention the "eventualities" were *caused* by the "responsible government," insisting on a no-deal Brexit. The only real hope was the discredited 'herd immunity' adopted by Boris the Butcher, could be achieved by a less lethal second wave than the Covid Delta variant, like a new Omicron strain discussed on page 426.

Tory insiders say the *Covid-19 No-Deal* report was drawn up so that Prime Minister Johnson could be prepared for "any eventuality", to duck away on holiday like he did during the 2011 London riots. You'll recall that while London burned from Tottenham to Peckham, Mayor Johnson was on holiday in Canada. When Covid-19 first hit Britain, newly elected Prime Minister Johnson sunbathed on a private Caribbean Island known as Mustique. Then, he missed five crucial COBRA meetings, held to address the Covid-19 crisis. Where was the prime minister while these vital meetings took place? He was at the luxury Chevening seventeenth-century mansion in Kent, partying with upper crust friends, Boris enjoyed the trappings of a king but had none of the wisdom. The costly Downing Street makeover that had seen Boris face investigations is already fraying, the gold £840 a roll wallpaper that Boris chose is peeling, and experts have been called in to rehang it. A grim portent of the Johnson tenure as Prime Minister; Britain begged for someone to down the charlatan Boris Johnson.

Under Tony Blair, the Labour Party won a majority in three elections. The first was in 1997, when Labour won by a landslide, ousting the Conservative Party which had been in power for 18 years. Blair's successor Gordon Brown lost his first election as leader, as did the next new commie-on-the-block, Red Ed Miliband - then came Commie Corbyn, who turned losing elections into an art form. After his trouncing in 2019 elections Commie Corbyn had to go, the Labour Party scratched around frantically for another communist, but they were a dying breed.

So, wise Lord Evil Neville contacted Labour lords, a campaign was launched to elect Sir Keir Starmer as the next leader of the Labour Party. At fifty-seven years of age, Sir Keir Rodney Starmer K.C.B., P.C., Q.C. is the man to stop the lawbreaker Boris Johnson,.

Sir Keir was knighted for his services as Head of Crown Prosecutions, he is the man to banish the anti-Semitism in the Labour Party; his barrister wife Victoria is Jewish and is raising her son and daughter in the Jewish faith. So, if Commie Corbyn is not careful he will be banished by Sir Keir. This is the man to call Boris Johnson to account, and his arrogant adviser Dominic Cummings, who flouted the lockdown rules he helped make!

Boris Johnson claims he followed the science, but he followed Cummings by adopting herd immunity, to avoid the politically harmful economic damage of a lockdown. His massive egoism cost Britain 20,000 needless deaths, and shockingly the P.M. then had the brazen cheek to excuse those who sniffed at lockdown rules! When the U.K prime minister's most senior adviser came under fire for travelling during lockdown, Boris defended him and arranged a press conference. Where Dominic Cummings lounged in the Downing Street rose garden, answering questions from journalists.

At the press conference Dominic Cummings made it crystal clear that, as described by George Orwell, all pigs are equal, but some are more equal than most. So, they could twice drive 260 miles from London to Durham to visit family, then take a scenic 60-mile excursion to Barnard Castle, to celebrate the wife's birthday. Neither Boris Johnson nor Cummings attempt to disguise their contempt for the law of the land. Cummings says: "There must be urgent action to correct the farce the judicial review has become," and he describes the courts as, "a perfect symbol of the British state's dysfunction." So, what Orwellian interpretation should we give to the draconian *2020 Coronavirus Act*, which contains powers to detain people not suspected of any crime? To ban gatherings, including protests and strikes, close borders, postpone elections and remove safeguards for the disabled? Is Boris so shameless that he first downplayed Covid, but is now using the Corbynvirus threat to divert media scrutiny from an unprecedented threat? Are official secrecy and lack of accountability in Whitehall combining with government cronyism, to represent an assault on the Britain's parliamentary democracy! Britain is respected worldwide as a bastion of democracy, yet they have a prime minister today who has more in common with dictators like Kim Jong-un and Robert Mugabe. Thanks to opposition leaders like Commie Corbyn, interested only in imposing a failed system on Parliament, rather than upholding the system they have. British values of honesty and trust are things of the past, did the E.U. really think Boris would honour the Brexit deal they negotiated? He'd broken British law, so why respect international law? Tony Blair suggests that to combat Boris Johnson there must be cooperation between

Labour and the Liberal Democrats; in 1997, such a pact led to a Conservative collapse, giving Blair a landslide victory. Yet, the defining issue of Blair's premiership was the Iraq War, which the Lib Dems vigorously opposed. Still, that must not stand in the way of an alliance. One doesn't wish to downplay the loss of 179 British soldiers killed in the Iraq War, but consider the 20,000 slaughtered by Butcher Boris, that should sober the voters up. Reflect also on the 2010 alliance of Tories and Lib Dems, resulting in a loss of 85% of Lib Dem MP's, and two thirds of their voters. Merging with Labour is a much sounder alternative; not just a tame electoral pact but a fully-fledged political unification, why don't the Lib Dems just fold into the Labour Party? They have already decided that under any circumstances, a Labour prime minister would be preferable to a Tory one, so why not just join the red team for real? The Lab Dems has a real nice ring to it, and if it gets Sir Keir Starmer into Number 10 in 2024, the advantages would be plentiful to sitting Lib Dem MPs and their top 2019 candidates.

COVID-19
PUBLIC INQUIRY

VOTE KEIR STARMER

LABOUR
DEMOCRATS

Liberal Party – Founded 9th June 1859

Liberal Democrats – Founded 3rd March 1988

Labour Party – Founded 27th February 1900

Labour Democrats – Founded 1st April 2021

A Labour Legacy

Labour Lords heeded Lord Neville's wise counsel, and the impact of the new Labour leader was felt immediately in Parliament, as bumbling Boris wilted under the forensic unpicking of the articulate Sir Keir Starmer. Gone were the tired, outdated communist platitudes of Jeremy Corbyn, as the new opposition leader put incompetent Tory MP's to the sword. Why was Britain performing so badly in test and trace systems? Germany carried out 50,000 tests daily, at a time when the U.K. could not achieve that weekly. When both countries entered lockdown, Germany had identified 27,000 cases, while snail's-pace Boris Britain confirmed just 9,000. Boris was heading for the highest European Covid-19 death rate of over 100,000, while Germany, with a larger population, was half that. If Boris had not played with discredited herd immunity, the British death toll would be closer to Germany's much lower count.

The May 6th 2021 local elections loomed, with 184 councils and 13 mayorships at stake – including London, where Sadiq Khan stood – 40 police chiefs in England and Wales, 60 Welsh MP's and 129 Scottish. If these elections didn't finish venal Boris Johnson, a Covid-19 Inquiry would, surely there was some morality in Britain? The May 2021 U.K. local elections hinged on a Brexit deal: should Boris not close a deal with E.U. head Ursula von der Leyen, the economic twin hit of Covid-19 and a no-deal would ensure huge Tory election losses. For, the joker in the game was Donald Trump, if he lost U.S. elections on November 3rd, then Boris would be out of aces.

Donald Trump and Boris Johnson scoffed at lockdowns and protective masks, resulting in both catching Covid-19 – kindred souls, who put politics before safety. Resulting in the U.S. Democratic Party despising Boris, who mocked President Obama as "part Kenyan", with "an ancestral dislike of the British empire," while Hillary Clinton was likened to "a sadistic nurse in a mental hospital."

"So last year 37,000 Americans died from the common Flu. It averages between 27,000 and 70,000 per year. Nothing is shut down; life & the economy go on. There are 546 confirmed cases of CoronaVirus, with 22 deaths."

Such tweets from Trump greatly encouraged Boris, given his Democratic Party insults and his contempt of the Irish, needless to say a proudly Irish President Joe Biden was a nightmare for Boris. The U.S. would thus be inclined to make trade deals with Europe, not Britain, strengthening the hand of E.U. negotiator Ursula von der Leyen. To avoid a ruinous **No Hard No Deal**, warned of in the Gematria, Boris must negotiate a deal before U.S. elections.

It was looking unlikely Boris could, still weak from his Covid-19 bout, his cockiness had gone. The P.M. was a haunted and harried man, beset by a nation's problems, as well as those from arrogant lawbreaker friends like Dominic Cummings, and even his own family. Disciplined families caring for their aged and their young are the backbone of great nations. The Jimmy Savile scandal showed the Tories view the young as celebrity sex toys, while the aged are disdained as part of a herd that can be culled, Boris himself was pretty skeptical about families. Although not his own, who he fiercely protected.

"In families on lower incomes, the women have no choice but to work, often with adverse consequences for family life and society as a whole, in that unloved and undisciplined children are more likely to become hoodies or a NEET, who mugs you on the street corner."

Boris Johnson, *Spectator Magazine,* 1995.

It appears that upper-class families also produced NEETS who naughtily don't wear hoodies, is this why Boris despised the elderly; was it because of the embarrassment of his own father?

"Let pensioners die," Johnson's advisers ordered, and the pensioners surely did. Of the 100,000 Britons killed, over half died in care homes, at the appalling rate of one in twenty.

"Care homes didn't follow procedures," Boris Johnson said, trying to wheedle his way out. His words sparked fury in the care home sector, with one charity boss calling them "cowardly".

Despite evidence of government's failure at national level, to obtain adequate P.P.E., Boris put the blame on care homes! This from the man who toyed with herd immunity, and allowed the elderly to be discharged from hospitals into care homes without being tested? *"Don't confuse me with facts"* was the mantra Boris had learned from bosom buddy Donald Trump, who now headed for 500,000 American deaths. Yet P.M. Boris Johnson didn't have it all his own way, because Sir Keir Starmer fought back and the fatberg fighters assisted. Influential Lord Neville advised his fellow Labour Lords to block the P.M.'s Internal Market Bill, which overrode key elements in the Brexit Withdrawal Agreement, so if the Bill was passed the EU would scrap talks and there would be a no-deal Brexit. Clever Boris would then sign trade deals with his pal Donald Trump, but even cleverer Lord Neville knew Trump would lose elections - because the Gematria said so!

It was therefore vital that the Internal Market Bill be blocked. You know from the House of Lords chapter that the Lords cannot scrap a bill, but Lord Neville's introduction of a Regret Amendment ensured the bill would face lengthy scrutiny. The voting list shows the biggest Tory rebellion in 20 years: with 39 Conservative peers among the 395 votes for Lord Neville, while just 169 voted against. The Archbishop of Canterbury Justin Welby, former Commons Speaker Baroness Boothroyd and past Tory leader Lord Howard all backed Lord Neville – against devious Boris Johnson. The P.M. liked to compare himself to celebrated war leader Winston Churchill, but had bumbling Boris been in charge of Britain in 1939, the British people would all be speaking German today! Boris fawning over the eccentric American President Donald Trump, was not only highly embarrassing for the British it was also a dangerous tactic, a Joe Biden win in America would be a knockout blow. Not only for Trump but bosom buddy Boris, who dragged his feet in Brexit talks, in the hope that Trump might win 2020 elections.

Both Trump and Boris adopted "herd immunity," let the virus kill the community but build up a national immunity in survivors, but what if a Covid variant emerged on page 482 that achieved herd immunity without major deaths? How would history view the barbarity of Trump and Johnson, why was it that the word Omicron circulated in Peter's dreams, was it a portent of such a variant virus? Omicron is the 15th letter of the Greek alphabet, in Greek numerals it has a value of 129, you can do the math's yourself.

OMICRON + 15 + 129 = 666

'Twas 2020 elections, and all over the land
The voters prepared to stake out their stand
'Tween the Challenger and President Orange
Who trumpeted loud while sucking a lozenge
The disease he'd denied hit him right square,
It flattened his friends and his own lady fair
Causing the Challenger to brand him a liar
Yet President Orange soon doused this fire
Through the land there arose such a clatter
I sprang to the T.V. to see what was the matter
Found the Challenger was a despicable crook
Who the famed F.B.I. would bring to book
A waterlogged computer brought in for repair
Had thrown the Challenger into deep despair
When an email revealed by the New York Post
Bugled the Challenger a lonely 'Last Post'
The email showed no header or no metadata
Yet it incited a gleeful Republican Cha-Cha
No evidence needed in the press gossip game
As foxy Fox News *now spread on more shame*

It had worked with Hillary so why not again
President Orange knew well how to defame
Foxy Fox News *quizzed a scion of business*
Who'd once served the Navy but not N.C.I.S.
Who met the Challenger in dark bar-rooms
Dug dirt from his friends in U.S. boardrooms
Although there was no other witness to this
The Challenger must tumble dentures in dust
Yet the U.S. media showed a fine press ethic
Causing President Orange to look pathetic
When the papers refused to report the scandal
Inciting President Orange to fly off the handle
So he ranted 'n' raved about press censorship
When the truth was a case of one-upmanship
For even Fox News *had conceded it clear-cut*
That it was clearly a case of Navy scuttlebutt
Elections came and the Challenger romped in
President Orange tried to stop vote counting
Naught could wilt the blooming lotus flower
Or curtail the crowning of new Queen Kamala

A Joe Biden Win = 666

Donald Trump's surrender of global leadership, to replace it with an inward-looking fortress mentality, was rejected because voters realized that a nation's strength stems from mutually gainful alliances with other countries – which went counter to Boris Johnson's egoism. He had sold Northern Ireland to the E.U. as slaves, in return for what he termed "an oven-ready deal," which still smouldered in the oven.

"A physical and emotional clone of Trump," Joe Biden once called Boris Johnson, with his Irish family roots Joe Biden would not tolerate Boris gerrymandering with the Irish, the E.U. watched with interest. The Trump election trouncing moved Europe to harden their Brexit terms; they knew Boris had lost his gamble and was out of aces.

The P.M. had toyed with passing an illicit Internal Market Bill, but Lord Neville stopped it, sensible people were taking note of the Gematria warning against a **No Hard No Deal.** Experts had warned Britain of the appalling consequences, and painted a picture of the perfect storm of a winter Covid-19 second wave, coinciding with a harmful no-deal Brexit. The Cabinet Office's E.U. Task Force gave MP's a PowerPoint horror show marked *"Official Sensitive"* – a doomsday document. Which feared that restrictions on trade sparked by a no-deal scenario, combined with a bad winter of flood, flu and Covid-19, would overwhelm hospitals. Britain would be hit by shortages of power and petrol, as 8,500 trucks got stuck at Dover, in Whitehall's *"reasonable worst-case scenario"*. Yet, still Boris toyed with a no-deal Brexit, he seemed fixated on it, perhaps it was only a threat but it was terribly dangerous. Adjacent, are some thoughts of really wise men, on the utterances of the British Prime minister.

"A disastrous no-deal Brexit will leave Prime Minister Boris Johnson as the most isolated leader in the entire British peacetime history, engaged in a bitter economic war with both Europe and America."

Gordon Brown.

"There is no doubt that a no-deal Brexit is a threat to the United Kingdom. It will greatly boost those supporting Scottish independence and be a threat to Unionists in Northern Ireland."

Tony Blair.

"Boris Johnson insists that the U.K. can 'prosper mightily' if it crashes out of the E.U. with an Australian-style no-deal. He must be careful what he wishes for. Australia has a deal with the E.U. on W.T.O. terms, but there are some large barriers to Australian trade with Europe, which I sought to address when I was Australian Prime Minister."

Malcolm Turnbull.

Not only humans but animals were affected by the reluctance of Boris to sign a Brexit deal, the R.S.P.C.A. reported an alarming increase in animals being abandoned; they were currently dealing with 33% more callouts than five years ago. The number of pets abandoned would be enough to fill Albert Hall 40 times over, Britain could not afford more economic damage caused by the no-deal uncertainty. The British pound ping-ponged in value, as the P.M. played Bashful Boris with the E.U., the battered British economy contracted even further.

Yet, needless to say, obese Prime Minister Johnson experienced no shortage; he feasted on the choicest cuisine, while his mentor Dominic Cummings fed his lapdog with titbits of Brexit no-deal dogma. The game was to show the British electorate that the demise of Boris's bosom-buddy Trump had not dented the Tory determination to forge a beneficial Brexit deal, or diminished their willingness to enter a harmful no-deal. It was all just pathetic political posturing; the E.U. would never concede a deal more favourable to the U.K. than its other 27 members - for each would then demand the same, and this could collapse the richest single market in the world. Britain fretted as Boris fiddled, so to cheer people up he again defied scientific advice, and allowed families to meet for Christmas. *"Too Late to Cancel Christmas"* a jolly headline in *Daily Telegraph*, while the *Daily Mail* cheered: *"Carry on Christmas"*; Boris the populist knew how to grab the headlines. Yet the *Guardian* wisely cautioned, *"Christmas Plans Still in the Balance"*, which soon came true when Boris flip-flopped on his promises. Then, the headlines changed dramatically:

Public Fury at New Boris Christmas Rules

The public fury increased when newspapers revealed, the true reason Boris the Grinch had cancelled Christmas, and the European Union acted accordingly. Only now did the P.M. reveal to his people, the impact of a new Covid 20 variant, which was 70% more infectious than the original strain. The harsher Christmas rules were due to the rapid spread of this new virus, which showed in laboratory tests an increased ability to infect. This was first detected way back in September, but Boris only revealed it in mid-December; by then, 80% of the London cases were this new mutation.

Yet, amazingly, Boris was still focused on his no-deal Brexit. That was until pathogen tracker Nextstrain, which traced the genetic codes of viruses, revealed that cases in Italy and Denmark came from the U.K. Boris had attained his Brexit dream of isolation from Europe, but traffic jams at ports caused by E.U. travel bans were a grim preview of a no-deal, which focused Tory attention on the truth: that a no-deal Brexit would hurt Britain far more than Europe.

"When the history of these troubled months comes to be written, it will not be kind to the current prime minister and his Tory cabinet."

Lord Stevenson of Balmacara.

Lord Stevenson was spot on for it was now clear, the Boris no-deal push was a criminal act of depraved indifference; with Trump out of the picture so was a no-deal Brexit. 50% of U.K. trade is with the EU, just 10% of theirs with Britain, mixing a no-deal with a new Covid 20 strain was a *Rocky Horror Boris Show.* Boris was forced to defy his zany Tory Brexit zealots, with their illusory bravado about *"breaking free"*, to return to some long-lost Imperial grandeur. Hardline Brexiteers like Dominic Cummings were axed as the Tories kowtowed to the E.U. Britain had finally realized they needed Europe more than Europe needed them; this time, not only Ireland but the whole of the U.K. was sold out! Cap in hand Boris slunk into Brussels to sign the withdrawal agreement, his failed gamesmanship had given the E.U. the upper hand.

The Brexit Withdrawal Agreement was officially signed on the 24th January 2020, to mark the occasion Britain brought out a set of commemorative postage stamps, while the French trawlers still freely looted British waters of their fish. Why was Boris so timid in defending British fishing rights, why did the French negotiators trample all over Boris, could it be the family French connection?

Even as his son negotiated a Brexit deal with an unyielding E.U., the unmasked shopper Stanley Johnson was negotiating a French passport – not surprising, for Stanley had been nicknamed "Froggy" by friends who knew him.

"I am French, my mother was born in France, her mother was totally French, as was her grandfather. So, really for me, it is about reclaiming what I already have, and that makes me very happy," Stanley (Froggy) Johnson told *R.T.L.* radio station in fluent French, which may go some way to explaining why French fishermen received such a bountiful Brexit deal, from his fishy French son Boris.

An Eton education in Latin and Greek served poorly in the Euro fish-fight; Boris promised that E.U. trawlers would forfeit 80% of their British catch, but settled for a meagre 25%. Nicola the Sturgeon was furious, because the British National Federation of Fishermen claimed "Boris bottled it" over sovereignty of U.K. fishing waters. It appeared that promises meant naught to Breton Boris; or perhaps his loyalties lay elsewhere? Boris "bottled it" on nearly every aspect of Brexit negotiations, the oft-quoted *"red line on U.K. sovereignty"* was breached, when Boris kept Britain tied to the European Court of Justice.

Boris Johnson is no Winston Churchill, but rather a gullible Neville Chamberlain, who lauds the return of U.K. sovereignty through a trade deal, where Euro bosses can impose punishing tariffs on U.K. trade disobeying E.U. laws. The Boris 2020 Christmas present to Britain was a Brexit deal lacking provision for the service sector, which comprises 80% of the U.K. economy, putting Britain in a worse position than before Brexit. When the Tories dispatched Boris to negotiate with a beautiful woman, what did they imagine would happen? The sordid history of the Johnson clan, is peppered with panting exposés of carnal lust, it's in their French/Turk blood. The Barfüsser Church mummy was linked to Boris Johnson by D.N.A. The *"sexual health care"* referred to *"great grand mummy"* dying of mercury poisoning, used to cure syphilis in the eighteenth century. The mummy is Anna Catharina Bischoff, whose daughter was married to Baron Pfeffel, leading to the Johnsons' syphilitic French ancestry.

Boris Johnson @BorisJohnson

Very excited to hear about my late great grand 'mummy' - a pioneer in sexual health care. Very proud bbc.co.uk/news/world-eur...

♡ 2,125 4:35 PM - Jan 25, 2018

THE NAT🏴ONAL

THE NEWSPAPER THAT SUPPORTS AN INDEPENDENT SCOTLAND

Stanley Johnson accused of groping women at Tory party conferences

A senior Tory MP Caroline Nokes said that Stanley Johnson forcefully smacked her on the backside, and bawled most manfully.

"Oh Romsey, you have a lovely seat," as Tory training ahead of running to be a MP in 2003. The allegation prompted Ailbhe Rea, a journalist for the

New Statesman magazine, to accuse Stanley Johnson of having "groped" her at the 2019 Tory conference. The French custom of *droit du seigneur* mentioned on page 347, appeared to be a tradition in the Johnson clan, pretty peasant women be on your guard.

British Prime Minister Alexander Boris de Pfeffel Johnson, is a curious crossbreed, born in New York of French/Turkish ancestry; Johnson is about as "unBritish" as you can get. *Spectator* journalist Petronella Wyatt, who Boris impregnated and promised to marry, but reneged on his promise forcing her to have an abortion – has written:

"He is inordinately proud of his Turkish ancestry and his views on matters such as monogamy are decidedly Eastern. He finds it genuinely unreasonable that men should be confined to one woman, and cannot understand the media's reaction to his personal affairs."

This tells you that marital fidelity is viewed with contempt by Boris the Turk, an unrepentant serial philanderer. Which also explains how easily the prime minister broke his solemn promises on a Brexit deal, and why he demonstrates no trace of a moral conscience whatsoever when foully betraying his nation. Of equal concern is his thirst for popularity, pointed out by journalist Petronella Wyatt:

"Boris is famous for being friendly yet he has few friends. I remarked on this after he kept introducing me to the same two people, who comprised his entire social circle."

Boris replied that he is not "clubbable", and does not enjoy mixing with "high-achieving men". Yet, according to Wyatt, he is obsessively driven; a despot craving to be adored by loyal minions.

"Like many loners, Boris has a fierce compensating need to be liked. There is an element in him that wants to be prime minister because the love of family and Tory voters is not enough; he wants to be loved by the world."

We scientists said lockdown but UK politicians refused to listen, for 11 fateful days in March 2020 government ignored the best coronavirus advice, they must learn from their fatal mistake.

Professor Helen Ward - Imperial College

Everyone wants to be loved, but when you are prime minister you must make tough decisions, not always liked by the people. Britain warily entered 2021 with the uncertainty of Brexit looming, and a Covid 20 second wave out of control. Labour leader Sir Keir Starmer called for an immediate national lockdown: "Not in a week, or two, or three, as the prime minister hints. Such delays have been the source of many problems." Sir Keir reminded of the early 2020 lockdown delay which caused 20,000 needless deaths, yet his gripping addiction to "being liked" made Boris Johnson hesitate again!

Being liked can quickly turn to being hated, ignoring the advice of Sir Keir Starmer was stupid, but ignoring the guidance of expert scientists was criminal. Prime Minister Boris Johnson should really have listened to the scientists and to Sir Keir Starmer, whose wisdom would prove a great blessing to Britain, especially on the forthcoming vaccine rollout? Yet the recalcitrance of the P.M. in September 2020, would once again prove deadly, and the proof of this is now emerging.

In a recent interview with BBC commentator Laura Kuenssberg, Dominic Cummings the ex-adviser to the Tories, sensationally claimed that Boris allowed Brits to die from Covid to save his political career. Cummings said both Sir Patrick Vallance and Chris Whitty, urged the P.M. to lockdown last September to stop a killer second wave, but Boris put political expedience before people's lives.

Boris once more ignored the advice of scientists, according to Cummings the P.M. told them "no no no." His attitude at that point in autumn 2020, was a 'mad scientist' mix of partly, "it's all nonsense and lockdowns don't work anyway." Dominic Cummings claims that the P.M. actually made this horrifying statement. "Well, this is terrible but people who are dying are essentially all over 80, and we can't kill the economy just because of people over 80 dying." At that stage the Tories became increasingly desperate to get rid of their irrational Prime Minister, but May 6th local elections loomed and polls bizarrely showed voters retaining a macabre fascination, for their mad scientist PM even as the death toll of his deadly experiments mounted? Einstein is reputed to have said that constantly repeating an action, and expecting a different result, is a definitive sign of insanity. As the world moved to 2021 every Briton fretted, not whether their Prime Minister was a bumbling buffoon, but was he in fact certifiably insane? Over a hundred thousand Britons died of Covid under the inept administration of Boris Johnson, while his rushed Brexit deal kept Britain closely tied to the EU, with no say in decision making? Yet it was not all bad news for the Fatberg was defeated, Doctor Zee had developed a Covid-19 vaccine at Oxford University, and there was always the rugby. Covid ensured it would be October 31st when England were crowned 2020 Six Nations Champions, Scotland finished in a fine fourth place consigning the Welsh to fifth, after beating them in Wales for the first time since 2002. Rampant Scotland combined this, with a fourth consecutive Murrayfield win over a powerful French side, the Scots rugby bagpipes blew strong in 2020. Yet still to come was the eagerly anticipated 2021 Lions rugby tour to South Africa, the combined British isles rugby teams versus the world champions, Professor Peter Watercloset and Lord Evil Neville licked their lips in eager anticipation.

Greatest Game

After Scotland's fine performance in the Six Nations, Laird Neville considered returning to his roots by dropping England and supporting Scotland, then came the calamitous British Lions tour and the Laird seriously considered no longer watching rugby? England rugby faded somewhat in 2021 but the British Lions fell shockingly apart, fans put it down to Boris Johnson breaking up the United Kingdom, for the Lions were the combined home nations teams. In 2013 the Lions thrashed Australia in a 2-1 series win, in 2017 the Lions drew their series with mighty New Zealand, four years on it was current world champions South Africa at home. Where it was not so much the Lions 2021 series loss, but the un-British way in which they lost, thanks to the outlandish shenanigans of their foreign coach? The Lions coach hailed from New Zealand, he'd never played international rugby, so he relied on vocal outbursts against referees.

It worked well in the first test where the ref was terrified to penalize the Lions, awaking the troglodytes of *World Rugby* to the necessity of a computer chipped rugby *smart ball*, yet in the last two tests the Springboks were ruthlessly dominant. Helped by the bitter ethnic squabbling amongst Lions players, due to the imminent Boris breakup of the United Kingdom, which meant the Lions would never again play as a united British team. Some Irishmen wanted the Lions to remain but others didn't, many Scottish players felt uneasy given the Nicola Sturgeon drive for independence, the English were derisive of everyone and the Welsh captain struggled to keep it together. Prime Minister Boris Johnson had killed a Lions rugby heritage that went back to 1888, that is his shameful historic legacy which matched the grubbiest game, he played daily in the Westminster parliament. Yet there was now a new voice, the House of Commons pulsed with raw energy as the articulate Sir Keir played the greatest game, the pitiful whining of Commie Corbyn was thankfully a thing of the past.

Sir Keir called for an inquiry on "corrupt Tory PPE contracts," Nicola Sturgeon raged, "every day more Tory sleaze and it stinks." The source of corruption lay in the Westminster reality, that luxury loving Tories could not live on £82k salaries, three times the national average. £9.2 million outside earnings were declared by all MPs, on the 2020 Register, of this Tory MPs earned more than £8 million.

Under Boris Johnson barely a week went by without some new dishonesty, his government had made 43 U-Turns since it came to power in December 2019, most motivated by disreputable dealings. Sir Keir Starmer accused the prime minister of "leading his troops through the sewer", reaffirming Labour's commitment to bar MPs from directorships and consultancies; along with restrictions to stop ministers joining companies through a corrupt revolving door. Another stink was a well-greased path to the House of Lords, the Metropolitan Police were urged to launch a "cash for honours investigation," after fresh scrutiny of the Tories award of peerages.

A *Sunday Times* report showed that disdaining the advice of the House of Lords Appointment Commission, 15 of the last 16 Conservative Party's treasurers had been offered a seat in the Lords, after each generously donated more than £3m to the Tories. May 2021 local elections arrived in Britain just as Dominic Cummings revealed the true depths of Tory iniquity, but voters were so used to Boris sleaze it hardly mattered, and Commie Corbyn still cast a dark shadow over |Labour?

It's been noted by the press that Sir Keir Starmer resembles Action Man, muscular body with iron jaw and a steely stare, his actions certainly matched his looks. His decision to suspend anti-Semite Commie Corbyn was done with Keir Hardie decisiveness, swiftly with no wavering just as the Labour Party founder would do, after whom Sir Keir is named. He was knighted for his services as head of Crown Prosecutions Service, when he speaks there is thought in what he says, he doesn't score points on personal issues but presents facts.

This is in stark contrast to the nonsensical babbling of Boris, which is why medical experts credit the effective British vaccine rollout to the intervention of Sir Keir, in correcting the many errors of inept Health Secretary Matt Hancock. Perhaps the only intelligent thing Boris Johnson did during the Covid pandemic, was accept the advice of Sir Keir Starmer, and offer the job of UK vaccine rollout chief to Doctor Zee Garbo. The *AsterixZee* vaccine trials were complete, so Doctor Zee considered the offer, United Kingdom vaccine chief was a hugely responsible position. Zee talked it over with her husband Peter and they consulted the Gematria, which revealed Zee had **An Aptitude** for such medical work, so Doctor Zee Garbo accepted the offer? In line with the Gematria guide **APTITUDE** became her mantra, the hopelessly inept Health Secretary Matt Hancock wasn't much help, so Dr. Zee began to work closely with Sir Keir Starmer. The Tory aligned media never mention this but the charts and picture overleaf, tell the true story of the successful vaccine rollout in Britain.

A - Approval – Early regulatory approval from the UK's drugs regulator (MHRA) was vital, so thanks to the timely intervention of *Vac Man* Sir Keir Starmer, the Pfizer/BioNTech vaccine was approved weeks before the EU - so the UK had a running start on the EU.

P – Production – British Vaccines Taskforce Chief Doctor Zee Garbo, held early talks with vaccine producers, getting ahead of the EU in the vaccination race. She signed in-principal agreements quickly, securing four types of vaccines, this was thanks to the special relationship that Sir Keir Starmer had with the pharma sector.

T – Targets – Sir Keir Starmer set a clear target to vaccinate 14 million by mid-February, this first phase concentrated on frontline health and social care workers; and then people age 70 or over.

I – Initial – Doctor Garbo prioritized the initial dose in contrast to the EU's two dose approach, her aim was to quickly give all 'at-risk' people an initial dose.

T – Tier - A tier system gave every UK citizen, a vaccination center within 10 miles of home.

U – Users - Appointments could be made online without the need for a GP consultation, unlike France with its snail pace consultant system.

D – Dissidents - Sir Keir Starmer was the first leader to devise communication campaigns, to counter propaganda by French vaccine sceptics.

E – Enlistees – Thanks to Sir Keir Starmer, the military and thousands of civvie volunteers ably assisted the NHS, but Boris Johnson naturally took all the credit.

How could voters believe that the incompetent health secretary was behind the successful vaccine rollout, you've just read of the litany of disaster under the watch of Matt Hancock, Dominic Cummings claims Boris described Hancock as "a total f…..g disaster." The PM only kept the health secretary on as a fall-guy, for a damaging Covid-19 Inquiry that would surely come, then Boris unexpectedly fired Hancock for breaching social distancing guidance by kissing an attractive colleague?

It's since been revealed that there was a CCTV camera, hidden in the smoke detector of Hancock's office, unbeknown to the Health Secretary otherwise he wouldn't have groped his colleague. Who gave the order for the camera to be installed, who leaked the picture to the *Sun* newspaper? This is against the Official Secrets Act so it's a crime, yet government shut the investigation down quickly, was Boris Johnson spying on his colleagues? Another example of the PM's lawbreaking, was Boris now a spymaster, and when would his shenanigans stop?

The firing of Matt Hancock puzzled the dissolute Tories, after all, Dominic Cummings got away with far more? Speculation arose, that it emanated from the P.M's jealousy. Although most people saw Boris as Doctor Evil, he fancied himself as the lover Austin Powers, how dare Hancock upstage him with a kiss blazoned front page on the *Sun*. The department of health was in chaos, so Sir Keir Starmer, now known as *Vac Man,* took the reins in the U.K vaccine rollout.

Doctor Zee could not credit Sir Keir for she was now a government ascribed scientist, but canny Lord Neville had the ear of the shrewd Nicola Sturgeon.

There was a woman who could take advice, and the success of the vaccine rollout in Scotland, resulted in a huge May 2021 election victory for the S.N.P. Scottish independence was now a certainty, while the Boris Irish Sea Border made Northern Ireland a defacto part of Europe, where British goods must undergo EU checks. Sadly, throughout the whole of Britain, the Boris Trade and Co-operation Agreement (TCA), hamstrung the economy. As noted already the deal covered EU-UK trade in goods not services, but this service sector forms 80% of the UK economy?

Sectors like banking, insurance, advertising, floundered as they awaited new rules. Britain was in for a torrid few years and voters would blame Boris, while Labour and the Lib Dems, would unite for 2024 general elections. That lay ahead but in the May 2021 local elections, the Conservatives made major gains - Scottish and Welsh voters took a moral stand but decadent England just shrugged, as Boris took the key Hartlepool seat. The justice chapter on page 78 did hint, that the monkey survived the hanging?

MONKEYSHINES DON'T LAST LONG

BIG BROTHER BBC = 666

Government mishandling of Covid-19 and the Brexit carnage had hit home, so British voting patterns started to change, the almighty **Big Brother BBC** Tory media arm appeared to be losing sway?

NEWS

Labour conference: Starmer sets out 'serious plan' for government

Labour conference: Starmer vows green new deal, skilled jobs revival and says UK needs plan to 'make Brexit work'

 INDEPENDENT

NEWS   INDEPENDENT TV   CLIMATE

Labour conference – live: Starmer attacks 'trickster' Boris Johnson as left-wing hecklers disrupt speech

According to a Sky News poll, Starmer surpasses Johnson in his first face-to-face speech as a Labor leader.  What people think, feel and do

Even the Big Brother BBC media clone of the Tories, were forced to admit that Sir Keir Starmer had presented a "serious plan," for there had been a seminal shift at the September 2021 Labour Conference. Under Commie Corbyn the leadership had centered around Corbyn and a communist clique of fanatic members, while the majority of his Labour MPs were marginalized in the most humiliating manner, for the ruling Corbyn clique was well to the left of most MPs. At this conference Sir Keir Starmer returned the Labour Party to its MPs, an historic shift of power that resulted from a pact between Sir Keir and the big trade unions, the left-wing would heckle but they could not stay this seminal change. New rules made it more difficult to throw out sitting MPs, by limiting the power of militant left-wing members to determine leadership elections, also toughening up disciplinary procedures against anti-Semites and other bigots. Sir Keir Starmer had made a calculation, that winning an election meant replacing the member centered rule of Corbyn, with British democracy.

From now on the party leader and elected MPs, would use their judgement to determine what is in the interests of the British people, even if this offends the sensibilities of communist Labour members. The "trickster" Boris Johnson was in trouble, he had launched himself into power with the trick slogan "get Brexit done," but now it was "make Brexit work" and Boris wasn't doing very well. The new Labour Party devised by Sir Keir Starmer was a deadly serious threat, Prime Minister Boris Johnson pondered as he crept back into Britain like a whipped dog, after his disastrous first state visit to America.

His UN Muppet speech where he expressed admiration for Miss Piggy, had caused Britain to cringe with embarrassment, yet he did it again but this time with Peppa Pig. In a speech to high-ranking British businessmen, Boris Johnson gushingly praised *Peppa Pig World,* compared himself to Moses and imitated the noise of an accelerating car, then he lost his place in the speech and muttered "forgive me" as he shuffled the printed pages on his podium.

Mail Online

'His advisers really are muppets!' Johnson is mocked over Kermit the Frog reference in climate speech to UN

Statler: "Wake up old fool, you slept thru the speech."

Waldorf: "Who's the old fool, you watched it."

Statler: "He says we'll drown cos of climate change."

Waldorf: "After this speech, it'd be an act of mercy."

Both: "Do-ho-ho-ho-ho!"

Boris: "Greta Thunberg has mocked my speech, Kermit."

Kermit: "Your jokes fell flat, it was embarrassing, Boris."

Boris: "I'm actually deadly serious about climate change."

Kermit: "Yet, in 2010 you denied climate change, Boris."

Both: "Do-ho-ho-ho-ho!"

"It's easy to be green" Boris assured Kermit in his speech, but it's not easy to be funny and Britain cringed as Boris floundered, before a stony UN Assembly who recalled his past environment record?

JANUARY 2010 - Johnson wrote an article in the *Telegraph* promoting the work of Piers Corbyn, rabid climate change denier and conspiracy theorist whose environmental views, were as bizarre as the political views of his brother Jeremy (Commie) Corbyn.

JANUARY 2013 – In another *Telegraph* column, Johnson wrote: "According to Piers Corbyn, global temperature depends not on concentrations of CO2, but on the mood of our celestial orb the sun."

DECEMBER 2015 - In an even stronger *Telegraph* rant Boris raged: "I can't stand this December heat, but it has nothing to do with global warming, humans always put ourselves center of cosmic events. Global leaders are driven by a primitive fear that the present ambient warm weather is somehow caused by humanity; and that fear – as far as I understand the science – is equally without foundation.

APRIL 2021 - Even after graduating to Number 10 Johnson still scoffed at the climate crisis, when asked if he would set a deadline for ending fossil fuels, Boris the comedian sneered: "Thanks to the Iron Lady Margaret Thatcher, who closed many coal mines across the country, we had an early start."

SEPTEMBER 2021

On his first state visit to America the Brit PM pushed for his AUKUS pipe-dream, where the UK/US built Australian nuclear submarines, for a nation disdaining nuclear power stations. Australia had 100 fossil fuel projects in the pipeline that could add 5% to global emissions, as a top exporter of coal and gas Australia relied on coal-fired power, making them one of the world's top CO2 polluting nations per capita. Pipe-dreamer Boris would soon host a Glasgow COP 26 climate conference, Greta Thunberg sorrowfully awaited the pantomime, from the now punch-drunk British government. A disastrous state visit to America, a scathing parliamentary inquiry into Covid 19, the Tories were slumped on the ropes.

House of Commons

Health and Social Care, and
Science and Technology
Committees

Sixth Report of the Health and Social
Care Committee and Third Report
of the Science and Technology
Committee of Session 2021–22

The Guardian

News website of the year

Culture   **Lifestyle**   More

Covid response 'one of UK's worst ever public health failures'

**Early handling and belief in 'herd immunity' led to
more deaths, Commons inquiry finds**

- Coronavirus - latest updates
- See all our coronavirus coverage

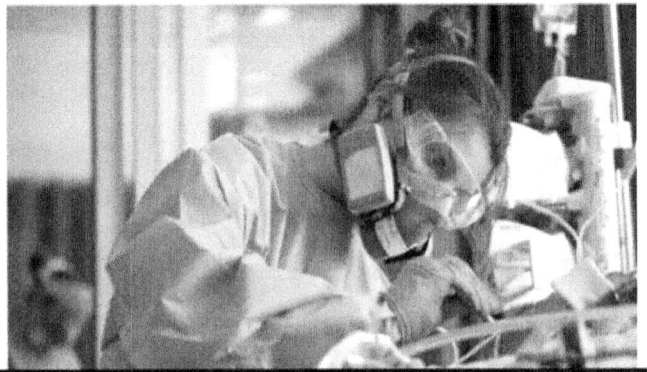

Could it get any worse, unbelievably it could when a video emerged, of government staff joking about a party that took place on 18 December 2020 - a day on which more than 400 Covid deaths were reported! An official investigation is currently focusing on three 2020 Christmas parties at Downing Street, that all breeched lockdown rules of the time, any potential criminality uncovered would be reported to the police. Sir Keir Starmer has called for the prime minister to resign, if he is found to have misled MPs about the parties, but as is Tory practice a spokeswoman has resigned over the video obtained by ITV News.

The Tories belong in jail not in government, while people exchanged gifts at motorway service stations at Christmas 2020, Boris and pals held a pub quiz. While parents missed the births of their own children, the Tories nibbled on cheese and wine, kidding themselves it was a meeting not a party. While grandparents spent their last Christmas alone, the PM's advisers laughed at them and filmed themselves doing it, millions of people up and down the country have had enough of Boris. A *Survation Poll* put Labour on 41%, a whopping 9-point lead over Boris Johnson's shameless Government, and the largest lead for Labour since 2014. While in an *Ipsos-MORI Poll*, disgruntled voters gave Sir Keir Starmer a 13-point lead over the bent Boris Johnson, on the question of who they'd prefer to be Prime Minister, the first lead for a Labour leader since 2008. The Tories themselves have had enough, already there is talk of the submission of 54 letters to the chair of the *1922 Committee,* sufficient to trigger a no-confidence vote in the Tory leader.

The damaging findings on previous pages regarding the Tories hypocritical handling of Covid 19, were enough to sink any government, especially if you combine this with the Brexit fiasco. Which had reduced King Boris to a pathetic Boris the Beggar, the Tories now realized that satirical journalists don't really make effective Prime Ministers, for they carry the baggage of nasty articles they've written?

Prime Minister Johnson slunk home empty handed from his first state visit to America, to be faced with a damaging parliamentary inquiry into his Covid-19 bungles, and revelations about 2020 Christmas parties. Coming on top of the Biden rejection it was a bitter blow, Boris had played "who's chicken" by backing Trump and insulting the Democratic Party, so the USA trade chickens flew the coop while UK Brexit chickens came home to roost. A shortage of European workers meant huge financial losses for UK companies, petrol queues at garages and empty supermarket shelves magnified, as Britain faced a chilly 2021 Christmas due to universal credit cuts and a gas shortage. The truck driver shortage was estimated at 100,000, by freight company Logistics UK, as access to European drivers faded. Desperate UK bosses offered new truckers £78k yearly, while farmers paid veg pickers £62k, or were forced to destroy produce. Boris Johnson pinned his hopes on Transatlantic free trade, but he became an object of ridicule after his UN speech, so Joe Biden stayed obdurate. He'd called Boris "a clone of Donald Trump," after the Boris barrage of insults recorded on page 420, little wonder then that the first Johnson state visit to America failed so dismally? President Biden dashed Boris's hopes of a free trade deal, to leave the UK facing a booby-prize pact, putting British firms on par with Mexican ones. UK inflation neared 5 percent, as ministers now pursued a fresh negotiation line, meekly begging to join an existing US-Canada-Mexico trade deal. As expected, President Joe Biden also laid down the law on the Northern Ireland protocol, Boris was out of aces for he'd wagered all Britain's cards on Trump winning American elections. Prime Minister Boris Johnson was a desperate man, not only had his wild Trump card gamble failed dismally, but his Tory MPs were now copying his dissolute ways. Despite Boris Johnson's best efforts to stifle the scandal, more and more of his Conservative MPs were now coming under scrutiny, for lucrative incomes from second jobs. Boris Johnson's personal approval rating plummeted to its lowest level on record, after his botched attempts to scrap parliaments standards system, to protect his errant MP's who used their positions to benefit from consultancy jobs. Sir Keir tore into the Tories with all the skill of the great prosecutor he was, and for the first time opinion polls showed him as preferred leader to sleazebag Boris, the political tide was turning against corrupt Tories.

The Tories were still reeling, from the Health and Science Committee page 472-473 findings, on their inept Covid-19 response. Calls for a public inquiry increased, after the Boris ham-fisted attempt, failed to tear up the MP's rule book. The rigged vote to scrap parliaments standards system was the last straw, the outrage built to a crescendo, that devious Prime Minister Johnson would not withstand. Even after the end of this book, from four corners of Great Britain would come clarion calls, for a Covid-19 Inquiry into the government handling of the pandemic.

Boris Johnson had gone too far, his clumsy attempt at censorship, had aroused a rage that would consume him. Then to compound the problems of the Tories a new virus struck, as predicted by the Gematria on page 426, the dreaded word Omicron had now entered the dictionary. Boris Johnson pressed the panic button, deathly afraid of killing thousands more, he imposed strict travel bans and announced Plan B restrictions. That's the problem with incompetence, it tends to overcompensate, for Doctor Zee Garbo had identified a dominant strain she called **Omicron X = 666.** If this Omicron variant proved to be mild as initial reports suggested, and it spread quicker than other Covid strains, **Omicron X** could actually help us on our way to the herd immunity that could wipe out Covid 19? What a boost that would be for Britain, first they had rid themselves of the Corbynvirus, now Covid 19 would follow. The living fatbergs had been eradicated, now it was time to get rid of Fatberg Boris Johnson, who had done far too much damage.

"Vote of no-confidence," roared Sir Keir.

Britain was fighting back for they are a winning nation, they would rid themselves of their charlatan PM, and repair the terrible damage he'd inflicted. Boris Johnson had not succeeded one whit, in dousing the indominable Brit fighting spirit, using their traditional common sense and discipline Britain would pull through. Brexit had become an exercise in quiet damage limitation, London and Brussels had arrived at an uneasy equilibrium, that was in everybody's interest to maintain. One man's self-centered foolhardiness would not sink the British, for in business and sport or in science, the little island of Great Britain remained a world beater. That is what this book is all about, that is what the mythical Gematria predicted, that heroic individuals would conquer collective neo-liberalism. Yes, our modern neo-liberalism is not about the rights of the individual, it's about empowering collective groups like the Tories to brutally control individuals.

"Down with the pigs," cheered George Orwell.

Loss of ultra-safe seat adds to huge pressures facing Boris Johnson

Lib Dem Helen Morgan delivered a fresh blow to the beleaguered Prime Minister, by taking the seat vacated by Tory MP Owen Paterson, who stepped down after becoming embroiled in the 'second jobs scandal.' The Lib Dems overturned a Conservative majority of 23,000, and won by a whopping 5,925 votes, a telling indication of how voters view the shenanigans of Boris Johnson.

FIRST TORY LOSS IN 200 YEARS

INDEPENDENT

NEWS   INDEPENDENT TV   CLIMATE   SPORT   VOICES   CULTURE   PREMIUM   INDY LIFE   INDYBEST   INDY100

The Lib Dem win in North Shropshire gives hope the Tories can be beaten

It shows there are consequences for Boris Johnsons' Conservatives, who've broken the very rules they asked our country to follow during the pandemic – **Ed Davey**

NEWS... BUT NOT AS YOU KNOW IT

Veteran Tory says Boris is on 'last orders' and 'one more strike and he's out'

The Telegraph Business Sport Opinion Politics World

UK news ˅   Coronavirus ˅   Royals ˅   Health   Defence   Science   Education

TORY WALK OF SHAME

Friday morning UK news briefing: Humiliation for Boris Johnson as Liberal Democrats win North Shropshire by-election

Dr. Zee Garbo had never looked so lovely, as she stood on the podium to receive the Nobel Prize for medicine, her work on the world's first Covid 19 pill had won her this high honour. In the audience, Professor Peter Watercloset and Lord Evil Neville listened proudly, as Zee made her Nobel acceptance speech. While outside the grand Stockholm Hall the world slowly healed. Yet, no pill could heal world economic inequality, and lack of vaccines in poorer countries could breed Covid variants to strike the world again. So, Dr. Zee Garbo gifted her vaccine to the planet. Her selflessness must become the mantra of all world leaders, self-serving Donald Trump and Boris Johnson taught us this lesson. They ignored scientists and delayed lockdowns, for an economic slump would hurt them politically; their narcissistic egoism caused hundreds of thousands to die unnecessarily. Now Trump is gone, and a Covid-19 Public Inquiry followed by 2024 elections, will see the end of Boris Johnson. Who misjudged badly, by betting all Britain's cards on Trump winning elections, but America thankfully came to her senses and so will Britain. That's why the Gematria predicted that people, not their rulers, would save the world.

The End

THE TIMES | Today's sections

Covid mistakes demand a swift, no-blame inquiry

Liam Smeeth   Wednesday August 19 2020, 12.01am, The Times

THE SCOTSMAN   News you can trust since 1817

Demand for Holyrood inquiry on Covid-19 handling after damning MP report

Holyrood should hold its own parliamentary inquiry into the Scottish Government's handling of Covid-19, Scottish Labour has said.

THE IRISH TIMES

NEWS | SPORT | BUSINESS | OPINION | LIFE & STYLE

Covid response 'one of UK's worst ever
public health failures', inquiry finds

Bereaved families call for public inquiry to be brought forward after cross-party report

the Leader

Holywell family joins the fight
for Wales Covid inquiry

About the Author

Patrick John Stevens was born in Johannesburg, in the same month Steve Bantu Biko was born. December 1946 was also the month that Alan Paton completed his book *Cry, the Beloved Country*, so some characters in *The Greatest Game* series derive from both sources. Today the author lives in England, but the river between Africa and Pat Stevens runs deep; his books are mostly set in Southern Africa. Back in the 'sixties, Pat Stevens met the author Alan Paton, whose son Jonathan Paton was a Parkwood neighbour, so Pat had the honour of introducing Alan Paton to *Amnesty International.* The organization was founded back in 1961 by Peter Benenson, and the early days were pretty rocky, because they infuriated the British government with allegations of military torture of the I.R.A. *Amnesty International* needed the backing of a world-famous writer, and apprentice Pat Stevens was working alongside a German exchange student, who was a member of the organization. This

German also possessed a neat NATO Air Force jacket, so Pat Stevens agreed to introduce the student to Paton, in exchange for his jacket. A meeting was arranged; peace-loving *Amnesty International* were introduced to peacenik Alan Paton, for the price of one war-like jacket. Pat Stevens wore the jacket throughout Africa, when he hit the construction trail, this afforded him the opportunity of observing the customs and traditions of the locals. Those are the Pat Stevens qualifications for writing African novels: knowledge of African people, forged by a lifetime of moving amongst African people.

THE GREATEST GAME REVIEWS

You have a writing talent and have written an original book, something new in SA writing.
Adrian Donker
AD Donker Publishers
Johannesburg

Stunningly original, a true parody of the South African scene from the sixties onward, reads well and has tremendous atmosphere.
Isabel Cooke
Literary Dynamics
Durban

Hugely original, a clever book, that brings to mind the novels of Joseph Heller and John Irving. Absurd; yet serious.
Kirsty Fawkes
Hodder & Stoughton
London

Picturesque and provocative, brash and funny, *The Greatest Game* does for South African politics what *Catch 22* did for World War 11.
Jim Mc Evoy
Janus Books
London

BIBLIOGRAPHY

THE GREATEST GAME SERIES OF BOOKS

Available at Amazon and at most book stores, the *Greatest Game* quartet of books are subtitled *Sixties*, *Seventies*, *Eighties* and *Nineties*. The storyline counterpoints the lives and loves of four main characters against the background of four turbulent decades, in a slowly changing South Africa, culminating in the historic 1994 democratic elections. Political events of such magnitude normally produce great novels, and these four books are serious contenders for that title, read them and see what you think. Unfortunately, only the books of pushy journalists receive attention in South Africa. So, *Sunday Times Book Awards* were restructured in 2015, grandly renamed *Barry Ronge Fiction Prize.*

The lesser prize is the non-fiction *Alan Paton Award*, for the novelist Alan Paton never rose to the heights of journalist Barry Ronge, who has two acclaimed books of newspaper cuttings on Amazon. They are called *Spit* and *Polish*. The *spit* is for famous writers like Alan Paton, the *polish* reserved for pushy journalists like Barry Ronge.

THE GREATEST GAME: Sixties

This first book of the *Greatest Game* quartet introduces you to a zany South African schoolboy named Rupertheimer, a man set apart, who would play a pivotal role in the 1994 transition to democracy. The novel describes his schooldays and military service, where young Rupertheimer shows early signs of the remarkable prescience, he would one day employ to guide his country to an embryonic democracy. The liberal press has covered this historic event extensively, but if you prefer your fiction laced with a semblance of historical truth, then the works of Pat Stevens are worth a read.

BALLAD OF STEVE BIKER: Seventies

Recounts an overseas holiday by the friends of Rupertheimer – called "The Pack" – where they all meet their future wives, and also come under the influence of a mysterious motorcyclist named Steve Biker. The politically articulate Biker has a profound impact on the Pack, especially on the young Zulu Peter Khumalo, who returns home to join "The Struggle", only to end up in a fierce standoff at Rupertheimer's wedding. These bizarre events seem to point the way for the pivotal role, Rupertheimer is destined to play in the historic 1994 transition to democracy, with the support of the ever-loyal Pack.

SONS AND DAUGHTERS: Eighties

Introduces you to *Robber Island*, where the terrorist Peter Khumalo has been incarcerated. Yet life must go on for the rest of the Pack, because there are now sons and daughters to be raised. Hofmeyr grapples gamely with technical problems at decrepit *Hospital Hill*, while Rupertheimer battles valiantly with the

Green Freaks, but Jarvis is unfortunately experiencing *Marital Blues.* Then Khumalo is released from prison in 1988, so he joins the mighty Rupertheimer Corporation as a labour lawyer, which he comes to bitterly regret, when Rupertheimer involves him in *Labour Pains.*

DEMOCRATIC DAWN: Nineties

The 1994 South African democratic election was a glorious achievement, unparalleled in history. Never before had a ruling elite willingly given up power, and never before had a single, bold individual achieved it. Now it can be revealed who the remarkable individual was, unheralded by the myopic liberal press, he secretly secured the release of Nelson Mandela and steered his country to an embryonic democracy. There are only two ways to change society: bloody revolution or peaceful negotiation, and Rupertheimer's chosen work was to negotiate a South Africa democracy.

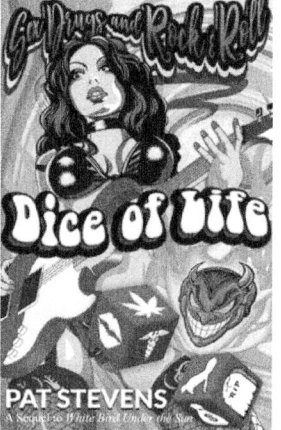

HERO OF THE STRUGGLE

In 2018 an explosive expose revealed that South African newspapers were disseminating fake news, this came as no surprise to political satirist Will Powers, who first uncovered the false newspaper headline that led to the arrest of Jacob Zuma. Will Powers struck back at the fascist press by revealing the *Spy Tapes,* phone taps proving media and political intrusion into a court case, so all charges were dropped. Will Powers had to fight against his own blood father, who refused to recognize his mixed-race son, for racist editor Pen Powers of the *Partisan* newspaper had been bribed by presidential hopeful Harry Hiroshima. Whose rival Jacob Zuma must be put to the sword, with savage satire Will Powers thwarted the Hiroshima presidential aspirations, so Cyril Ramaphosa replaced Jacob Zuma as president. Will Powers then concentrated on Zimbabwe, while myopic opposition leader Helen Zille harangued President Mbeki to invade Zimbabwe, Will convinced Mbeki to mediate a unity government.

Which paved the way for the ultimate removal of Robert Mugabe, then Will Powers replaced war mongering Helen Zille with moderate Mmusi Maimane. Will Powers then urged his father to focus his *Partisan* newspaper, on racial imbalances in platinum mines, but Will was ignored resulting in strikes leading to the Marikana Massacre. Undeterred by this, Helen Zille removed all black leaders, including Mmusi Maimane from the opposition. Now known as *Illez the Witch* she then convinced her puppet ruling Kritarchy of Judges, to jail her hated enemy Jacob Zuma, causing another bloody massacre worse than Marikana.

ZULU VAMPIRE

Captain Jake Smit loved the Zulu, he loved the easy laughter that bubbled so readily to the surface, and he respected the long-standing traditions and culture of the Zulu people. Jake Smit was an Afrikaner who had being brought up amongst the Zulu; he spoke Zulu fluently and was recognized by Zululand police, as being something of an authority on Zulu traditions.

Together with his trusted Zulu sergeant Peter Khumalo, Captain Jake flanked the local rugby team and kept the peace in rural Umuzi. But that isn't always easy to do, for the Zulu are a volatile people. Captain Jake Smit loved the Zulu, but he hated the superstition that permeates their society; as a police captain he saw the worst of the witchcraft murders and ritual killings. Now he has to deal with an outbreak of killing which had frozen the district in fear, because the slaughter is reputed to be the work of the dreaded *Impundulu*, a legendary "lightning bird" that strikes lightning from its talons and feeds on human blood. Flaring the rising hysteria is the lanky American, who has stirred the story in the local newspaper. Journalist Marlin Madison is a highly attractive woman, so Captain Jake looks forward to reasoning with her, together they trace the source of the killings to a local AIDS clinic. Under the guise of testing patients, Doctor Silvio Sarkoy is identifying suitable doners, then murdering them to harvest their organs.

WHITE BIRD UNDER THE SUN

Is a coming-of-age novel set in Africa, although based partly on the author's own upbringing; this is not a biography but rather a passage in a young boy's life. The story starts right in the womb where he is startled to discover, a greedy twin sister crowding the rather limited space, then comes the traumatic birth into 'fifties Johannesburg where the White Bird absorbs the music and movies of the time. He then leaves Johannesburg when the family travels to cowboy country, Northern Rhodesia. The flight of the White Bird is not a solitary journey; there is the warmth of a close-knit family, and the inevitable rivalry between siblings. Yet, through the journey of life the White Bird is supported by loyal Twiny who, despite the early struggle in the womb, turns into a loyal aide and willing assistant in her brother's madcap schemes. The book takes you on an odyssey through 'fifties Africa, which will both charm and amuse you, as it recounts the wonder of a boyhood spent in the lush Rhodesian bush. This is not a tale of high adventure or romantic love, but lifetime memories that are engendered, as your first tiger fish tugs at your line, or your first buck lies dead at your feet. Fly with the White Bird and share his memories, as the author unveils the wonder of an African boyhood. This book describes the reverent wonder you feel, when you first set eyes on the magnificent Victoria Falls, or watch a fish eagle swoop down on the mighty Zambezi River. Share the African memories that can never be felt again, as the White Bird unveils the wonder of Africa, as seen through the entranced eyes of a young boy.

DICE OF LIFE

A coming-of-age novel set in 'seventies South Africa. The story revolves around a group of apprentices and deals with the complexity of a racist society, examining the old apartheid South Africa through the eyes of protagonist Harry Cheals, counterpointing his concerns against the blasé attitudes of his friends. Who are the privileged white elite, who enjoy life to its fullest. Harry senses that the dice of life will roll a payback, and he attempts to warn his carefree friends, but they are oblivious to the many ills which plague South Africa. Both Warthog and Wilfred concentrate rather on their individual needs, while Harry Cheals is friendly with both of them, he is scornfully dismissive of their selfish and uncaring attitudes. Harry is acutely aware of worldwide revulsion for apartheid, but he feels nothing can be done, so he grows a cynical shell, which hardens after his betrayal by the beautiful but wayward Liza. This drives heartbroken Harry to drunkenness, until he meets a wise Afrikaner Seer who teaches, that life is not a random throw of the dice but a deliberately chosen course The Seer also predicts a coming liberal system in South Africa, more repressive than the apartheid it will replace, a system dominated by the media and civil society groups. Who use their influence to direct a ruling Kritarchy of Judges, who make decisions often against the will of the people, making democracy just a hollow farce. This prophecy of the Seer shocks Harry, and motivates him to reform his life, to fight against this coming system of neoliberalism.

CLOUD EATER

The Zulu people have colourful names for their children, which often come to resemble the nature of the child – and so it was with young Thulani. His name means "Be Still" in Zulu, and his parents often wished he were, for Thulani was a lively boy who loved telling wild tales. These tales bestowed on him the nickname Amnyama Idla, which means "Cloud Eater" in the Zulu tongue. The name perfectly described the boy's dreamy nature; because his stories were as mysterious and gossamer as the clouds themselves. Thulane was in fact a traditional Zulu seer. All the Zulu men loved listening to the fabulous tales of the Cloud Eater. The boy was also a firm favourite of the women, for there was an ancient African wisdom in young Thulani. Although his stories were wildly implausible, there was always a moral imparted by his tales, and that is the essence of African storytelling. They are called the "Eaters of Clouds" in Africa. Whimsical philosophers who are the lifeblood of African culture, for history and traditions are passed on orally by Africans, there is no writing culture in traditional Africa. In the African folk tales, the stories reflect a culture where animals abound; animals appear frequently in the stories along with a birds and spiders - taking on human characteristics of greed, jealousy, honesty, crookedness, etc. Through their behavior, many valuable lessons are learned from the animals. This is your opportunity to read the tales of Thulani. They are in fact cautionary fables, and culminate in a modern fable relevant to South Africa today.

PARABLES AND POEMS

Is an anthology of short works, some of which are featured in other books by Pat Stevens, yet are included here to reinforce points of view. The pieces range from brief, humorous essays to longer, satirical articles, covering a wide spectrum of problems, but concentrating mainly on Southern Africa. The author has attempted to sequence the articles, so the content of each complements the previous, in order to create an interlinking theme. There is a light-hearted thrust at sport which, due to the interference of the liberal press, is a heavy-hearted subject. The pathetic Protea cricketers are a tragic example: the pushy liberal press insisted on dropping the Springbok emblem, since then cricket and its pretty flower has never won a world cup, while the rugby Springboks have won three. The most recent been in 2019, and Springbok rugby culminated this, with an historic win over the British Lions in 2021. South African cricketers have been referenced as 'chokers' by Wikipedia, and more damaging are the allegations of racism currently swirling around, the press obsession on killing the Springbok has cost cricket dearly. While abolishing the death penalty and introducing criminal-friendly laws, are more serious examples of the liberal press interference, which bedevils South Africa and has turned the country into a felon friendly crime hellhole. Neoliberalism is satirized in four amusing allegories, attacking the liberal penchant for total social control, and noting their sway over the Kritarchy of Judges who rule South Africa.

THE GREATEST BOOK EVER WRITTEN

The Bible is a great inspiration to Pat Stevens, for it is the greatest book ever written, so important that mankind divided time into before and after the birth of the Messiah. The teaching of Jesus is narrated in the *New Testament*, while the *Old Testament* is a marvelous tapestry of amazing ancestors. Among these the author drew his inspiration for *Absalom's Tomb*, in which the King James English is retained for the dialogue, while a modern writing style is used for the narrative, overlaying a lovely Shakespearian veneer on the story. *Absalom's Tomb* then continues the Davidic line with *Solomon's Sons* – namely Haile Selassie of Ethiopia, and his historic links to the Rastafarian movement. The Rasta believe that neoliberals are the Babylon Whore, a belief strongly supported by the author who explores this through a Gematria, also featured in the novel *Boris and the Fatberg*. A Gematria is an ancient Babylonian system of numerology, later adopted by the Jews, it is used by Pat Stevens to zero in on noxious neoliberalism. The book also features a novel concept of the *Big Bang,* which counterpoints the creation account in *Genesis* against Darwin's Theory of Evolution, the author calls this *Old Earth Creationism.* Because it uses science to explain the Biblical account of creation, it accepts evolution as part of creation because ancient man was there before Adam and Eve, that's why the creation of man is mentioned twice in Genesis? This is known as the *Gap Theory,* Adam and Eve were not the first humans but start of the *Messianic Line,* created thousands of years after the first Homo sapiens. Yet if Albert Einstein was correct that time is relative to speed, then Godspeed makes a seven-day creation timeframe possible, that's what the science says?

ACKNOWLEDGMENTS

The publishers and authors would like to thank Russell Spencer, Matt Vidler, Susan Woodard, Leonard West, Lianne Baily Woodward and Laura Jayne Humphrey for their work, without which this book would not have been possible.

ABOUT THE PUBLISHER

L.R. Price Publications is dedicated to publishing books by unknown authors. We use a mixture of both traditional and modern publishing options, to bring our authors' words to the wider world.

We print, publish, distribute and market books in a variety of formats including paper and hardback, electronic books, digital audiobooks and online.

If you are an author interested in getting your book published, or a book retailer interested in selling our books, please contact us.

www.lrpricepublications.com

L.R. Price Publications Ltd,

27 Old Gloucester Street,

London, WC1N 3AX.

020 3051 9572

publishing@lrprice.com

Printed in Great Britain
by Amazon